THE SPOOK'S CURSE

Also by Joseph Delaney

THE WARDSTONE CHRONICLES

BOOK ONE: THE SPOOK'S APPRENTICE
BOOK TWO: THE SPOOK'S CURSE
BOOK THREE: THE SPOOK'S SECRET

THE SPOOK'S CURSE

Joseph Delaney

Illustrated by David Wyatt

RED FOX

THE SPOOK'S CURSE
A RED FOX BOOK : 9780099456469

First published in Great Britain by The Bodley Head,
an imprint of Random House Children's Books

The Bodley Head edition published 2005
Red Fox edition published 2006

3 5 7 9 10 8 6 4

Copyright © Joseph Delaney, 2005
Illustrations copyright © David Wyatt, 2005

The right of Joseph Delaney to be identified as the author of this work has been
asserted in accordance with the Copyright, Designs and Patents Act 1988.

Papers used by Random House Children's Books are natural, recyclable products
made from wood grown in sustainable forests. The manufacturing processes
conform to the environmental regulations of the country of origin.

Set in 10.5/16.5 Palatino by Falcon Oast Graphic Art Ltd.

The Random House Group Limited makes every effort to ensure that the
papers used in its books are made from trees that have been legally
sourced from well-managed and credibly certified forests. Our paper
procurement policy can be found at: www.randomhouse.co.uk/paper.htm.

Red Fox Books are published by Random House Children's Books,
61–63 Uxbridge Road, London W5 5SA,
a division of The Random House Group Ltd

Addresses for companies within The Random House Group Limited
can be found at: www.randomhouse.co.uk/offices.htm

THE RANDOM HOUSE GROUP Limited Reg. No. 954009
www.kidsatrandomhouse.co.uk

A CIP catalogue record for this book is available from the British Library.

Printed and bound in Great Britain by
Cox & Wyman Ltd, Reading, Berkshire

For Marie

THE HIGHEST POINT IN THE COUNTY
IS MARKED BY MYSTERY.
IT IS SAID THAT A MAN DIED THERE IN A
GREAT STORM, WHILE BINDING AN EVIL
THAT THREATENED THE WHOLE WORLD.
THEN THE ICE CAME AGAIN, AND WHEN IT
RETREATED, EVEN THE SHAPES OF THE
HILLS AND THE NAMES OF THE TOWNS
IN THE VALLEYS WERE CHANGED.
NOW, AT THAT HIGHEST POINT ON
THE FELLS, NO TRACE REMAINS OF WHAT
WAS DONE SO LONG AGO,
BUT ITS NAME HAS ENDURED.
THEY CALL IT –

THE WARDSTONE.

CHAPTER
1
THE HORSHAW RIPPER

When I heard the first scream, I turned away and covered my ears with my hands, pressing hard until my head hurt. At that moment I could do nothing to help. But I could still hear it, the sound of a priest in torment, and it went on for a long time before finally fading away.

So I shivered in the dark barn, listening to rain drumming on the roof, trying to gather my courage. It was a bad night and it was about to get worse.

Ten minutes later, when the rigger and his mate arrived, I rushed across to meet them in the doorway. Both of them were big men and I barely came up to their shoulders.

'Well, lad, where's Mr Gregory?' asked the rigger, an edge of impatience in his voice. He lifted the lantern he was holding and peered about suspiciously. His eyes were shrewd and intelligent. Neither of the men looked like they would stand any nonsense.

'He's been taken badly,' I said, trying to control the nerves that were making my voice sound weak and wobbly. 'He's been in bed with a bad fever this past week so he's sent me in his place. I'm Tom Ward. His apprentice.'

The rigger looked me up and down quickly, like an undertaker measuring me up for future business. Then he raised one eyebrow so high that it disappeared under the peak of his flat cap, which was still dripping with rain.

'Well, Mr Ward,' he said, an edge of sarcasm sharp in his voice, 'we await your instructions.'

I put my left hand into my breeches pocket and pulled out the sketch that the stonemason had made. The rigger set the lantern down on the earthen floor and then, with a world-weary shake of his head and a glance at his mate, accepted the sketch and began to examine it.

The mason's instructions gave the dimensions of the pit that needed to be dug, and the measurements of the stone that would be lowered into place.

After a few moments the rigger shook his head again and knelt beside the lantern, holding the paper very close to it. When he came to his feet, he was frowning. 'The pit should be nine feet deep,' he said. 'This only says six.'

The rigger knew his job all right. The standard boggart pit is six feet deep but for a ripper, the most dangerous boggart of all, nine feet is the norm. We were certainly facing a ripper – the priest's screams were proof of that – but there wasn't time to dig nine feet.

'It'll have to do,' I said. 'It has to be done by morning or it'll be too late and the priest will be dead.'

Until that moment they'd both been big men wearing big boots, oozing confidence from every pore. Now, suddenly, they looked nervous. They knew the situation from the note I'd sent summoning them to the barn. I'd used the Spook's name to make sure they came right away.

'Know what you're doing, lad?' asked the rigger. 'Are you up to the job?'

I stared straight back into his eyes and tried hard not to blink. 'Well, I've made a good start,' I said. 'I've hired the best rigger and mate in the County.'

It was the right thing to say and the rigger's face cracked into a smile. 'When will the stone arrive?' he asked.

'Well before dawn. The mason's bringing it himself. We have to be ready.'

The rigger nodded. 'Then lead the way, Mr Ward. Show us where you want it dug.'

This time there was no sarcasm in his voice. His tone was business-like. He wanted the job over and done with. We all wanted the same, and time was short so I pulled up my hood and, carrying the Spook's staff in my left hand, led the way out into the cold, heavy drizzle.

Their two-wheel cart was outside, the equipment covered with a waterproof sheet, the patient horse between the shafts steaming in the rain.

We crossed the muddy field, then followed the blackthorn hedge to the place where it thinned, beneath the branches of an ancient oak on the boundary of the churchyard. The pit would be close to holy ground, but not too close. The nearest gravestones were just twenty paces away.

'Dig the pit as close as you can get to that,' I said, pointing towards the trunk of the tree.

Under the Spook's watchful eye I'd dug lots of practice pits. In an emergency I could have done the job myself but these men were experts and they'd work fast.

As they went back for their tools, I pushed through the hedge and weaved between the gravestones towards the old church. It was in a bad state of repair: there were slates missing from the roof and it hadn't seen a lick of paint for years. I pushed open the side door, which yielded with a groan and a creak.

5

The old priest was still in the same position, lying on his back near the altar. The woman was kneeling on the floor close to his head, crying. The only difference now was that the church was flooded with light. She'd raided the vestry for its hoard of candles and lit them all. There were a hundred at least, clustered in groups of five or six. She'd positioned them on benches, on the floor and on window ledges but the majority were on the altar.

As I closed the door, a gust of wind blew into the church and the flames all flickered together. She looked up at me, her face running with tears.

'He's dying,' she said, her echoing voice full of anguish. 'Why did it take you so long to get here?'

Since the message reached us at Chipenden, it had taken me two days to arrive at the church. It was over thirty miles to Horshaw and I hadn't set off right away. At first the Spook, still too ill to leave his bed, had refused to let me go.

Usually the Spook never sends apprentices out to work alone until he's been training them for at least a year. I'd just turned thirteen and had been his apprentice for less than six months. It was a difficult, scary trade, which often involved dealing with what we call 'the dark'. I'd been learning how to cope with witches, ghosts, boggarts and things that go bump in the night. But was I ready for this?

There was a boggart to bind which, if done properly, should be pretty straightforward. I'd seen the Spook do it twice. Each time he'd hired good men to help and the job had gone smoothly. But this job was a little different. There were complications.

You see, this priest was the Spook's own brother. I'd seen him just once before when we'd visited Horshaw in the spring. He'd glared at us and made a huge sign of the cross in the air, his face twisted with anger. The Spook hadn't even glanced in his direction because there'd been little love lost between them and they hadn't spoken for over forty years. But family was family and that's why he'd eventually sent me to Horshaw.

'Priests!' the Spook had raved. 'Why don't they stick

to what they know? Why do they always have to meddle? What was he thinking of, trying to tackle a ripper? Let me get on with my business and other folks get on with theirs.'

At last he'd calmed down and spent hours giving me detailed instructions on what had to be done and telling me the names and addresses of the rigger and mason I had to hire. He'd also named a doctor, insisting that only he would do. That was another nuisance because the doctor lived some distance away. I'd had to send word and I just hoped that he'd set off immediately.

I looked down at the woman, who was dabbing very gently at the priest's forehead with a cloth. His greasy, lank white hair was pulled back from his face and his eyes were rolling feverishly in his head. He hadn't known that the woman was going to send to the Spook for help. If he had, he would have objected so it was a good job that he couldn't see me now.

Tears were dripping from the woman's eyes and sparkling in the candlelight. She was his housekeeper, not even family, and I remember thinking that he must have been really kind to her to make her get so upset.

'The doctor'll be here soon,' I said, 'and he'll give him something for the pain.'

'He's had pain all his life,' she answered. 'I've been a big trouble to him too. It's made him terrified of dying. He's a sinner and he knows where he's going.'

Whatever he was or had done, the old priest didn't deserve this. Nobody did. He was certainly a brave man. Either brave or very stupid. When the boggart had got up to its tricks, he'd tried to deal with it himself by using the priest's tools: bell, book and candle. But that's no way to deal with the dark. In most cases it wouldn't have mattered because the boggart would just have ignored the priest and his exorcism. Eventually it would have moved on and the priest, as often happens, would have taken the credit.

But this was the most dangerous type of boggart we ever have to deal with. Usually, we call them 'cattle-rippers' because of their main diet, but when the priest had started meddling, *he* had become the boggart's victim. Now it was a full-blown 'ripper' with a taste for human blood and the priest would be lucky to escape with his life.

There was a crack in the flagged floor, a zigzag crack that ran from the foot of the altar to about three paces beyond the priest. At its widest point it was more a chasm and almost half a hand's span wide. After splitting the floor, the boggart had caught the old priest by his foot and dragged his leg down into the ground almost as far as his knee. Now, in the darkness below, it was sucking his blood, drawing the life from him very slowly. It was like a big fat leech, keeping its victim alive as long as possible to extend its own enjoyment.

Whatever I did, it would be touch and go whether or not the priest survived. In any case, I had to bind the boggart. Now that it had drunk human blood it would no longer be content with ripping cattle.

'Save him if you can,' the Spook had said, as I prepared to leave. 'But whatever else you do, make sure you deal with that boggart. That's your first duty.'

* * *

I started making my own preparations.

Leaving the rigger's mate to carry on digging the pit, I went back to the barn with the rigger himself. He knew what to do: first of all he poured water into the large bucket they'd brought with them. That was one advantage of working with people who had experience of the business: they provided the heavy equipment. This was a strong bucket, made of wood, bound with metal hoops and large enough to deal with even a twelve-foot pit.

After filling it about half full with water, the rigger began to shake brown powder into it from the large sack he'd brought in from the cart. He did this a little at a time and then, after each addition, began to stir it with a stout stick.

It soon became hard work as, very gradually, the mixture turned into a thick goo which became more and more difficult to mix. It stank as well, like something that had been dead for weeks, which wasn't really surprising seeing as the bulk of the powder was crushed bone.

The end result would be a very strong glue, and the longer the rigger stirred, the more he began to sweat and gasp. The Spook always mixed his own glue, and he'd made me practise doing the same, but time was very short and the rigger had the muscles for the job. Knowing that, he'd started work without even being asked.

When the glue was ready, I began to add iron filings and salt from the much smaller sacks I'd brought with me, stirring slowly to ensure they were spread evenly right through the mixture. Iron is dangerous to a boggart because it can bleed away its strength, while the salt burns it. Once a boggart is in the pit, it will stay there because the underside of the stone and the sides of the pit are coated with the mixture, forcing it to make itself small and stay within the boundaries of the space inside. Of course, the problem is getting the boggart into the pit in the first place.

For now I wasn't worrying about that. At last the rigger and I were both satisfied. The glue was ready.

* * *

As the pit wasn't finished yet, I had nothing to do but wait for the doctor in the narrow, crooked lane that led into Horshaw.

The rain had stopped and the air seemed very still. It was late September and the weather was changing for the worse. We were going to have more than just rain soon, and the sudden, first, faint rumble of thunder from the west made me even more nervous. After about twenty minutes I heard the sound of hooves pounding in the distance. Riding as though all the hounds of Hell were on his tail, the doctor came round the corner, his horse at full gallop, his cloak flying behind him.

I was holding the Spook's staff so there was no need for introductions, and in any case the doctor had been riding so fast he was out of breath. So I just nodded at him and he left his sweating horse munching at the long grass in front of the church and followed me round to the side door. I held it open out of respect so that he could go in first.

My dad's taught me to be respectful to everyone, because that way they'll respect you back. I didn't know this doctor but the Spook had insisted on him so I knew he'd be good at his job. His name was Sherdley and he was carrying a black leather bag. It looked almost as heavy as the Spook's, which I'd brought with me and left in the barn. He put it down about six feet from his patient and, ignoring the housekeeper, who was still heaving with dry sobs, he began his examination.

I stood just behind him and to one side so that I had the best possible view. Gently he pulled up the priest's black cassock to reveal his legs.

His right leg was thin, white and almost hairless but the left, the one gripped by the boggart, was red and swollen, bulging with purple veins that darkened the closer they were to the wide crack in the floor.

The doctor shook his head and let out his breath very slowly. Then he spoke to the housekeeper, his voice so low that I barely caught the words.

'It'll have to come off,' he said. 'That's his only hope.'

At that, the tears started running down her cheeks

again and the doctor looked at me and pointed to the door. Once outside, he leaned back against the wall and sighed.

'How long before you're ready?' he asked.

'Less than an hour, Doctor,' I replied, 'but it depends on the mason. He's bringing the stone himself.'

'If it's much longer, we'll lose him. The truth is, I don't really give much for his chances anyway. I can't even give him anything for the pain yet because his body won't stand two doses and I'll have to give him something just before I amputate. Even then, the shock could kill him outright. Having to move him straight afterwards makes it even worse.'

I shrugged. I didn't even like to think about it.

'You do know exactly what has to be done?' the doctor asked, studying my face carefully.

'Mr Gregory explained everything,' I said, trying to sound confident. In fact, if he'd explained it once, the Spook had explained it a dozen times. Then he'd made me recite it back to him over and over again until he was satisfied.

'About fifteen years ago we dealt with a similar case,' the doctor said. 'We did what we could but the man died anyway and he was a young farmer, fit as a butcher's dog and in the prime of life. Let's just cross our fingers. Sometimes the old ones are a lot tougher than you think.'

There was a long silence then, which I broke by checking something I'd been worrying about.

'So you know that I'll need some of his blood.'

'Don't tell your grandfather how to suck eggs,' the doctor growled, then he gave me a tired smile and pointed down the lane towards Horshaw. 'The mason's on his way so you'd better get off and do your job. You can leave the rest to me.'

I listened and heard the distant sound of a cart approaching, so I headed back through the gravestones to see how the riggers were getting on.

The pit was ready and they'd already assembled the wooden platform under the tree. The rigger's mate had climbed up into the tree and was fixing the block and tackle onto a sturdy branch. It was a device the size of a man's head, made out of iron and hanging with chains and a big hook. We would need it to support the weight of the stone and position it very precisely.

'The mason's here,' I said.

Immediately, both men left what they were doing and followed me back towards the church.

Now another horse was waiting in the lane, the stone resting in the back of the cart. No problems so far, but the mason didn't look too happy and he avoided my eyes. Still, wasting no time, we brought the cart round the long way to the gate that led into the field.

Once close to the tree, the mason slipped the hook into the ring in the centre of the stone and it was lifted off the cart. Whether or not it would fit precisely, we'd have to wait and see. The mason had certainly fitted the ring correctly because the stone hung horizontally from the chain in perfect balance.

It was lowered into a position about two paces from the edge of the pit. Then the mason gave me the bad news.

His youngest daughter was very ill with a fever, the one that had swept right through the County, confining the Spook to his bed. His wife was by her bedside and he had to get back right away.

'I'm sorry,' he said, meeting my eyes properly for the first time. 'But the stone's a good 'un and you'll have no problems. I can promise you that.'

I believed him. He'd done his best and had worked on the stone at short notice, when he'd rather have been with his daughter. So I paid him and sent him on his way with the Spook's thanks, my thanks and best wishes for the recovery of his daughter.

Then I turned back to the business in hand. As well as chiselling stone, masons are experts at positioning it so I'd rather he'd stayed in case anything went wrong. Still, the rigger and mate were good at their job. All I had to do was keep calm and be careful not to make any silly mistakes.

First I had to work fast and coat the sides of the pit with the glue; then, finally, the underside of the stone, just before it was lowered into position.

I climbed down into the pit and, using a brush and working by the light of a lantern held by the rigger's mate, I got to work. It was a careful process. I couldn't afford to miss the tiniest spot because that would be enough to let the boggart escape. And with the pit only being six feet deep rather than the regulation nine, I had to be extra careful.

The mixture keyed itself into the soil as I worked, which was good, because it wouldn't easily crack and flake off as the soil dried out in summer. The bad thing was that it was difficult to judge just how much to apply so that a thick enough outer coat was left on the soil. The Spook had told me that it was something that would come with experience. Up to now he'd been there to check my work and add a few finishing touches. Now, I would have to do the job right myself. First time.

Finally I climbed out of the pit and attended to its upper edge. The top thirteen inches, the thickness of the stone, were longer and broader than the pit itself, so there was a ledge for the stone to rest on without leaving the slightest crack for the boggart to slip through. This needed very careful attention because it was where the stone made its seal with the ground.

As I finished there was a flash of lightning and, seconds later, a heavy rumble of thunder. The storm had moved almost directly overhead.

I went back to the barn to get something important from my bag. It was what the Spook called a 'bait-dish'. Made out of metal, it was specially crafted for the job and had three small holes drilled at equal distances from each other, close to its rim. I eased it out, polished it on my sleeve, then ran to the church to tell the doctor that we were ready.

As I opened the door there was a strong smell of tar and, just left of the altar, a small fire was blazing. Over it, on a metal tripod, a pot bubbled and spat. Dr Sherdley was going to use the tar to stop the bleeding. Painting the stump with it would also prevent the rest of the leg from going bad afterwards.

I smiled to myself when I saw where the doctor had got his wood from. It was wet outside, so he'd gone for the only dry kindling available. He'd chopped up one of the church pews. No doubt the priest wouldn't be too happy, but it might just save his life. In any case he was now unconscious, breathing very deeply, and would stay that way for several hours until the effects of the potion wore off.

From the crack in the floor came the noise of the boggart feeding. It was a nasty gulping, slurping sound as it continued to draw blood from the leg. It was too preoccupied to realize that we were close by and about to bring its meal to an end.

We didn't speak. I just nodded at the doctor and he nodded back. I handed him the deep metal dish to catch the blood I needed, and he took a small metal saw from his bag and laid its cold, shiny teeth against the bone just below the priest's knee.

The housekeeper was still in the same position but her eyes were squeezed tight shut and she was muttering to herself. She was probably praying and it was obvious she wouldn't be much help. So, with a shiver, I knelt down beside the doctor.

He shook his head. 'There's no need for you to see this,' he said. 'No doubt you'll witness worse one day but it needn't be now. Go on, lad. Back to your own business. I can deal with this. Just send the other two back to give me a hand getting him up onto the cart when I've finished.'

I'd been gritting my teeth ready to face it but I didn't need to be told twice. Full of relief, I went back to the pit. Even before I reached it, a loud scream cut through the air followed by the sound of anguished weeping. But it wasn't the priest. He was unconscious. It was the housekeeper.

The rigger and his mate had already hoisted the stone aloft again and were busy wiping off the mud. Then, as they went back to the church to help the doctor, I dipped the brush into the last of the mixture and gave the underside of the stone a thorough coating.

I'd hardly time to admire my handiwork before the mate came back at a run. Behind him, moving much more slowly, came the rigger. He was carrying the dish with the blood in it, being careful not to spill a single drop. The bait-dish was a very important piece of equipment. The Spook had a store of them back in Chipenden and they'd been made according to his own specifications.

I lifted a long chain from the Spook's bag. Fastened to a large ring at one end were three shorter chains, each ending in a small metal hook. I slipped the three hooks into the three holes close to the rim of the dish.

When I lifted the chain, the bait-dish hung below it in perfect balance, so it didn't need that much skill to lower it into the pit and set it down very gently at its centre.

No, the skill was in freeing the three hooks. You had to be very careful to relax the chains so that the hooks dropped away from the dish without tipping it over and spilling the blood.

I'd spent hours practising this, and despite being very nervous I managed to get the hooks out at my very first attempt.

Now it was just a question of waiting.

* * *

As I said, rippers are some of the most dangerous boggarts of all because they feed on blood. Their minds are usually quick and very crafty, but while they're feeding they think very slowly and it takes them a long time to work things out.

The amputated leg was still jammed into the crack in the church floor and the boggart was busily slurping blood from it, but sucking very slowly so as to make it last. That's the way with a ripper. It just slurps and sucks, thinking of nothing else until it slowly realizes that less and less blood is reaching its mouth. It wants more blood, but blood comes in lots of different flavours and it likes the taste of what it's been sucking. It likes it very much.

So it wants more of the same, and once it works out that the rest of the body has been separated from the leg, it goes after it. That's why the riggers had to lift the priest up onto the cart. By now the cart would have reached the edge of Horshaw, every *clip-clop* of the horse's hooves taking it further from the angry boggart, desperate for more of that same blood.

A ripper's like a bloodhound. It would have a good idea of the direction in which the priest was being taken. It would also realize that he was getting further and further away. Then it would be aware of something else. That more of what it needed was very close by.

That's why I'd put the dish into the pit. That was why it was called a 'bait-dish'. It was the snare to lure the ripper into the trap. Once it was in there, feeding, we had to work fast and we couldn't afford to make a single mistake.

I looked up. The mate was standing on the platform, one hand on the short chain, ready to start lowering the stone. The rigger was standing opposite me, his hand on the stone, ready to position it as it came down. Neither of them looked in the least bit afraid, not even nervous, and suddenly it felt good to be working with people like that. People who knew what they were doing. We'd all played our part, all done what had to be done as quickly and efficiently as possible. It made me feel good. It made me feel a part of something.

Quietly we waited for the boggart.

After a few minutes I heard it coming. At first it sounded just like the wind whistling through the trees.

But there was no wind. The air was perfectly still and, in a narrow band of starlight between the edge of the thundercloud and the horizon, the crescent moon was visible, adding its pale light to that cast by the lanterns.

The rigger and his mate could hear nothing, of course, because they weren't seventh sons of seventh sons like me. So I had to warn them.

'It's on its way,' I said. 'I'll tell you when.'

By now the sound of its approach had become more shrill, almost like a scream, and I could hear something else too: a sort of low, rumbling growl. It was coming across the graveyard fast, heading straight for the dish of blood inside the pit.

Unlike a normal boggart, a ripper is slightly more than a spirit, especially when it's just been feeding. Even then, most people can't see it but they can feel it all right, if it ever gets a grip on their flesh.

Even I didn't see much – just something shapeless and a sort of pinky red. Then I felt a movement of the air close to my face and the ripper went down into the pit.

I said 'When' to the rigger who, in turn, nodded to his mate, who tightened his grip upon the short chain. Even before he pulled it there came a sound from the pit. This time it was loud and all three of us heard it. I glanced quickly at my companions and saw their eyes widen and mouths tighten with the fear of what was below us.

The sound we heard was the boggart feeding from the dish. It was like the greedy lapping of some monstrous tongue, combined with the ravenous snuffling and snorting of a big carnivorous animal. We had less than a minute or so before it finished it all. Then it would sense our blood. It was rogue now and we were all on the menu.

The mate began to loosen the chain and the stone came down steadily. I was adjusting one end, the rigger the other. If they'd dug the pit accurately and the stone was exactly the size specified on the sketch, there should be no problem. That's what I told myself – but I kept thinking of the Spook's last apprentice, poor Billy Bradley, who'd died trying to bind a boggart like this. The stone had jammed, trapping his fingers under its edge. Before they could lift it free, the boggart had bitten his fingers off and sucked his blood. Later he'd died of shock. I couldn't get him out of my mind no matter how hard I tried.

The important thing was to get the stone into the pit first time – and, of course, to keep my fingers out of the way.

The rigger was in control, doing the job of the mason. At his signal, the chain halted when the stone was just a fraction of an inch clear. He looked at me then, his face very stern, and raised his right eyebrow. I looked down and moved my end of the stone very slightly so that it seemed to be in perfect position. I checked again just to make sure, then nodded to the rigger, who signalled to his mate.

A few turns of the short chain and the stone eased down into position first time, sealing the boggart into the pit. A scream of anger came from the ripper and we all heard it. But it didn't matter because it was trapped now and there was nothing more to be scared of.

'Job's a good 'un!' shouted the mate, jumping down from the platform, a grin splitting his face from ear to ear. 'It's a perfect fit!'

'Aye,' said the rigger, joking drily, 'It could've been made for the job.'

I felt a huge sense of relief, glad that it was all over. Then, as the thunder crashed and the lightning flashed directly overhead to illuminate the stone, I noticed, for the first time, what the mason had carved there and suddenly felt very proud.

Ward

The large Greek letter beta, crossed with a diagonal line, was the sign that a boggart had been laid under it. Below it, to the right, the Roman numeral for one meant that it was a dangerous boggart of the first rank. There were ten ranks in all and those from one to four could kill. Then, underneath, was my own name, *Ward*, which gave me the credit for what had been done.

I'd just bound my first boggart. And it was a ripper at that!

CHAPTER 2
THE SPOOK'S PAST

Two days later, back at Chipenden, the Spook made me tell him everything that had happened. When I'd finished, he made me repeat it. That done, he scratched at his beard and gave a great big sigh.

'What did the doctor say about that daft brother of mine?' the Spook asked. 'Does he expect him to recover?'

'He said he seemed to be over the worst but it was too early to tell.'

The Spook nodded thoughtfully. 'Well, lad, you've done well,' he said. 'I can't think of one thing you could have done better. So you can have the rest of the day off. But don't let it go to your head. Tomorrow it's business as usual. After all that excitement you need to get back into a steady routine.'

The following day he worked me twice as hard as usual. Lessons began soon after dawn and included what he called 'practicals'. Even though I'd now bound a boggart for real, that meant practising digging pits.

'Do I really have to dig another boggart pit?' I asked wearily.

The Spook gave me a withering look until I dropped my eyes, feeling very uncomfortable.

'Think you're above all that now, lad?' he asked. 'Well, you're not, so don't get complacent! You've still a lot to learn. You may have bound your first boggart but you'd good men helping. One day you might have to dig the pit yourself and do it fast in order to save a life.'

After digging the pit and coating it with salt and iron, I had to practise getting the bait-dish down into the pit without spilling a single drop of blood. Of course, because it was only part of my training, we used water rather than blood but the Spook took it very seriously and usually got annoyed if I didn't manage to do it first time. But on this occasion he didn't get the chance. I'd managed it at Horshaw and I was just as good in practice, succeeding ten times in a row. Despite that, the Spook didn't give me one word of praise and I was starting to feel a bit annoyed.

Next came one practical I really enjoyed – using the Spook's silver chain. There was a six-foot post set up in the western garden and the idea was to cast the chain over it. The Spook made me stand at various distances from it and practise for over an hour at a time, keeping in mind that at some point it might be a real witch I'd be facing, and if I missed, I wouldn't get another chance. There was a special way to use the chain. You coiled it over your left hand and cast it with a flick of your wrist so that it spun widdershins, falling in a left-handed spiral to enclose the post and tighten against it. From a distance of eight feet I could now get the chain over the post nine times out of ten but, as usual, the Spook was grudging with his praise.

'Not bad, I suppose,' he said. 'But don't get smug,

lad. A real witch won't oblige you by standing still while you throw that chain. By the end of the year I'll expect ten out of ten and nothing less!'

I felt more than a bit annoyed at that. I'd been working hard and had improved a lot. Not only that, I'd just bound my first boggart and done it without any help from the Spook. It made me wonder if he'd done any better during his own apprenticeship!

In the afternoon the Spook allowed me into his library to work by myself, reading and making notes, but he only let me read certain books. He was very strict about that. I was still in my first year, so boggarts were my main area of study. But sometimes, when he was off doing something else, I couldn't help having a glance at some of his other books too.

So, after reading my fill of boggarts, I went to the three long shelves near the window and chose one of the large leather-bound notebooks from the very top shelf. They were diaries, some of them written by spooks hundreds of years ago. Each one covered a period of about five years.

This time I knew exactly what I was looking for. I chose one of the Spook's earliest diaries, curious to see how he'd coped with the job as a young man and whether he'd shaped up better than me. Of course, he'd been a priest before training to be a spook so he'd have been really old for an apprentice.

Anyway, I picked a few pages at random and started to read. I recognized his handwriting, of course, but a stranger reading an extract for the first time wouldn't have guessed the Spook had written it. When he talks, his voice is typical County, down to earth and without a hint of what my dad calls 'airs and graces'. When he writes it's different. It's as if all those books he's read have altered his voice, whereas I mostly write the way I talk: if my dad were ever to read my notes he'd be proud of me and know I was still his son.

At first what I read didn't seem any different from the Spook's more recent writings, apart from the fact that he made more mistakes. As usual he was very honest, and each time explained just how he'd gone wrong. As he was always telling me, it was important to write everything down and so learn from the past.

He described how, one week, he'd spent hours and hours practising with the bait-dish and his master had got angry because he couldn't manage a better average than eight out of ten! That made me feel a lot better. And then I came to something that lifted my spirits even further. The Spook hadn't bound his first boggart until he'd been an apprentice for almost eighteen months. What's more, it had only been a hairy boggart, not a dangerous ripper!

That was the best I could find to cheer me up: clearly the Spook had been a good, hard-working apprentice. A lot of what I found was routine so I skipped through the pages quickly until I reached the point when my master became a spook, working on his own. I'd seen all I really needed to see and was just about to close the book when something caught my eye. I flipped back to the start of the entry just to make sure, and this is what I read. It's not exactly word for word but I have a good memory and it's pretty close. And after reading what he'd written, I certainly wasn't going to forget it.

Late in the autumn I journeyed far to the north of the County, summoned there to deal with an abhuman, a creature who had brought terror to the district for far too long. Many families in the locality had suffered at its cruel hands and there had been many deaths and maimings.

I came down into the forest at dusk. All the leaves had fallen and were rotten and brown on the ground, and the tower was like a black demon finger pointing at the sky. A girl had been seen waving from its solitary window, beckoning frantically for aid. The creature had seized her for its own and now held her as its plaything, imprisoning her within those dank stone walls.

Firstly I made a fire and sat gazing into its flames while gathering my courage. Taking the whetstone from my bag, I sharpened my blade until my fingers could not touch its edge without yielding blood. Finally, at midnight, I went to the tower and hammered out a challenge upon the door with my staff.

The creature came forth brandishing a great club and roared out in anger. It was a foul thing dressed in the skins of animals, reeking of blood and animal fat, and it attacked me with terrible fury.

At first I retreated, waiting my chance, but the next time it hurled itself at me I released the blade from its recess in my staff and, using all my strength, drove it deep into its head. It fell stone-dead at my feet but I had no regrets at taking its life, for it would have killed again and again and would never have been sated.

It was then that the girl called out to me, her siren voice luring me up the stone steps. There, in the topmost room of the tower, I found her upon a bed of straw, bound fast with a long silver chain. With skin like milk and long fair hair, she was by far the prettiest woman that my eyes had ever seen. Her name was Meg and she pleaded to be released from the chain and her voice was so persuasive that my reason fled and the world spun about me.

No sooner had I unbound her from the coils of the chain than she fastened her lips hard upon mine own. And so sweet were her kisses that I almost swooned away in her arms.

I awoke with sunlight streaming through the window and saw her clearly for the first time. She was one of the lamia witches, and the mark of the snake was upon her. Fair of face though she was, her spine was covered with green and yellow scales.

Full of anger at her deceit, I bound her again with the chain, and carried her at last to the pit at Chipenden. When I released her, she struggled so hard that I barely overcame her and I was forced to pull her by her long hair through the trees, while she ranted and screamed fit to wake the dead. It was raining hard and she slipped on the wet grass but I carried on dragging her along the ground, though her bare arms and legs were scratched by brambles. It was cruel but it had to be done.

But when I started to tip her over the edge into the pit, she clutched at my knees and began to sob pitifully. I stood there for a long time, full of anguish, about to topple over the edge myself, until at last I made a decision that I may come to regret.

I helped her to her feet and wrapped my arms about her and we both wept. How could I put her into the pit, when I realized that I loved her better than my own soul?

I begged her forgiveness and then we turned together and, hand in hand, walked away from the pit.

From this encounter I have gained a silver chain, an expensive tool which otherwise would have taken many long months of hard work to acquire. What I have lost, or might yet lose, I dare not think about. Beauty is a terrible thing; it binds a man tighter than a silver chain about a witch.

I couldn't believe what I'd just read! The Spook had warned me about pretty women more than once, but here he'd broken his own rule! Meg was a witch and yet he hadn't put her into the pit!

I quickly leafed through the rest of the notebook, expecting to find another reference to her, but there was nothing – nothing at all! It was as if she'd ceased to exist.

I knew quite a bit about witches, but had never heard of a lamia witch before so I put the notebook back and searched the next shelf down, where the books were arranged in alphabetical order. I opened the book labelled *Witches* but there was no reference to a Meg. Why hadn't the Spook written about her? What had happened to her? Was she still alive? Still out there, somewhere in the County?

I was really curious and I had another idea; I pulled a big book out from the lowest shelf. This was entitled *The Bestiary* and was an alphabetical listing of all sorts of creatures, witches included. At last I found the entry I wanted: *Lamia witches*.

It seemed that lamia witches weren't native to the County but came from lands across the sea. They shunned sunlight, but at night they preyed upon men and drank their blood. They were shape-shifters and belonged to two different categories: the feral and the domestic.

The feral were lamia witches in their natural state, dangerous and unpredictable and with little physical resemblance to humans. All had scales rather than skin and claws rather than fingernails. Some scuttled across the ground on all fours, while others had wings and

43

feathers on their upper bodies and could fly short distances.

But a feral lamia could become a domestic lamia by closely associating with humans. Very gradually, it took a woman's form and looked human but for a narrow line of green and yellow scales that could still be found on its back, running the length of its spine. Domestic lamias had even been known to grow to share human beliefs. Often they ceased to be malevolent and became benign, working for the good of others.

So had Meg eventually become benign? Had the Spook been right not to bind her in the pit?

Suddenly I realized how late it was and I ran out of the library to my lesson, my head whirling. A few minutes later my master and I were out on the edge of the western garden, under the trees with a clear view of the fells, the autumn sun dropping towards the horizon. I sat on the bench as usual, busy making notes while the Spook paced back and forth dictating. But I couldn't concentrate.

We started with a Latin lesson. I had a special notebook to write down the grammar and new vocabulary the Spook taught me. There were a lot of lists and the book was almost full.

I wanted to confront the Spook with what I'd just read, but how could I? I'd broken a rule myself by not keeping to the books he'd specified. I wasn't supposed to have been reading his diaries and now I wished I hadn't. If I said anything to him about it, I knew he'd be angry.

Because of what I'd read in the library, I found it harder and harder to keep my mind on what he was saying. I was hungry too and couldn't wait until it was supper time. Usually the evenings were mine and I was free to do what I wanted, but today he'd been working me very hard. Still, there was less than an hour before the sun went down and the worst of the lessons were over.

And then I heard a sound that made me groan inside.

It was a bell ringing. Not a church bell. No, this had the higher, thinner note of a much smaller bell – the one that was used by our visitors. Nobody was allowed up to the Spook's house so people had to go to the crossroads and ring the bell there to let my master know they needed help.

'Go and see to it, lad,' the Spook said, nodding in the direction of the bell. Generally we would both have gone but he was still quite weak from his illness.

I didn't rush. Once out of sight of the house and gardens, I settled down to a stroll. It was too close to dusk to do anything tonight, especially with the Spook still not properly recovered, so nothing would get done until morning anyway. I would bring back an account of the trouble and tell the Spook the details during supper. The later I got back, the less writing there'd be. I'd done enough for one day and my wrist was aching.

Overhung by willow trees, which we in the County call 'withy trees', the crossroads was a gloomy place even at noon and it always made me nervous. For one thing, you never knew who might be waiting there; for another, they almost always had bad news because that's why they came. They needed the Spook's help.

This time a lad was waiting there. He wore big miners' boots and his fingernails were dirty. Looking even more nervous than I felt, he dashed off his tale so quickly that my ears couldn't keep up and I had to ask him to repeat it. When he left, I set off back towards the house.

I didn't stroll, I ran.

The Spook was standing by the bench with his head bowed. When I approached, he looked up and his face seemed sad. Somehow I guessed that he knew what I was going to say, but I told him anyway.

'It's bad news from Horshaw,' I said, trying to catch my breath. 'I'm sorry but it's about your brother. The doctor couldn't save him. He died yesterday morning, just before dawn. The funeral's on Friday morning.'

The Spook gave a long, deep sigh and didn't speak for several minutes. I didn't know what to say so I just kept silent. It was hard to guess what he was feeling. As they hadn't spoken for over forty years, they couldn't have been that close, but the priest was still his brother and he must have had some happy memories of him – perhaps from before they'd quarrelled or when they were children.

At last the Spook sighed again and then he spoke.

'Come on, lad,' he said. 'We might as well have an early supper.'

We ate in silence. The Spook picked at his food and I wondered if that was because of the bad news about his brother or because he still hadn't got his appetite back since being ill. He usually spoke a few words, even if they were just to ask me how the meal was. It was almost a ritual because we had to keep praising the Spook's pet boggart, which prepared all the meals, or it got sulky. Praise at supper was very important or the bacon would end up burned the following morning.

'It's a really good hotpot,' I said at last. 'I can't remember when I last tasted one so good.'

The boggart was mostly invisible but sometimes took on the shape of a big ginger cat; if it was really pleased, it would rub itself against my legs under the kitchen table. This time there wasn't even so much as a faint purr. Either I hadn't sounded very convincing or it was keeping quiet because of the bad news.

The Spook suddenly pushed his plate away and scratched at his beard with his left hand. 'We're going to Priestown,' he said suddenly. 'We'll set off first thing tomorrow.'

Priestown? I couldn't believe what I was hearing. The Spook shunned the place like the plague and had once told me that he would never set foot within its boundaries. He hadn't explained the reason and I'd never asked because you could always tell when he didn't want to explain something. But when we'd been within spitting distance of the coast and needed to cross the river Ribble, the Spook's hatred of the town had been a real nuisance. Instead of using the Priestown bridge we'd had to travel miles inland to the next one so that we could steer clear of it.

'Why?' I asked, my voice hardly more than a whisper, wondering if what I was saying might make him angry. 'I thought we might be going to Horshaw, for the funeral.'

'We *are* going to the funeral, lad,' the Spook said, his voice very calm and patient. 'My daft brother only worked in Horshaw, but he was a priest: when a priest dies in the County, they take his body back to Priestown and hold a funeral service in the big cathedral there before laying his bones to rest in the churchyard.

'So we're going there to pay our last respects. But that's not the only reason. I've unfinished business in that godforsaken town. Get out your notebook, lad. Turn to a clean page and make this heading . . .'

I hadn't finished my hotpot but I did what he asked right away. When he said 'unfinished business', I knew he meant spook's business so I pulled the bottle of ink out of my pocket and placed it on the table next to my plate.

Something clicked in my head. 'Do you mean that ripper I bound? Do you think it's escaped? There just wasn't time to dig nine feet. Do you think it's gone to Priestown?'

'No, lad, you did fine. There's something far worse than that there. That town is cursed! Cursed with something that I last faced over twenty long years ago. It got the better of me then and put me in bed for almost six months. In fact I almost died. Since then I've never been back, but as we've a need to visit the place, I might as well attend to that unfinished business. No, it's not some straightforward ripper that plagues that cursed town. It's an ancient evil spirit called "the Bane" and it's the only one of its kind. It's getting stronger and stronger so something needs to be done and I can't put it off any longer.'

I wrote '*Bane*' at the top of a new page but then, to my disappointment, the Spook suddenly shook his head and followed that with a big yawn.

'Come to think of it, this'll save until tomorrow, lad. You'd better finish up your supper. We'll be making an early start in the morning so we'd best be off to bed.'

CHAPTER 3
THE BANE

We set off soon after dawn, with me carrying the Spook's heavy bag as usual. But within an hour I realized the journey would take us two days at least. Usually the Spook walked at a tremendous pace, making me struggle to keep up, but he was still weak and kept getting breathless and stopping to rest.

It was a nice sunny day with just a touch of autumn chill in the air. The sky was blue and the birds were singing but none of that mattered. I just couldn't stop thinking about the Bane.

What worried me was the fact that the Spook had already nearly been killed once trying to bind it. He was older now and if he didn't get his strength back soon, how could he possibly hope to beat it this time?

So at noon, when we stopped for a long rest, I decided to ask him all about this terrible spirit. I didn't ask him right away because, to my surprise, as we sat down together on the trunk of a fallen tree, he pulled a loaf and a big hunk of ham from his bag and cut us a very generous portion each. Usually, when on the way to a job, we made do with a measly nibble of cheese because you have to fast before facing the dark.

Still, I was hungry, so I didn't complain. I supposed that we'd have time to fast once the funeral was over and that the Spook needed food now to build up his strength again.

At last, when I'd finished eating, I took a deep breath, got out my notebook and finally asked him about the Bane. To my surprise he told me to put the book away.

'You can write this up later when we're on our way back,' he said. 'Besides, I've a lot to learn about the Bane myself so there's no point in writing down something that you might need to change later.'

I suppose my mouth dropped open at that. I mean, I'd always thought the Spook knew almost everything there was to know about the dark.

'Don't look so surprised, lad,' he said. 'As you know, I still keep a notebook myself and so will you, if you live to my age. We never stop learning in this job, and the first step towards knowledge is to accept your own ignorance.

'As I said before, the Bane is an ancient, malevolent spirit that has so far got the better of me, I'm ashamed to admit. But hopefully not this time. Our first problem will be to find it,' continued the Spook. 'It lives in the catacombs down under Priestown cathedral – there are miles and miles of tunnels.'

'What are the catacombs for?' I asked, wondering who would build so many tunnels.

'They're full of crypts, lad, underground burial chambers that hold ancient bones. Those tunnels existed long before the cathedral was built. The hill was already a holy site when the first priests came here in ships from the west.'

'So who built the catacombs?'

'Some call the builders the "Little People" on account of their size but their true name was the Segantii; not that much is known about them apart from the fact that the Bane was once their god.'

'It's a god?'

'Aye, it was always a powerful force, and the earliest Little People recognized its strength and worshipped it. Reckon the Bane would like to be a god again. You see, it used to roam free in the County. Over the centuries it grew corrupt and evil and terrorized the Little People night and day, turning brother against brother, destroying crops, burning homes, slaughtering innocents. It liked to see people existing in fear and poverty, beaten down until life was hardly worth living. Those were dark, terrible times for the Segantii.

'But it wasn't just the poor people it plagued. The Segantii's king was a good man called Heys. He'd defeated all his enemies in battle and tried to make his people strong and prosperous. But there was one enemy they couldn't beat: the Bane. It suddenly demanded an annual tribute from King Heys. The poor man was ordered to sacrifice his seven sons, starting with the eldest. One son each year until none remained alive. It was more than any father could bear. But somehow Naze, the very last son, managed to bind the Bane to the catacombs. I don't know how he did it – perhaps if I did it would be easier to defeat this creature. All I know is that its way was blocked by a locked silver gate: like many creatures of the dark it has a vulnerability to silver.'

'And so it's still trapped down there after all this time?'

'Yes, lad. It's bound down there until someone opens that gate and sets it free. That's fact and it's something that all the priests know. It's knowledge passed down from generation to generation.'

'But isn't there any other way out? How can the Silver Gate keep it in?' I asked.

'I don't know, lad. All I know is that the Bane is bound in the catacombs, and is only able to leave through that gate.'

I wanted to ask what was wrong with just leaving it there if it was bound and unlikely to escape, but he answered before I could voice the question. The Spook knew me well by now and was good at guessing what I was thinking.

'But we can't just leave things as they are, I'm afraid, lad. You see, it's growing stronger again now. It wasn't always just a spirit. That only happened after it was bound. Before that, when it was very powerful, it had a physical form.'

'What did it look like?' I asked.

'You'll find out tomorrow. Before you enter the cathedral for the funeral service, look up at the stone carving directly above the main doorway. It's as good a representation of the creature as you're likely to see.'

'Have you seen the real thing then?'

'Nay, lad. Twenty years ago, when I first tried to kill the Bane, it was still a spirit. But there are rumours that its strength has grown so much that it's now taking the shape of other creatures.'

'What do you mean?'

'I mean it's started shape-shifting and it won't be long before it's strong enough to take on its original true form. Then it'll be able to make almost anyone do what it wants. And the real danger is that it might force somebody to unlock the Silver Gate. That's the most worrying thing of all!'

'But where's it getting its strength from?' I wanted to know.

'Blood mainly.'

'Blood?'

'Aye. The blood of animals – and humans. It has a terrible thirst. But fortunately, unlike a ripper, it can't take the blood of a human being unless it's given freely—'

'Why would anyone want to *give* it their blood?' I asked, astonished at the very idea.

'Because it can get inside people's minds. It tempts them with money, position and power – you name it. If it can't get what it wants by persuasion, it terrorizes its victims. Sometimes it lures them down to the catacombs and threatens them with what we call "the press".'

'The press?' I asked.

'Aye, lad. It can make itself so heavy that some of its victims are found squashed flat, their bones broken and their bodies smeared into the ground – you have to scrape them up for burial. They've been "pressed" and it's not a pleasant sight. The Bane cannot rip our blood against our will, but remember we're still vulnerable to the press.'

'I don't understand how it can make people do these things when it's trapped in the catacombs,' I said.

'It can read thoughts, shape dreams, weaken and corrupt the minds of those above ground. Sometimes it even sees through their eyes. Its influence extends up into the cathedral and presbytery, and it terrorizes the priests. It's been working its mischief that way through Priestown for years.'

'With the priests?'

'Yes – especially those who are weak-minded. Whenever it can it gets them to spread its evil. My brother Andrew works as a locksmith in Priestown, and more than once he's sent warnings to me about what's happening. The Bane drains the spirit and the will. It makes people do what it wants, silencing the voices of goodness and reason: they become greedy and cruel, abuse their power, robbing the poor and sick. In Priestown tithes are now collected twice a year.'

I knew what a tithe was. A tenth of our farm's income for the year and we had to pay it as a tax to the local church. It was the law.

'Paying it once is bad enough,' the Spook continued, 'but twice and it's hard to keep the wolf from the door. Once again, it's beating the people down into fear and poverty, just as it did to the Segantii. It's one of the purest and most evil manifestations of the dark I've ever met. But the situation can't go on much longer. I've got to put a stop to it once and for all before it's too late.'

'How will we do that?' I asked.

'Well, I'm not sure I rightly know just yet. The Bane

is a dangerous and clever foe; it may be able to read our minds and know just what we're thinking before we realize it ourselves.

'But apart from silver, it does have one other serious weakness. Women make it very nervous and it tries to avoid their company. It can't abide being near them. Well, I can understand that easily enough, but how to use it to our advantage needs some thinking about.'

The Spook had often warned me to beware of girls, and for some reason, particularly those who wore pointy shoes. So I was used to him saying things like that. But now I knew about him and Meg I wondered if she'd played some part in making him talk the way he did.

Well, my master had certainly given me a lot to think about. And I couldn't help wondering about all those churches in Priestown, and the priests and congregations, all believing in God. Could they all be wrong? If their God was so powerful why didn't He do something about the Bane? Why did He allow it to corrupt the priests and spread evil out into the town?

My dad was a believer, even though he never went to church. None of our family did because farming didn't stop on Sunday and we were always too busy milking or doing other chores. But it suddenly made me wonder what the Spook believed, especially knowing what Mam had told me – that the Spook had once been a priest himself.

'Do you believe in God?' I asked him.

'I used to believe in God,' the Spook replied, his expression very thoughtful. 'When I was a child I never doubted the existence of God for a single moment, but eventually I changed. You see, lad, when you've lived as long as I have, there are things that make you wonder. So now I'm not so sure but I still keep an open mind.

'But I'll tell you this,' he went on. 'Two or three times in my life I've been in situations so bad that I never expected to walk away from them. I've faced the dark and almost, but not quite, resigned myself to death. Then, just when all's seemed lost, I've been filled with new strength. Where it came from I can only guess. But with that strength came a new feeling. That someone or something was at my side. That I was no longer alone.'

The Spook paused and sighed deeply. 'I don't believe in the God they preach about in church,' he said. 'I don't believe in an old man with a white beard. But there's something watching what we do, and if you live your life right, in your hour of need it'll stand at your side and lend you its strength. That's what I believe. Well, come on, lad. We've dawdled here long enough and had best be on our way.'

I picked up his bag and followed him. Soon we left the road and took a short cut through a wood and across a wide meadow. It was pleasant enough but we stopped long before the sun set. The Spook was too exhausted to continue and should really have been back at Chipenden, recuperating after his illness.

I had a bad feeling about what lay ahead, a strong sense of danger.

CHAPTER 4
PRIESTOWN

Priestown, built on the banks of the river Ribble, was the biggest town I'd ever visited. As we came down the hill, the river was like a huge snake gleaming orange in the light from the setting sun.

It was a town of churches, with spires and towers rising above the rows of small terraced houses. Set right on the summit of a hill, near the centre of the town, was the cathedral. Three of the largest churches I'd seen in my whole life would have easily fitted inside it. And its steeple was something else. Built from limestone, it was almost white and so high that I guessed on a rainy day the cross at its top would be hidden by clouds.

'Is that the biggest steeple in the world?' I asked, pointing in excitement.

'No, lad,' the Spook answered with a rare grin. 'But it's the biggest steeple in the County, as well it might be with a town that boasts so many priests. I only wish there were fewer of them but we'll just have to take our chance.'

Suddenly the grin faded from his face. 'Talk of the Devil!' he said, clenching his teeth before pulling me through a gap in the hedge into the adjoining field. There he placed his forefinger against his lips for silence and made me crouch down with him, while I listened to the sound of approaching footsteps.

It was a good, thick hawthorn hedge and it still had most of its leaves, but through it I could just make out a black cassock above the boots. It was a priest!

We stayed there for quite a while even after the footsteps had faded into the distance. Only then did the Spook lead us back onto the path. I couldn't work out what all the fuss was about. On our travels we'd passed lots of priests. They hadn't been

65

too friendly but we'd never tried to hide before.

'We need to be on our guard, lad,' the Spook explained. 'Priests are always trouble but they represent a real danger in this town. You see, Priestown's bishop is the uncle of the High Quisitor. No doubt you'll have heard of him.'

I nodded. 'He hunts witches, doesn't he?'

'Aye, lad, he does that. When he catches someone he considers to be a witch or warlock, he puts on his black cap and becomes the judge at their trial – a trial that's usually over very quickly. The following day he puts on a different hat. He becomes the executioner, and organizes the burning. He's a reputation for being good at that and a big crowd usually gathers to watch. They say he positions the stake carefully so that the poor wretch takes a very long time to die. The pain is supposed to make a witch sorry for what she's done, so she'll beg God's forgiveness and, as she dies, her soul will be saved. But that's just an excuse. The Quisitor lacks the knowledge a spook has and wouldn't know a real witch if she reached up from her grave and grabbed his ankle! No, he's just a cruel man who likes to inflict pain. He enjoys his work and he's grown rich from the money he makes selling the homes and property of those he condemns.

'Aye, and that brings me to the problem for us. You see, the Quisitor counts a spook as a warlock. The Church doesn't like anyone to meddle with the dark, even if they're fighting it. They think only priests should be allowed to do that. The Quisitor has the power of arrest, with armed churchwardens to do his bidding – but cheer up, lad, because that's just the bad news.

'The good news is that the Quisitor lives in a big city way to the south, far beyond the boundaries of the County, and rarely comes north. So if we're spotted and he's summoned, it would take him more than a week to arrive, even on horseback. Also my arrival here should be a surprise. The last thing anyone will expect is that I'll be attending the funeral of a brother I haven't spoken to in forty years.'

But his words were of little comfort. As we moved off down the hill, I shivered at what he'd said. Entering the town seemed full of risks. With his cloak and staff he was unmistakably a spook. I was just about to say as much when he gestured left with his thumb and we walked off the road into a small wood. After about thirty paces or so my master came to a halt.

'Right, lad,' he said. 'Take off your cloak and give it to me.'

I didn't argue; from the tone of his voice I realized that he meant business, but I did wonder what he was up to. He took off his own cloak with its attached hood and laid his staff on the ground.

'Right,' he said. 'Now find me some thin branches and twigs. Nothing too heavy, mind.'

A few minutes later I'd done as he asked and I watched him place his staff amongst the branches and wrap the whole lot up with our cloaks. Of course, by then I'd already guessed what he was up to. Sticks were poking out of each end of the bundle and it just looked like we'd been out gathering firewood. It was a disguise.

'There are lots of small inns close to the cathedral,'

he said, tossing me a silver coin. 'It'll be safer for you if we don't stay at the same one, because if they came for me, they'd arrest you too. Best if you don't know where I am either, lad. The Quisitor uses torture. Capture one of us and he'd soon have the other. I'll set off first. Give me ten minutes, then follow.

'Choose any inn that hasn't got anything to do with churches in its title, so we don't end up in the same one by accident. Don't have any supper either because we'll be working tomorrow. The funeral's at nine in the morning but try to be early and sit near the back of the cathedral; if I'm there already, keep your distance.'

'Working' meant spook's business and I wondered if we'd be going down into the catacombs to face the Bane. I didn't like the idea of that one little bit.

'Oh, and one more thing,' the Spook added as he turned to go. 'You'll be looking after my bag, so what should you remember when carrying it in a place like Priestown?'

'To carry it in my right hand,' I said.

He nodded in agreement, then lifted the bundle up

onto his right shoulder and left me waiting in the wood.

We were both left-handed, something that priests didn't approve of. Left-handers were what they called 'sinister', those most easily tempted by the Devil or even in league with him.

I gave him ten minutes or more, just to be sure there was enough distance between us, then, carrying his heavy bag, I set off down the hill, heading for the steeple. Once in the town I started to climb again towards the cathedral, and when I got close, I began my search for an inn.

There were plenty of them all right; most of the cobbled streets seemed to have one, but the trouble was that all of them seemed to be linked to churches in some way or other. There was the Bishop's Crook, the Steeple Inn, the Jolly Friar, the Mitre and the Book and Candle, to name but a few. The last one reminded me of the reason we'd come to Priestown in the first place. As the Spook's brother had found to his cost, books and candles didn't usually work against the dark. Not even when you used a bell as well.

I soon realized that the Spook had made it easy for himself but very difficult for me, and I spent a long time searching Priestown's maze of narrow streets and the wider roads that linked them. I walked along Fylde Road and then up a wide street called Friargate, where there was no sign of a gate at all. The cobbled streets were full of people and most of them seemed to be in a rush. The big market near the top of Friargate was closing for the day, but a few customers still jostled and haggled with traders for good prices. The smell of fish was overpowering and a big flock of hungry seagulls squawked overhead.

Every so often I saw a figure dressed in a black cassock and I would change direction or cross the road. I found it hard to believe that one town could have so many priests.

Next I walked down Fishergate Hill until I could see the river in the distance, and then all the way back again. Finally I came round in a circle, but without any success. I couldn't just ask somebody to direct me to an inn whose name had nothing to do with churches because they'd have thought me mad. Drawing attention to myself was the last thing I wanted. Even though I was carrying the Spook's heavy black leather bag in my right hand, it still attracted too many curious glances my way.

At last, just as it was getting dark, I found somewhere to stay not too far from the cathedral where I'd first begun my search. It was a small inn called the Black Bull.

Before becoming the Spook's apprentice I'd never stayed at an inn, never having any cause to wander far from my dad's farm. Since then I'd spent the night in maybe half a dozen. It should have been a lot more, for we were often on the road, sometimes for several days at a time, but the Spook liked to save his money, and unless the weather was really bad he thought a tree or an old barn good enough shelter for the night. Still, this was the first inn I'd ever stayed in alone, and as I pushed my way in through the door, I felt a little nervous.

The narrow entrance opened out into a large gloomy

room, lit only by a single lantern. It was full of empty tables and chairs, with a wooden counter at the far end. The counter smelled strongly of vinegar but I soon realized it was just stale ale that had soaked into the wood. There was a small bell hanging from a rope to the right of the counter, so I rang it.

Presently a door behind the counter opened and a bald man came out, wiping his big hands on a large dirty apron.

'I'd like a room for the night, please,' I said, adding quickly, 'I might be staying longer.'

He looked at me as if I were something he'd just found on the bottom of his shoe, but when I pulled out the silver coin and put it on the counter, his expression became a lot more pleasant.

'Will you be wanting supper, master?' he asked.

I shook my head. I was fasting anyway, but one glance at his stained apron had made me lose my appetite.

Five minutes later I was up in my room with the door locked. The bed looked a mess and the sheets were dirty. I knew the Spook would have complained but I just wanted to sleep and it was still a lot better than a draughty barn. However, when I looked through the window, I felt homesick for Chipenden.

Instead of the white path leading across the green lawn to the western garden and my usual view of Parlick Pike and the other fells, all I could see was a row of grimy houses opposite, each with a chimneypot sending dark smoke billowing down into the street.

So I lay on top of the bed and, still gripping the handles of the Spook's bag, quickly fell asleep.

Just after eight the next morning I was heading for the cathedral. I'd left the bag locked inside my room because it would have looked odd carrying it into a funeral service. I was a bit anxious about leaving it at the inn but the bag had a lock and so did the door and both keys were safely in my pocket. I also carried a third key.

The Spook had given it to me when I went to Horshaw to deal with the ripper. It had been made by his other brother, Andrew the locksmith, and it opened most locks as long as they weren't too complex. I should have given it back but I knew the Spook had more than one, and as he hadn't asked, I'd kept it. It was very useful to have, just like the small tinderbox my dad gave me when I started my apprenticeship. I always kept that in my pocket too. It had belonged to his dad and was a family heirloom but a very useful one for someone who followed the Spook's trade.

Before long I was climbing the hill, with the steeple to my left. It was a wet morning, a heavy drizzle falling straight into my face, and I'd been right about the steeple. At least the top third of it was hidden by the dark grey clouds that were racing in from the south-west. There was a bad smell of sewers in the air too, and every house had a smoking chimney, most of the smoke finding its way down to street level.

A lot of people seemed to be rushing up the hill. One woman went by almost running, dragging two children faster than their little legs could manage. 'Come on! Hurry up!' she scolded. 'We're going to miss it.'

For a moment I wondered if they were going to the funeral too but it seemed unlikely because their faces were filled with excitement. Right at the top the hill flattened out and I turned left towards the cathedral. Here an excited crowd was eagerly lining both sides of the road, as if waiting for something. They were blocking the pavement and I tried to ease my way through as carefully as possible. I kept apologizing, desperate to avoid stepping on anyone's toes, but eventually the people became so thickly packed that I had to come to a halt and wait with them.

I didn't wait long. Sounds of applause and cheers had suddenly erupted to my right. Above them I heard the *clip-clop* of approaching hooves. A large procession was moving towards the cathedral, the first two riders dressed in black hats and cloaks and wearing swords at their hips. Behind them came more riders, these armed with daggers and huge cudgels, ten, twenty, fifty, until eventually one man appeared riding alone on a gigantic white stallion.

He wore a black cloak, but underneath it expensive

chain mail was visible at neck and wrists and the sword at his hip had a hilt encrusted with rubies. His boots were of the very finest leather and probably worth more than a farm labourer earned in a year.

The rider's clothes and bearing marked him out as a leader, but even if he'd been dressed in rags, there would have been no doubt about it. He had very blond hair, tumbling from beneath a wide-brimmed red hat, and eyes so blue they put a summer's sky to shame. I was fascinated by his face. It was almost too handsome to be a man's, but it was strong at the same time, with a jutting chin and a determined forehead. Then I looked again at the blue eyes and saw the cruelty glaring from them.

He reminded me of a knight I'd once seen ride past our farm, when I was a young lad. He hadn't so much as glanced our way. To him we didn't exist. Well, that's what my dad said anyway. Dad also said that the man was noble, that he could tell by looking at him that he came from a family that could trace its ancestors back for generations, all of them rich and powerful.

At the word 'noble' my dad spat into the mud and told me that I was lucky to be a farmer's lad with an honest day's work in front of me.

This man riding through Priestown was also clearly noble and had arrogance and authority written all over his face. To my shock and dismay I realized that I must be looking at the Quisitor, for behind him was a big open cart pulled by two shire horses and there were people standing in the back bound together with chains.

Mostly they were women but there were a couple of men too. The majority of them looked as if they hadn't eaten properly for a long time. They wore filthy clothes and many had clearly been beaten. All were covered in bruises and one woman had a left eye that looked like a rotten tomato. Some of the women were wailing hopelessly, tears running down their cheeks. One screeched again and again at the top of her voice that she was innocent. But to no avail. They were all captives, soon to be tried and burned.

A young woman suddenly darted towards the cart,

reaching up towards one of the male prisoners and trying desperately to pass him an apple. Perhaps she was a relative of the prisoner – maybe a daughter.

To my horror, the Quisitor simply turned his horse and rode her down. One moment she was holding out the apple; the next she was on her side on the cobbles howling in pain. I saw the cruel expression on his face. He'd enjoyed hurting her. As the cart trundled past, followed by an escort of even more armed riders, the crowd's cheers turned to howls of abuse and cries of 'Burn them all!'

It was then that I saw the girl chained amongst the other prisoners. She was no older than me and her eyes were wide and frightened. Her black hair was streaked across her forehead with the rain, which was dribbling from her nose and the end of her chin like tears. I looked at the black dress she was wearing, then glanced down at her pointy shoes, hardly able to believe what I was seeing.

It was Alice. And she was a prisoner of the Quisitor.

CHAPTER 5
THE FUNERAL

My head was whirling with what I'd witnessed. It was several months since I'd last seen Alice. Her aunt, Bony Lizzie, was a witch the Spook and I had dealt with, but Alice, unlike the rest of her family, wasn't really bad. In fact she was probably the closest I'd ever come to having a friend, and it was thanks to her that a few months back I'd managed to destroy Mother Malkin – the most evil witch in the County.

No, Alice had just been brought up in bad company. I couldn't let her be burned as a witch. Somehow I had to find a way to rescue her, but at that moment I didn't have the slightest clue how it could be done. I decided that as soon as the funeral was over, I'd have to try and persuade the Spook to help.

And then there was the Quisitor. What terrible timing that our visit to Priestown should coincide with his arrival. The Spook and I were in grave danger. Surely now my master wouldn't stay here after the funeral. A huge part of me hoped he'd want to leave right away and not face the Bane. But I couldn't leave Alice behind to die.

When the cart had gone by, the crowd surged forward and began to follow the Quisitor's procession. Jammed in shoulder to shoulder, I'd little choice but to move with them. The cart continued past the cathedral and halted outside a big three-storey house with mullioned windows. I assumed that it was the presbytery – the priests' house – and that the prisoners were about to be tried there. They were taken down from the cart and dragged inside but I was too far away to see Alice properly. There was nothing I could do but I'd have to think of something quickly before the burning, which was bound to take place soon.

Sadly, I turned away and pushed through the crowd until I reached the cathedral and Father Gregory's funeral. The building had big buttresses and tall, pointy stained-glass windows. Then, remembering what the Spook had told me, I glanced upwards at the large stone gargoyle above the main door.

This was a representation of the original form of the Bane, the shape it was slowly trying to return to as it grew stronger down there in the catacombs. The body, covered in scales, was crouching with tense, knotted muscles, long sharp talons gripping the stone lintel. It looked ready to leap down.

I've seen some terrifying things in my time but I'd never seen anything uglier than that huge head. It had an elongated chin that curved upwards almost as far as its long nose, and wicked eyes that seemed to follow me as I walked towards it. Its ears were strange too, and wouldn't have been out of place on a big dog or even a wolf. Not something to face in the darkness of the catacombs!

Before I went in, I glanced back desperately towards

the presbytery once more, wondering if there was any real hope of rescuing Alice.

The cathedral was almost empty so I found a place near the back. Close by, a couple of old ladies were kneeling in prayer with bowed heads, and an altar boy was busy lighting candles.

I had plenty of time to look around. The cathedral seemed even bigger on the inside, with a high roof and huge wooden beams; even the slightest cough seemed to echo for ever. There were three aisles – the middle one, which led right up to the altar steps, was wide enough to take a horse and cart. This place was grand all right: every statue in sight was gilded and even the walls were covered in marble. It was worlds away from the little church in Horshaw where the Spook's brother had gone about his business.

At the front of the central aisle stood Father Gregory's open coffin, with a candle at each corner. I'd never seen such candles in my life. Each one, set in a big brass candlestick, was taller than a man.

People had started to drift into the church. They

entered in ones and twos and, like me, selected pews close to the back. I kept looking for the Spook but there was no sign of him yet.

I couldn't help glancing around for evidence of the Bane. I certainly didn't feel its presence, but perhaps a creature so powerful would be able to feel mine. What if the rumours were true? What if it did have the strength to take on a physical form and was sitting here in the congregation! I looked about nervously but then relaxed when I remembered what the Spook had told me. The Bane was bound to the catacombs far below, so for now, surely, I was safe.

Or was I? Its mind was very strong, my master had said, and it could reach up into the presbytery or the cathedral to influence and corrupt the priests. Maybe at this very moment it was trying to get inside my head!

I looked up, horrified, and caught the eye of a woman returning to her seat after paying her last respects to Father Gregory. I recognized her instantly as his weeping housekeeper and she knew me in the same moment. She stopped at the end of my pew.

'Why were you so late?' she demanded in a raised whisper. 'If you'd come when I first sent for you he'd still be alive today.'

'I did my best,' I said, trying not to attract too much attention to us.

'Sometimes your best ain't good enough then, is it?' she said. 'The Quisitor's right about your lot, you're nowt but trouble and deserve all that's coming to you.'

At the Quisitor's name I started but lots of people had begun to stream in, all of them wearing black cassocks and coats. Priests – dozens of them! I'd never thought to see so many in one place at a time. It was as if all the clergymen in the whole world had come together for the funeral of old Father Gregory. But I knew that wasn't true and that they were only the ones who lived in Priestown – and maybe a few from the surrounding villages and towns. The housekeeper said nothing more and hurriedly returned to her pew.

Now I was really afraid. Here I was, sitting in the cathedral, just above the catacombs that were home to the most fearsome creature in the County, at a time when the Quisitor was visiting – and I'd been recognized. I desperately wanted to get as far from that place as possible and looked anxiously around for any sign of my master, but I couldn't see him. I was just deciding that I should probably leave, when suddenly the big doors of the church were flung back wide and a long procession entered. There was no escape.

At first I thought the man at the head was the Quisitor for he had similar features. But he was older and I remembered the Spook saying that the Quisitor had an uncle who was the bishop of Priestown; I realized it must be him.

The ceremony began. There was a lot of singing and we stood up, sat down and knelt endlessly. No sooner had we settled in one position than we had to move again. Now if the funeral service had been in Greek I might have understood a bit more of what was going on because my mam taught me that language when I was little. But most of Father Gregory's funeral was in Latin. I could follow some of it but it made me realize I'd have to work a lot harder at my lessons.

The bishop spoke of Father Gregory being in Heaven, saying that he deserved to be there after all the good work he'd done. I was a little surprised that he made no mention of how Father Gregory had died, but I suppose the priests wanted to keep that quiet. They were probably reluctant to admit that his exorcism had failed.

At last, after almost an hour, the funeral service was over and the procession left the church, this time with six priests carrying the coffin. The four big priests holding the candles had the harder job because they were staggering under their weight. It was only as the last one passed by, walking behind the coffin, that I noticed the triangular base of the big brass candlestick.

On each of its three faces was a vivid representation of the ugly gargoyle that I'd seen above the cathedral door. And although it was probably caused by the flickering of the flame, once again its eyes seemed to follow me as the priest carried the candle slowly by.

All the priests filed out to join the procession and

most of the people at the back followed them, but I stayed inside the church for a long time, wanting to keep clear of the housekeeper.

I was wondering what to do. I hadn't seen the Spook and I had no idea where he was staying or how I was supposed to meet up with him again. I needed to warn him about the Quisitor – and now the housekeeper.

Outside, the rain had stopped and the yard at the front of the cathedral was empty. Glancing to my right, I could just see the tail of the procession disappearing round the back of the cathedral where I supposed the graveyard must be.

I decided to go the other way, through the front gate and out into the street, but I was in for a shock. Across the road two people were having a heated conversation. More precisely, most of the heat was coming from an angry, red-faced priest with a bandaged hand. The other man was the Spook.

They both seemed to notice me at the same time. The Spook gestured with his thumb, signalling me to start walking right away. I did as I was told and my master followed me, keeping to the opposite side of the road.

The priest called out after him, 'Think on, John, before it's too late!'

I risked a glance back and saw that the priest hadn't followed us but seemed to be staring at me. It was hard to be sure, but I thought he suddenly seemed far more interested in me than in the Spook.

We walked downhill for several minutes before the ground levelled out. At first there weren't many people around but the streets soon became narrower and much busier, and after changing direction a couple of times we came to the flagged market. It was a big, bustling square, full of stalls, which were sheltered by wooden frames draped with grey waterproof awnings. I followed the Spook into the crowd, at times not far from his heels. What else could I do? It would have been easy to lose him in a place like that.

There was a large tavern at the northern edge of the market with empty benches outside and the Spook headed straight for it. At first I thought he was going in and wondered if we were going to buy lunch. If he intended to leave because of the Quisitor, there'd be no need to fast. But instead he turned into a narrow, cobbled blind alley, led me to a low stone wall and wiped the nearest section with his sleeve. When he'd got most of the beads of water off, he sat himself down and gestured that I should do the same.

I sat down and looked around. The alley was deserted and the walls of warehouses hemmed us in on three sides. There were few windows and they were cracked and smeared with grime so at least we were out of the way of prying eyes.

The Spook was out of breath with walking and this gave me a chance to get the first word in.

'The Quisitor's here,' I told him.

The Spook nodded. 'Aye, lad, he's here all right. I was standing on the opposite side of the road but you were too busy gawping at the cart to notice me.'

'But didn't you see her? Alice was in the cart—'

'Alice? Alice who?'

'Bony Lizzie's niece. We have to help her . . .'

As I mentioned before, Bony Lizzie was a witch

we'd dealt with in the spring. Now the Spook had her imprisoned in a pit, back in his garden in Chipenden.

'Oh, that Alice. Well, you'd best forget her, lad, because there's nothing to be done. The Quisitor has at least fifty armed men with him.'

'But it's not fair,' I said, hardly able to believe that he could stay so calm. 'Alice isn't a witch.'

'Little in this life is fair,' the Spook replied. 'The truth is, none of them were witches. As you well know, a real witch would have sniffed the Quisitor coming from miles away.'

'But Alice is my friend. I can't leave her to die!' I protested, feeling the anger rising inside me.

'This is no time for sentiment. Our job is to protect people from the dark, not to get distracted by pretty girls.'

I was furious – especially as I knew the Spook himself had once been distracted by a pretty girl – and that one *was* a witch. 'Alice helped save my family from Mother Malkin, remember!'

'And why was Mother Malkin free in the first place, lad, answer me that!'

I hung my head in shame.

'Because you got yourself mixed up with that girl,' he continued, 'and I don't want it happening again. Especially not here in Priestown, with the Quisitor breathing down our necks. You'll be putting your own life in danger – and mine. And keep your voice down. We don't want to attract any unwelcome attention.'

I looked about me. But for us, the alley was deserted. A few people could be seen passing the entrance but they were some distance away and didn't so much as glance in our direction. Beyond them I could see the rooftops at the far side of the market square and, rising above the chimneypots, the cathedral steeple. But when I spoke again, I did lower my voice.

'What's the Quisitor doing here anyway?' I asked. 'Didn't you say that he did his work down south and only came north when he was sent for?'

'That's mostly true but sometimes he mounts an expedition up north to the County and even beyond.

Turns out that for the last few weeks he's been sweeping the coast, picking up the poor dregs of humanity he had chained up in that cart.'

I was angry that he'd said Alice was one of the dregs because I knew it wasn't true. It wasn't the right time to continue the argument though, so I kept my peace.

'But we'll be safe enough in Chipenden,' continued the Spook. 'He's never yet ventured up towards the fells.'

'Are we going home now then?' I asked.

'No, lad, not yet. I told you before, I've got unfinished business in this town.'

My heart sank and I looked towards the alley entrance uneasily. People were still scurrying past, going about their business, and I could hear some stall-holders calling out the price of their wares. But although there was a lot of noise and bustle, we were thankfully out of sight. Despite that, I still felt uneasy. We were supposed to be keeping our distance from each other. The priest outside the cathedral had known the Spook. The housekeeper knew me. What if someone else walked down the alley and recognized us and we were both arrested? Many priests from County parishes would be in town and they'd know the Spook by sight. The only good news was that at the moment they were probably all still in the churchyard.

'That priest you were talking to before, who was he? He seemed to know you so won't he tell the Quisitor you're here?' I asked, wondering if anywhere was really safe. For all I knew that red-faced priest outside the cathedral could even direct the Quisitor to Chipenden. 'Oh, and there's something else. Your brother's housekeeper recognized me at the funeral. She was really angry. She might tell somebody that we're here.'

It seemed to me that we were taking a serious risk in staying in Priestown while the Quisitor was in the area.

'Calm yourself, lad. The housekeeper won't tell a soul. She and my brother weren't exactly without sin themselves. And as for that priest,' said the Spook with a faint smile, 'that's Father Cairns. He's family, my cousin. A cousin who meddles and gets a bit excited at times but he means well all the same. He's always trying to save me from myself and get me on the path of "righteousness". But he's wasting his breath. I've chosen my path – and right or wrong it's the one I tread.'

At that moment I heard footsteps and my heart lurched into my mouth. Someone had turned into the alley and was walking directly towards us!

'Anyway, talking of family,' the Spook said, totally unconcerned, 'here comes another member. This is my brother Andrew.'

A tall man with a thin body and sad, bony face was approaching us across the cobbles. He looked even older than the Spook and reminded me of a well-dressed scarecrow, for although he was wearing good quality boots and clean clothes, his garments flapped in the wind. He looked more in need of a good breakfast than I did.

Without bothering to brush away the beads of water, he sat on the wall on the other side of the Spook.

'I thought I'd find you here. A sad business, brother,' he said gloomily.

'Aye,' said the Spook. 'There's just the two of us left now. Five brothers dead and gone.'

'John, I must tell you, the Quis—'

'Yes, I know,' said the Spook, an edge of impatience in his voice.

'Then you must be going. It's not safe for either of you here,' said his brother, acknowledging me with a nod.

'No, Andrew, we're not going anywhere until I've done what needs to be done. So I'd like you to make me a special key again,' the Spook told him. 'For the gate.'

Andrew started. 'Nay, John, don't be a fool,' he said, shaking his head. 'I wouldn't have come here if I'd known you wanted that. Have you forgotten the curse?'

'Hush,' said the Spook. 'Not in front of the boy. Keep your silly superstitious nonsense to yourself.'

'Curse?' I asked, suddenly curious.

'See what you've done?' my master hissed angrily to his brother. 'It's nothing,' he said, turning to me. 'I don't believe in such rubbish and neither should you.'

'Well, I've buried one brother today,' said Andrew. 'Get yourself home now, before I find myself burying another. The Quisitor would love to get his hands on the County Spook. Get back to Chipenden while you still can.'

'I'm not leaving, Andrew, and that's final. I've got a job to do here, Quisitor or no Quisitor,' the Spook said firmly. 'So are you going to help or not?'

'That's not the point, and you know it!' Andrew insisted. 'I've always helped you before, haven't I? When have I ever let you down? But this is madness. You risk burning just by being here. This isn't the time to meddle with that thing again,' he said, gesturing towards the alley entrance and raising his eyes towards the steeple. 'And think of the boy – you can't drag him into this. Not now. Come back again in the spring when the Quisitor's gone and we'll talk again. You'd be a fool to attempt anything now. You can't take on the Bane *and* the Quisitor – you're not a young man, nor a well one by the looks of you.'

As they spoke, I looked up at the steeple myself. I suspected that it could be seen from almost anywhere in the town and that the whole town was also visible from the steeple. There were four small windows right near the top, just below the cross. From there you'd be able to see every rooftop in Priestown, most of the streets and a lot of the people, including us.

The Spook had told me that the Bane could use people, get inside their heads and peer out through their eyes. I shivered, wondering if one of the priests was up there now, the Bane using him to watch us from the darkness inside the spire.

But the Spook wasn't for changing his mind. 'Come on, Andrew, think on! How many times have you told me that the dark's getting stronger in this town? That the priests are becoming more corrupt, that people are afraid? And think about the double tithes and the Quisitor stealing land, and burning innocent women and girls. What's turned the priests and corrupted them so much? What terrible force makes good men inflict such atrocities or stand by and let them happen?

'Why, this very day the lad here has seen his friend carted off to certain death. Aye, the Bane is to blame, and the Bane must be stopped now. Do you really think I can let this go on for half a year more? How many more innocent people will have been burned by then, or will perish this winter through poverty, hunger and cold if I don't do something? The town is rife with rumours of sightings down in the catacombs. If they're true then the Bane is growing in strength and power, turning from a spirit into a creature clothed in flesh. Soon it could return to its original form, a manifestation of the evil spirit that tyrannized the Little People. And then where will we all be? How easy will it be then for it to terrify or trick someone into opening that gate? No, it's as plain as the nose on your face. I've got to act now to rid Priestown of the dark, before the Bane's power grows any stronger. So I'll ask you again, one more time. Will you make me a key?'

For a moment the Spook's brother buried his face in

his hands just like one of the old women saying her prayers in church. Finally he looked up and nodded. 'I still have the mould from last time. I'll have the key ready first thing tomorrow morning. I must be dafter than you,' he said.

'Good man,' replied the Spook. 'I knew you wouldn't let me down. I'll call for it at first light.'

'This time I hope you know what you're doing when you get down there!'

The Spook's face reddened with anger. 'You do your job, brother, and I'll do mine!' he said.

With that, Andrew stood up, gave a world-weary sigh and walked off without even a backward glance.

'Right, lad,' said the Spook, 'you leave first. Go back to your room and stay there till tomorrow. Andrew's shop is down Friargate. I'll have collected the key and will be ready to meet you about twenty minutes after dawn. There shouldn't be many people about that early. Remember where you were standing earlier when the Quisitor rode by?'

I nodded.

'Be on the nearest corner, lad. Don't be late. And remember, we must continue to fast. Oh, and one more thing: don't forget my bag. I think we might be needing it.'

My mind whirled on the way back to the inn. What should I fear most: a powerful man who would hunt me down and burn me at the stake? Or a fearsome creature that had beaten my master in his prime and, through the eyes of a priest, might be watching me at this very moment from the windows high in the steeple?

As I glanced up at the cathedral my eye caught the blackness of a priest's cassock nearby. I averted my gaze but not before I'd noted the priest: Father Cairns. Luckily the pavement was busy and he was staring straight ahead and didn't even glance in my direction. I was relieved, for had he seen me here, so close to my inn, it wouldn't have taken much for him to work out where I might be staying. The Spook had said he was harmless but I couldn't help thinking the fewer people who knew who we were and where we were staying, the better. But my relief was short-lived for when I got back to my room there was a note pinned to the door.

Thomas,
If you would save your master's life, come to my confessional this evening at seven. After that it will be too late.

Father Cairns

I felt a sickening unease. How had Father Cairns found out where I was staying? Had someone been following me? Father Gregory's housekeeper? Or the innkeeper? I hadn't liked the look of him at all. Had he sent a message to the cathedral? Or the Bane? Did that creature know my every movement? Had it told Father Cairns where to find me? Whatever had happened, the priests knew where I was staying and if they told the Quisitor he could come for me at any moment.

I hurriedly opened my bedroom door and locked

it behind me. Then I closed the shutters, hoping desperately to keep out the prying eyes of Priestown. I checked that the Spook's bag was where I'd left it then sat on my bed, not knowing what to do. The Spook had told me to stay in my room until morning. I knew he wouldn't really want me to go and see his cousin. He'd said he was a priest who meddled. Was he just going to meddle again? On the other hand he'd told me that Father Cairns meant well. But what if the priest really did know something that threatened the Spook? If I stayed, my master might end up in the hands of the Quisitor. Yet if I went to the cathedral, I was walking right into the lair of the Quisitor and the Bane! The funeral had been dangerous enough. Could I really push my luck again?

What I really should have done was tell the Spook about the message. But I couldn't. For one thing he hadn't told me where he was staying.

'Trust your instincts,' the Spook had always taught me, so at last I made up my mind. I decided to go and speak to Father Cairns.

CHAPTER 6
A PACT WITH HELL

Giving myself plenty of time, I walked slowly through the damp, cobbled streets. My palms were clammy with nerves and my feet seemed reluctant to move towards the cathedral. It was as if they were wiser than I was and I had to keep forcing one foot in front of the other. But the evening was chilly, and luckily there weren't many people about. I didn't pass even one priest.

I arrived at the cathedral at about ten minutes to seven and as I walked through the gate into the big flagged forecourt, I couldn't help glancing up at the gargoyle over the main door. The ugly head seemed bigger than ever and the eyes still seemed wick with life; they followed me as I walked towards the door. The long chin curved upwards so much that it almost met the nose, making it unlike any creature I'd ever seen. As well as the dog-like ears and a long tongue protruding from its mouth, two short horns curved upwards from its skull and it suddenly reminded me of a goat.

I looked away and entered the cathedral, shivering at the sheer strangeness of the creature. Inside the building it took a few moments for my eyes to adjust to the gloom, and to my relief I saw that the place was almost empty.

I was afraid though for two reasons. Firstly I didn't like being in the cathedral, where priests could appear at any moment. If Father Cairns was tricking me then I had just walked straight into his trap. Secondly I was now in the Bane's territory. Soon the day would draw in, and once the sun went down the Bane, like all creatures of the dark, would be at its most dangerous. Perhaps then its mind might reach up from the catacombs and seek me out. I had to get this business over with as quickly as possible.

Where was the confessional? There were just a couple of old ladies at the back of the cathedral, but an old man was kneeling near the front, close to the small door of a wooden box that stood with its back to the stone wall.

That told me what I wanted to know. There was an identical box a bit further along. The confessional boxes. Each had a candle fixed above it set within a blue glass holder. But only the one near the kneeling man was lit.

I walked down the right-hand aisle and knelt in the pew behind him. After a few moments the door to the confessional box opened and a woman wearing a black veil came out. She crossed the aisle and knelt in a pew further back while the old man went inside.

After a few moments I could hear him muttering. I'd never been to confession in my life but I had a pretty good idea of what went on. One of Dad's brothers had become very religious before he'd died. Dad always called him 'Holy Joe' but his real name was Matthew. He went to confession twice a week and after hearing his sins the priest gave him a big penance. That meant that afterwards he had to say lots of prayers over and over again. I supposed the old man was telling the priest about his sins.

The door stayed closed for what seemed an age and I started to grow impatient. Another thought struck me: what if it wasn't Father Cairns inside but some other priest? I really would have to make a confession then or it would seem very suspicious. I tried to think of a few sins that might sound convincing. Was greed a sin? Or did you call it gluttony? Well, I certainly liked my food but I'd had nothing to eat all day and my belly was starting to rumble. Suddenly it seemed madness to be doing this. In moments I could end up a prisoner.

I panicked and stood up to leave. It was only then that I noticed with relief a small card slotted into a holder on the door. A name was written on it: FATHER CAIRNS.

At that moment the door opened and the old man came out, so I took his place in the confessional and closed the door behind me. It was small and gloomy inside, and when I knelt down, my face was very close to a metal grille. Behind the grille was a brown curtain and, somewhere beyond that, a flickering candle. I couldn't see a face through the grille, just the shadowy outline of a head.

'Would you like me to hear your confession?' The priest's voice had a strong County accent and he breathed loudly.

I just shrugged. Then I realized that he couldn't see me properly through the grille. 'No, Father,' I said, 'but thank you for asking. I'm Tom, Mr Gregory's apprentice. You wanted to see me.'

There was a slight pause before Father Cairns spoke. 'Ah, Thomas, I'm glad you came. I asked you here because I need to talk to you. I need to tell you something very important, so I want you to stay here until I've finished. Will you promise me that you won't leave until I've said what I have to say?'

'I'll listen,' I replied doubtfully. I was wary of making promises now. In the spring I'd made a promise to Alice and it had got me in a whole lot of trouble.

'That's a good lad,' he said. 'We've made a good start to an important task. And do you know what that task is?'

I wondered whether he was talking about the Bane but thought it best not to mention that creature so close to the catacombs, so I said, 'No, Father.'

'Well, Thomas, we have to put together a plan. We have to work out how we can save your immortal soul. But you know what you have to do to begin the process, don't you? You must walk away from John Gregory. You must cease practising that vile trade. Will you do that for me?'

'I thought you wanted to see me about helping Mr Gregory,' I said, starting to feel angry. 'I thought he was in danger.'

'He is, Thomas. We are here to help John Gregory but we must begin by helping you. So will you do what I ask?'

'I can't,' I said. 'My dad paid good money for my

apprenticeship and my mam would be even more disappointed. She says I've a gift and I have to use it to help people. That's what spooks do. We go round helping people when they're in danger from things that come out of the dark.'

There was a long silence. All I could hear was the priest's breathing. Then I thought of something else.

'I helped Father Gregory, you know,' I blurted out. 'He died later, it's true, but I saved him from a worse death. At least he died in bed, in the warmth. He tried to get rid of a boggart,' I explained, raising my voice a little. 'That's what got him into trouble in the first place. Mr Gregory could have sorted it out for him. He can do things that a priest can't. Priests can't get rid of boggarts because they don't know how. It takes more than just a few prayers.'

I knew that I shouldn't have said that about prayers and I expected him to get very angry. He didn't. He kept calm and that made it seem a whole lot worse.

'Oh, yes, it takes much more,' Father Cairns

answered quietly, his voice hardly more than a whisper. 'Much, much more. Do you know what John Gregory's secret is, Thomas? Do you know the source of his power?'

'Yes,' I said, my own voice suddenly much calmer. 'He's studied for years, for the whole of his working life. He's got a whole library full of books and he did an apprenticeship like me and he listened carefully to what his master said and wrote it down in notebooks, just like I do now.'

'Don't you think that we do the same? It takes long, long years to train for the priesthood. And priests are clever men being trained by even cleverer men. So how did you accomplish what Father Gregory couldn't, despite the fact that he read from God's holy book? How do you explain the fact that your master routinely does what his brother could not?'

'It's because priests have the wrong kind of training,' I said. 'And it's because my master and I are both seventh sons of seventh sons.'

The priest made a strange noise behind the grille. At

first I thought he was choking; then I realized I could hear laughter. He was laughing at me.

I thought that was very rude. My dad always says that you should respect other people's opinions even if they sometimes seem daft.

'That's just superstition, Thomas,' Father Cairns said at last. 'Being the seventh son of a seventh son means nothing. It's just an old wives' tale. The true explanation for John Gregory's power is something so terrible that it makes me shudder just to think about it. You see, John Gregory has made a pact with Hell. He's sold his soul to the Devil.'

I couldn't believe what he was saying. When I opened my mouth, no words came out so I just kept shaking my head.

'It's true, Thomas. All his power comes from the Devil. What you and other County folk call boggarts are just lesser devils who only yield because their master bids them do that. It's worth it to the Devil because, in return, one day he'll get hold of John Gregory's soul. And a soul is precious to God, a thing of brightness and splendour, and the Devil will do anything to dirty it with sin and drag it down into the eternal flames of Hell.'

'What about me?' I said, getting angry again. 'I've not sold my soul. But I saved Father Gregory.'

'That's easy, Thomas. You're a servant of the Spook, as you call him, who, in turn, is a servant of the Devil. So the power of evil is on loan to you while you serve. But of course, if you were to complete your training in evil and prepare to practise your vile trade as master rather than apprentice, then it would be your turn. You too would have to sign away your soul. John Gregory hasn't yet told you this because you're too young, but he would certainly do so one day. And when that day arrived, it would come as no surprise because you'd remember my words to you now. John Gregory has made many serious mistakes in his life and has fallen a long, long way from grace. Do you know that he was once a priest?'

I nodded. 'I know that already.'

'And do you know how, just fresh from ordination

as a priest, he came to leave his calling? Do you know of his shame?'

I didn't reply. I knew that Father Cairns was going to tell me anyway.

'Some theologians have argued that a woman does not have a soul. That debate continues, but of one thing we can be certain – a priest cannot take a wife, because it would distract him from his devotion to God. John Gregory's failing was doubly bad: not only was he distracted by a woman but that woman was already betrothed to one of his own brothers. It tore the family apart. Brother turned against brother over a woman called Emily Burns.'

By now I didn't like Father Cairns one little bit and knew that if he'd talked to my mam about women not having souls, she'd have flayed him with her tongue to within an inch of his life. But I was curious about the Spook. Firstly I'd heard about Meg and now I was being told that, even earlier, he'd been involved with this Emily Burns. I was astonished and wanted to know more.

'Did Mr Gregory marry Emily Burns?' I asked, spitting my question right out.

'Never in the eyes of God,' answered the priest. 'She came from Blackrod, where our family has its roots, and lives there alone to this day. Some say they quarrelled, but whatever the case John Gregory eventually took another woman, whom he met in the far north of the County and brought south. Her name was Margery Skelton, a notorious witch. The locals knew her as Meg, and in time she became feared and loathed across the breadth of Anglezarke Moor and the towns and villages to the south of the County.'

I said nothing. I know that he expected me to be shocked. I was, at everything he'd said, but reading the Spook's diary back in Chipenden had prepared me for the worst.

Father Cairns gave another deep sniff then coughed deep in his throat. 'Do you know which of his six brothers John Gregory wronged?'

I'd already guessed. 'Father Gregory,' I answered.

'In devout families such as the Gregorys, it is the

tradition that one son takes Holy Orders. When John threw away his vocation, another brother took his place and began training for the priesthood. Yes, Thomas, it was Father Gregory, the brother we buried today. He lost his betrothed and he lost his brother. What else could he do but turn to God?'

When I'd arrived, the church had been almost empty, but as we'd talked I'd become aware of sounds outside the confessional box. There'd been footsteps and the increasing murmur of voices. Now, suddenly, a choir began to sing. It would be well after seven by now and the sun would already have set. I decided to make an excuse and leave but just as I opened my mouth I heard Father Cairns come to his feet.

'Come with me, Thomas,' he said. 'I want to show you something.'

I heard him open his door and go out into the church, so I followed.

He beckoned me towards the altar where, led by another priest, neatly arranged in three rows of ten, a choir of altar boys was standing on the steps. Each wore a black cassock and white surplice.

Father Cairns halted and put his bandaged hand on my right shoulder.

'Listen to them, Thomas. Don't they sound like holy angels?'

I'd never heard an angel sing so I couldn't answer, but they certainly made a better noise than my dad, who used to start singing as we got near to the end of the milking. His voice was bad enough to turn the milk sour.

'You could have been a member of that choir, Thomas. But you've left it too late. Your voice is already beginning to deepen and a chance to serve has been lost.'

He was right about that. Most of the boys were younger than me and their voices were more like girls' than lads'. In any case, my singing wasn't much better than my dad's.

'Still, there are other things you can do. Let me show you . . .'

He led the way past the altar, through a door and along a corridor. Then we went out into the garden at the rear of the cathedral. Well, it was more the size of a field than a garden, and rather than flowers and roses, vegetables grew there.

It was already beginning to get dark but there was still enough light to see a hawthorn hedge in the distance with the gravestones of the churchyard just visible beyond it. In the foreground a priest was on his knees, weeding with a trowel. It was a big garden and only a small trowel.

'You come from a family of farmers, Thomas. It's good, honest work. You'd be at home working here,' he said, pointing to the kneeling priest.

I shook my head. 'I don't want to be a priest,' I said firmly.

'Oh, *you* could never be a priest!' Father Cairns said, his voice filled with shock and indignation. 'You've been too close to the Devil for that and now will have to be watched closely for the rest of your life lest you slip back. No, that man is a brother.'

'A brother?' I asked, puzzled, thinking he was family or something.

The priest smiled. 'At a big cathedral like this, priests have assistants who offer support. We call them brothers because, although they can't administer the sacraments, they do other vital tasks and are part of the family of the Church. Brother Peter is our gardener and very good at it too. What do you say, Thomas? Would you like to be a brother?'

I knew all about being a brother. With being the youngest of seven, I'd been given all the jobs that nobody else wanted to do. It looked like it was the same here. In any case, I already had a job and I didn't believe what Father Cairns had told me about the Devil and the Spook. It had made me think a bit, but deep down I knew it couldn't be true. Mr Gregory was a good man.

It was getting darker and chillier by the moment so I decided it was time to go.

'Thanks for talking to me, Father,' I said, 'but could you tell me about the danger to Mr Gregory now, please?'

'All in good time, Thomas,' he said, giving me a little smile.

Something in that smile told me that I'd been tricked. That he had no intention at all of helping the Spook.

'I'll think about what you've told me but I've got to be getting back now or I'll miss my supper,' I told him. It seemed a good excuse at the time. He'd no way of knowing that I was fasting because I had to be ready to deal with the Bane.

'We've got supper for you here, Thomas,' said Father Cairns. 'In fact we'd like you to stay the night.'

Two other priests had come out of the side door and were walking towards us. They were big men and I didn't like the expressions on their faces.

There was a moment when I could probably have got away, but it seemed silly to run when I wasn't really sure what was going to happen.

Then it was too late because the priests stood on each side of me, gripping me firmly by my upper arms and shoulders. I didn't struggle because there was no point. Their hands were big and heavy and I felt that if I stayed in the same spot too long, I'd start to sink into the earth. Then they walked me back into the vestry.

'This is for your own good, Thomas,' Father Cairns said, as he followed us inside. 'The Quisitor will seize John Gregory tonight. He'll have a trial, of course, but the outcome is certain. Found guilty of dealing with the Devil, he will be burned at the stake. That's why I can't let you go back to him. There's still a chance for you. You're just a boy and your soul can still be saved without burning. But if you're with him when he's arrested then you'll suffer the same fate. So this is for your own good.'

'But he's your cousin!' I blurted out. 'He's family. How can you do this? Let me go and warn him.'

'Warn him?' asked Father Cairns. 'Do you think I haven't tried to warn him? I've been warning him for most of his adult life. Now I need to think about his soul more than his body. The flames will cleanse him. By means of pain, his soul can be saved. Don't you see? I'm doing it to help him, Thomas. There are much more important things than our brief existence in this world.'

'You've betrayed him! Your own flesh and blood. You've told the Quisitor we're here!'

'Not both of you, just John. So join us, Thomas. Your soul will be cleansed through prayer and your life will no longer be in danger. What do you say?'

There was no point in arguing with someone who was so sure that he was right, so I didn't waste my breath. The only sound to be heard was the echo of our footsteps and the jangle of keys as they led me further and further into the gloom of the cathedral.

CHAPTER 7
ESCAPE AND CAPTURE

They locked me in a small damp room without a window and didn't bring me the supper they'd mentioned. For a bed there was just a small heap of straw. When the door closed I stood there in the dark, listening to the key being turned in the lock and the footsteps echoing away down the corridor.

It was too dark to see my hands before my face but that didn't worry me much. After nearly six months as the Spook's apprentice I'd become a lot braver. Being a seventh son of a seventh son, I'd always seen things that others couldn't but the Spook had taught me that most of them couldn't do you much harm. It was an old cathedral and there was a big graveyard beyond

123

the garden so that meant there would be things about – unquiet things like ghasts and ghosts – but I wasn't afraid of them.

No, what bothered me was the Bane below in the catacombs! The thought of it reaching into my mind was terrifying. I certainly didn't want to face that, and if it was now as strong as the Spook suspected, it would know exactly what was going on. In fact it had probably corrupted Father Cairns, turning him against his own cousin. It might have worked its evil amongst the priests and been listening to their conversations. It was bound to know who I was and where I was and it wouldn't be too friendly to say the least.

Of course, I didn't plan on staying there all night. You see, I still had the three keys in my pocket and I intended to use the special one Andrew had made. Father Cairns wasn't the only one with tricks up his sleeve.

The key wouldn't get me beyond the Silver Gate, because you needed something far more subtle and well-crafted to open that lock, but I knew it would get me out into the corridor and through any door of the cathedral. I just had to wait a while until everyone was asleep and then I could sneak out. If I went too early, I'd probably be caught. On the other hand, if I delayed, I'd be too late to warn the Spook and might get a visit from the Bane, so it was a judgement I couldn't afford to get wrong.

As darkness fell and the noises outside faded, I decided to take my chance. The key turned in the lock without a hint of resistance, but just before I opened the door I heard footsteps. I froze and held my breath as, gradually, they receded into the distance and everything returned to silence.

I waited a long time, listening very carefully. Finally I drew in a slow breath and eased open the door. Fortunately, it opened without a single creak and I stepped out into the corridor, pausing and listening again.

I didn't know for sure that there was anybody left in the cathedral and its side buildings. Perhaps they'd all gone back to the big, priests' house? But I couldn't believe they wouldn't have left somebody on guard, so I tiptoed along the dark corridor, afraid to make even the slightest sound.

When I came to the side door of the vestry, I had a shock. I didn't need my key. It was already open.

The sky was clear now and the moon was up, bathing the path in a silver light. I stepped outside and moved cautiously. Only then did I sense somebody behind me; someone standing to the side of the door, hidden in the shadow of one of the big stone buttresses that shored up the sides of the cathedral.

For a moment I froze. Then, my heart pounding so loudly I could hear it, I slowly turned round. The shadowy figure stepped out into the moonlight. I recognized him straight away. Not a priest, but the brother who'd been on his knees tending the garden earlier. Gaunt of face, Brother Peter was almost totally bald, with just a thin collar of white hair below his ears.

Suddenly he spoke. 'Warn your master, Thomas,' he

said. 'Go quickly! Get away from this town while you both can!'

I didn't reply. I just turned and ran down the path as fast as I could. I only stopped running when I reached the streets. I walked so as not to draw too much attention to myself and I wondered why Brother Peter hadn't tried to stop me. Wasn't that his job? Hadn't he been left on guard?

But I didn't have time to think about that properly. I had to warn the Spook of his cousin's betrayal before it was too late. I didn't know which inn the Spook was staying at but perhaps his brother would know. That was a start because I knew where Friargate was: it was one of the roads I'd walked down while searching for an inn, so Andrew's shop wouldn't be too difficult to find. I hurried through the cobbled streets, knowing that I didn't have much time; that the Quisitor and his men would already be on their way.

Friargate was a wide, hilly road with two rows of shops and I found the locksmith's easily. The name above the shop said ANDREW GREGORY but the premises were in darkness. I had to knock three times before a light flickered in the upstairs room.

Andrew opened the door and held a candle up to my face. He was wearing a long nightshirt and his face held a mixture of expressions. He looked puzzled, angry and weary.

'Your brother's in danger,' I said, trying to keep my voice as low as possible. 'I would have warned him myself, but I don't know where he's staying . . .'

He beckoned me in without a word and led me through into his workshop. The walls were festooned with keys and locks of every possible shape and size. One large key was as long as my forearm and I wondered at the size of the lock it belonged to. Quickly I explained what had happened.

'I told him he was a fool to stay here!' he exclaimed, thumping his fist down hard on the top of a workbench. 'And damn that treacherous, two-faced cousin of ours! I knew all along he wasn't to be trusted. The Bane must have finally got to him, twisting his mind to get John out of the way – the one person in the whole County who still poses a real threat to it!'

He went upstairs but it didn't take him long to get dressed. Soon we were heading back through the empty streets, taking a route that led us back in the direction of the cathedral.

'He's staying at the Book and Candle,' muttered Andrew Gregory, shaking his head. 'Why on earth didn't he tell you that? You could have saved time by going straight there. Let's hope we're not too late!'

But we *were* too late. We heard them from several streets away: men's voices raised in anger and someone thumping a door loud enough to wake the dead.

We watched from a corner, taking care not to be seen. There was nothing we could do now. The Quisitor was there on his huge horse and he had about twenty armed men at his command. They had cudgels and some of them had drawn their swords as if they expected resistance. One of the men hammered on the inn door again with the hilt of his sword.

'Open up! Open up! Be quick about it!' he shouted. 'Or we'll break down the door!'

There was the sound of bolts being drawn back and the innkeeper came to the door in his nightshirt, holding a lantern. He looked bewildered, as if he'd just woken up from a very deep sleep. He saw only the two armed men facing him, not the Quisitor. Perhaps that was why he made a big mistake: he began to protest and bluster.

'What's this?' he cried. 'Can't a man get some sleep after a hard day's work? Disturbing the peace at this time of night! I know my rights. There's laws against such things.'

'Fool!' shouted the Quisitor angrily, riding closer to the door. 'I *am* the law! A warlock sleeps within your walls. A servant of the Devil! Sheltering a known enemy of the Church carries dire penalties. Stand aside or pay with your life!'

'Sorry, lord. Sorry!' wailed the innkeeper, holding up his hands in supplication, a look of terror on his face.

In answer the Quisitor simply gestured to his men, who seized the innkeeper roughly. Without ceremony he was dragged into the street and hurled to the ground.

Then, very deliberately, with cruelty etched on his face, the Quisitor rode his white stallion over the innkeeper. A hoof came down hard on his leg and I clearly heard the bone snap. My blood ran cold. The man lay screaming on the ground while four of the guards ran into the house; their boots thumped up the wooden stairs.

When they dragged the Spook outside, he looked old and frail. Perhaps a little afraid too, but I was too far away to be sure.

'Well, John Gregory, you're mine at last!' cried the Quisitor, in a loud, arrogant voice. 'Those dry old bones of yours should burn well!'

The Spook didn't answer. I watched them tie his hands behind his back and lead him away down the street.

'All these years, then it comes to this,' muttered Andrew. 'He always meant well. He doesn't deserve to burn.'

I couldn't believe it was happening. I had a lump in my throat so big that, until the Spook had been taken round the corner and out of sight, I couldn't even speak. 'We've got to do something!' I said at last.

Andrew shook his head wearily. 'Well, boy, have a think about it and then tell me just what we're supposed to do. Because I haven't a clue. You'd better come back to my place and at first light get as far away from here as possible.'

CHAPTER 8
BROTHER PETER'S TALE

The kitchen was at the back of the house, overlooking a small flagged yard. As the sky grew lighter, Andrew offered me some breakfast. It wasn't much, just an egg and a slice of toasted bread. I thanked him but had to refuse because I was still fasting. To eat would mean I'd accepted that the Spook was gone and that we wouldn't be facing the Bane together. Anyway, I didn't feel the slightest bit hungry.

I'd done what Andrew had suggested. Since the Spook had been taken I'd spent every single moment thinking of how we could save him. I thought about Alice too. If I didn't do something, they were both going to burn.

'Mr Gregory's bag is still in my room at the Black Bull,' I suddenly remembered, turning to the locksmith. 'And he must have left his staff and our cloaks in his room at the inn. How will we get them back?'

'Well, that's one thing I can help you with,' Andrew said. 'It's too risky for either of us to go, but I know someone who could pick them up for you. I'll see to it later.'

While I watched Andrew eating, a bell started to ring somewhere in the distance. It had a single dull tone and there was a long pause between each chime. It sounded mournful, like the tolling of a funeral bell.

'Is that from the cathedral?' I asked.

Andrew nodded and carried on chewing his food very slowly. He looked as if he'd as little appetite as I had.

I wondered if it was calling people to an early morning service, but before I could say as much Andrew swallowed his piece of toast and told me, 'It means another death at the cathedral or at some other church in the town. Either that or a priest's died somewhere else in the County and the news has only just got here. It's a common sound here these days. I'm afraid any priests who question the darkness and corruption in our town are swiftly dealt with.'

I shuddered. 'Does everybody in Priestown know it's the Bane that's the cause of the dark times?' I asked. 'Or just the priests?'

'The Bane's common enough knowledge. In the area closest to the cathedral most folk have had the doors to their cellars bricked up, and fear and superstition are rife. Who can blame the townsfolk when they can't even rely on their own priests to protect them? No wonder congregations are dwindling,' Andrew said, shaking his head sadly.

'Did you finish the key?' I asked him.

'Aye,' he said, 'but poor John won't be needing it now.'

'We could use it,' I said, speaking quickly so that I could finish what I was saying before he stopped me. 'The catacombs run right under the cathedral and presbytery, so there could be a way up into them. We could wait until dark, when everyone's asleep, and get up into the house.'

'That's just foolishness,' Andrew said, shaking his head. 'The presbytery's huge, with a lot of rooms both above and below ground. And we don't even know where the prisoners are being held. Not only that, there are armed men guarding them. Do you want to burn as well? I certainly don't!'

'It's worth a try,' I insisted. 'They won't expect anyone to come up into the house from below with the Bane down there. We'll have surprise on our side and maybe the guards will be asleep.'

'No,' Andrew said, shaking his head firmly. 'It's madness. It's not worth two more lives.'

'Then give me the key and I'll do it.'

'You'd never find your way without me. It's a maze of tunnels down there.'

'So you do know the way?' I said. 'You've been down there before?'

'Aye, I know the way as far as the Silver Gate. But that's as far as I'd ever want to go. And it's twenty years since I went down there with John. That thing down there nearly killed him. It could kill us too. You heard John: it's changing from a spirit, shape-shifting into God knows what. We could meet anything down there. Folk have spoken of ferocious black dogs with huge, snarling teeth; venomous serpents. The Bane can read your mind, remember, take the shape of your worst fears. No, it's too dangerous. I don't know which fate is worse – being burned alive at the stake by the Quisitor or pressed to death by the Bane. They're not choices a young lad should be making.'

'Don't worry about that,' I said. 'You deal with the locks and I'll do my job.'

'If my brother couldn't cope, then what hope have you? He was still in his prime then and you're just a boy.'

'I'm not daft enough to try and destroy the Bane,' I said. 'I'd just do enough to get the Spook to safety.'

Andrew shook his head. 'How long have you been with him?'

'Nearly six months,' I said.

'Well,' said Andrew, 'that tells us everything, doesn't it? You mean well, I know that, but we'd just be making things worse.'

'The Spook told me that burning's a terrible death. The worst death of all. That's why he doesn't hold with burning a witch. Would you let him suffer that? Please, you've got to help. It's his last chance.'

This time Andrew didn't say anything. He sat for a long time, deep in thought. When he did get up from his chair, all he said was that I should stay out of sight.

That seemed a good sign. At least he hadn't sent me packing.

I sat in the back, kicking my heels, as the morning slowly wore on. I hadn't slept at all and I was tired, but sleep was the last thing on my mind after the events of the night.

Andrew was working. Most of the time I could hear him in his workshop, but sometimes there was a tinkle from the doorbell as a customer entered or left the shop.

It was almost noon before Andrew came back into the kitchen. There was something different in his face. He looked thoughtful. And walking right behind him was someone else!

I came to my feet, ready to run, but the back door was locked and the two men were between me and the other doorway. Then I recognized the stranger and relaxed. It was Brother Peter and he was carrying the Spook's bag and staff and our cloaks!

'It's all right, boy,' Andrew said, walking up and laying his hand on my shoulder in reassurance. 'Take that anxious look off your face and sit yourself back down. Brother Peter is a friend. Look, he's brought you John's things.'

He smiled and handed me the bag, staff and cloaks. I accepted them with a nod of thanks and put them in the corner before sitting down. Both men pulled chairs out from the table and sat facing me.

Brother Peter was a man who'd spent most of his life working in the open air and the skin on his head was weathered by the wind and sun to an even shade of brown. He was as tall as Andrew but didn't stand as upright. His back and shoulders were bent, perhaps with too many years working away at the earth with a trowel or hoe. His nose was his most distinctive feature; it was hooked like a crow's beak, but his eyes were set wide apart and had a kindly twinkle. My instincts told me that he was a good man.

'Well,' he said, 'you were lucky it was me doing the rounds last night and not one of the others or you'd have found yourself back in that cell! As it was, Father Cairns summoned me just after dawn and I'd a few awkward questions to answer. He wasn't happy and I'm not sure that he's finished with me yet!'

'I'm sorry,' I said.

Brother Peter smiled. 'Don't worry, lad. I'm just a gardener with a reputation for being hard of hearing. He won't bother himself for long about me. Not when the Quisitor's got so many others ready for burning!'

'Why did you let me escape?' I asked.

Brother Peter raised his eyebrows. 'Not all priests are under the control of the Bane. I know he's your cousin,' he said, turning to Andrew, 'but I don't trust Father Cairns. I think the Bane may have got to him.'

'I've been thinking as much myself,' said Andrew. 'John was betrayed and I'm sure the Bane must have been behind it all. It knows John's a threat to it so it got that weak cousin of ours to get rid of him.'

'Aye, I think you're right. Did you notice his hand? He says it's bandaged because he burned himself on a candle, but Father Hendle had an injury in a similar place after the Bane got to him. I think Cairns has given that creature his blood.'

I must have looked horrified because Brother Peter came over and put an arm around my shoulders. 'Don't worry, son. There are still some good men left in that cathedral and I may just be a lowly brother but I count myself one of them and do the Lord's work whenever I can. I'll do everything in my power to help you and your master. The dark hasn't won yet! So let's get down to business. Andrew tells me that you're brave enough to go down into the catacombs. Is that right?' he asked, rubbing the end of his nose thoughtfully.

'Somebody has to do it, so I'm willing to try,' I told him.

'And what if you come face to face with . . .'

He didn't finish the sentence. It was almost as if he couldn't bring himself to say 'the Bane'.

'Has anyone told you what you could be facing? About the shape-shifting, and the mind reading and the . . .' He hesitated and looked over his shoulder before whispering, 'Pressing?'

'Yes, I've heard,' I said, sounding a lot more confident than I felt. 'But there are things I could do. It doesn't like silver . . .'

I unlocked the Spook's bag, reached into it and showed them the silver chain. 'I could bind it with this,' I said, staring straight into Brother Peter's eyes and trying not to blink.

The two men looked at each other and Andrew smiled. 'Practised a lot, have you?' he asked.

'For hours and hours,' I told him. 'There's a post in Mr Gregory's garden at Chipenden. I can cast this chain at it from eight feet away and drop it clean over it nine times out of ten.'

'Well, if you could somehow get past that creature and reach the presbytery tonight, one thing would be on your side. It would certainly be quieter than normal,' Brother Peter said. 'The death last night was at the cathedral so the body's already here, rather than out of town. Tonight nearly all the priests will be in there keeping a vigil.'

From my Latin lessons I knew that 'vigil' meant 'awake'. It still didn't tell me what they'd be up to.

'They say prayers and watch over the body,' Andrew said, smiling at the puzzlement on my face. 'Who was it who died, Peter?'

'Poor Father Roberts. Took his own life. Threw himself from the roof. That's five suicides this year already,' he said, glancing at Andrew then staring right back at me. 'It gets inside their minds, you see. Makes them do things that are against God and against their conscience. And that's a very hard thing for a priest who's taken holy orders to serve God. So when he can't stand it any longer he sometimes takes his own life. And that's a terrible thing to do. To take one's life is a mortal sin, and the priests know they can never go to Heaven, never be with God. Think how bad it must be to drive them to that! If only we could be rid of this terrible evil before there's nothing good left in the town for it to corrupt.'

There was a short silence, as if we were all thinking, but then I saw Brother Peter's mouth moving and I thought that he might be praying for the poor dead priest. When he made the sign of the cross I was sure of it. Then the two men glanced at each other and they both nodded. Without speaking, they'd reached an agreement.

'I'll go with you as far as the Silver Gate,' Andrew said. 'After that, Brother Peter here might be able to help . . .'

Was Brother Peter going with us? He must have read the expression on my face because he held up both hands, smiled and shook his head.

'Oh, no, Tom. I lack the courage to go anywhere near the catacombs. No, what Andrew means is that I can help in another way: by giving you directions. You see, there's a map of the tunnels. It's mounted in a frame just inside the presbytery entrance – the one that leads directly to the garden. I've lost count of the hours I've spent waiting there for one of the priests to come down and give me my duties for the day. Over the years I've got to know every inch of that map. Do you want to write this down, or can you remember it?'

'I've got a good memory,' I told him.

'Well, just tell me if you want me to repeat anything. As Andrew said, he'll guide you as far as the Silver Gate. Once through it, just keep going until the tunnel forks. Follow the left-hand passage until you reach some steps. They lead up to a door, beyond which is the big wine cellar of the presbytery. It'll be locked but that should cause no problem at all when you've a friend like Andrew. There's only one other door that leads from the cellar and it's on the far wall in the right-hand corner.'

'But can't the Bane follow me through into the wine cellar and escape?' I asked.

'No – it can only leave the catacombs through the Silver Gate, so you're quite safe from it once you've gone through the door into the wine cellar. Now, before you leave the cellar there's something you should do. There's a trapdoor in the ceiling to the left of the door. It leads up to the path that runs along the north wall of the cathedral – the delivery men use it to get the wine and ale down there. Unlock it before you go any further. It should prove a faster escape route than going back to the gate. Is that clear so far?'

'Wouldn't it be a lot easier to use that trapdoor to get down?' I asked. 'That way I could avoid the Silver Gate and the Bane!'

'I only wish it were so easy,' said Brother Peter. 'But it's too risky. The door is visible from the road and from the presbytery. Someone might see you going in.'

I nodded thoughtfully.

'Although you can't use it to get in, there's another good reason why you should try to get out that way,' Andrew said. 'I don't want John to risk coming face to face with the Bane again. You see, deep down I think he's afraid – so afraid that he couldn't possibly win—'

'Afraid?' I asked indignantly. 'Mr Gregory's not afraid of anything that belongs to the dark.'

'Not so as he'd admit it,' continued Andrew. 'I'll give you that all right. He probably wouldn't even admit it to himself. But he was cursed long ago and—'

'Mr Gregory doesn't believe in curses,' I interrupted again. 'He told you that.'

'If you'll let me get a word in edgeways, I'll explain,' insisted Andrew. 'This was a dangerous and powerful curse. As big as they ever get. Three whole covens of Pendle witches came together to do it. John had been interfering too much in their business, so they put aside their own quarrels and grievances and cursed him. It was a blood sacrifice and innocents were slaughtered. It happened on Walpurgis Night, the eve of the first of May, twenty years ago, and afterwards they sent it to him on a piece of parchment splattered with blood. He once told me what was written there: *You will die in a dark place, far underground with no friend at your side!*'

'The catacombs . . .' I said, my voice hardly more than a whisper. If he faced the Bane alone down in the catacombs, then the conditions of the curse would be fulfilled.

'Aye, the catacombs,' Andrew said. 'As I said, get him away through the hatch. Anyway, Brother Peter, sorry to have interrupted . . .'

Peter gave a bleak smile and continued. 'Once you've unlocked the hatch, go through the door into a corridor. This is the risky part. There's a cell at the far end which they use to hold prisoners. That's where you should find your master. But to get to it, you'll have to pass the guardroom. It's a dangerous business but it's damp and chilly down there. They'll have a big fire blazing away in the grate and, if God's willing, the door will be closed against the cold. So there you have it! Release Mr Gregory and get him out through the trapdoor and away from this town. He'll have to come back and deal with that foul creature another time, when the Quisitor's gone.'

'Nay!' said Andrew. 'After all this I wouldn't have him coming back here.'

'But if he doesn't fight the Bane, then who can?' asked Brother Peter. 'I don't believe in curses either. With God's help, John can defeat that evil spirit. You know it's getting worse. No doubt I'll be next.'

'Not you, Brother Peter,' Andrew said. 'I've met few men as strong-minded as you.'

'I do my best,' he said, shuddering. 'When I hear it whispering inside my head, I just pray harder. God gives us the strength we need – that's if we've the sense to ask for it. But something has to be done. I don't know how it's all going to end.'

'It'll end when the townsfolk have had enough,' said Andrew. 'You can only push people so far. I'm surprised they've stood the Quisitor's wickedness for so long. Some of those for burning have relatives and friends here.'

'Maybe and maybe not,' said Brother Peter. 'There are lots of people love a burning. We can only pray.'

CHAPTER 9
THE CATACOMBS

Brother Peter went back to his duties at the cathedral while we waited for the sun to go down. Andrew told me that the best way into the catacombs was through the cellar of an abandoned house close to the cathedral; we were less likely to be noticed after dark.

As the hours passed, I began to grow more and more nervous. When talking to Andrew and Brother Peter, I'd tried to sound confident, but the Bane really scared me. I kept rummaging through the Spook's bag, looking for anything that might be of some help.

Of course, I took the long silver chain that he used to bind witches and tied it around my waist, hidden under my shirt. But I knew it was one thing to be able to cast it over a wooden post and quite another to do it to the Bane. Next were salt and iron. After transferring my tinderbox to my jacket pocket, I filled my breeches pockets – the right pocket with salt, the left with iron. The combination worked against most things that haunted the dark. That was how I'd finally dealt with the old witch, Mother Malkin.

I couldn't see it being enough to finish off something as powerful as the Bane; if it had been, the Spook would have dealt with it last time, once and for all. However, I was desperate enough to try anything, and just having that and the silver chain made me feel better. After all, I wasn't planning to destroy the Bane this time, but to fend it off long enough to rescue my master.

At last, with the Spook's staff in my left hand and his bag with our cloaks in my right, I was following Andrew through the darkening streets in the direction of the cathedral. Above, the sky was heavy with clouds and it smelled as if rain wasn't very far away. I was learning to hate Priestown, with its narrow cobbled streets and walled back yards. I missed the fells and the wide open spaces. If only I were in Chipenden, back in the routine of my lessons with the Spook! It was hard to accept that my life there might be over.

As we approached the cathedral, Andrew led us into one of the narrow passages that ran between the backs of the terraced houses. He halted at a door, slowly lifted the latch and nodded me through into the small back yard. After closing the yard door carefully, he went up to the back door of the house, which was all in darkness.

A moment later he turned a key in the lock and we were inside. Locking the door behind us, he lit two candles and handed one to me.

'This house has been deserted for well over twenty years,' he said, 'and it'll stay like this too, for as you've realized, those like my brother aren't welcome in this town. It's haunted by something pretty nasty so most people keep well away and even dogs avoid it.'

He was right about there being something nasty in

the house. The Spook had carved a sign on the inside of the back door.

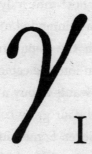

I

It was the Greek letter gamma, which was used for either a ghast or a ghost. The number to the right was a one, meaning it was a ghost of the first rank, dangerous enough to push some people to the edge of insanity.

'His name was Matty Barnes,' Andrew said, 'and he murdered seven people in this town, maybe more. He had big hands and he used them to choke the life from his victims. They were mainly young women. They say he brought them back here and squeezed the life from them in this very room. Eventually one of the women fought back and stabbed him through the eye with a hat pin. He died slowly of blood poisoning. John was going to talk his ghost into moving on but thought better of it. He always intended to come back here one day and deal with the Bane and wanted to make sure this way down into the catacombs would still be available. Nobody wants to buy a haunted house.'

Suddenly I felt the air grow colder and our candle flames began to flicker. Something was close by and getting nearer by the second. Before I could take another breath, it arrived. I couldn't actually see it but I sensed something lurking in the shadows in the far corner of the kitchen; something staring at me hard.

That I couldn't actually see it made things worse. The most powerful of ghosts can choose whether or not to make themselves visible. The ghost of Matty Barnes was showing me just how strong it was by keeping hidden, yet letting me know that it was watching me. What's more, I could sense its malevolence. It wished us ill and the sooner we were out of there the better.

'Am I imagining it, or has it suddenly got very chilly in here?' asked Andrew.

'It's cold all right,' I said, not mentioning the presence of the ghost. There was no need to make him more nervous than he already was.

'Then let's move on,' Andrew said, leading the way towards the cellar steps.

The house was typical of many terraced houses in the County's towns: a simple two rooms upstairs and two rooms down with an attic under the eaves. And the cellar door in the kitchen was in exactly the same position as the one in Horshaw, where the Spook had taken me on the first night after I'd become his apprentice. That house had been haunted by a ghast, and to see if I was up to doing the job the Spook had ordered me to go down to the cellar at midnight. It wasn't a night I'd forget; thinking about it now still makes me shiver.

Andrew and I followed the steps down into the cellar. The flagged floor was empty but for a pile of old rugs and carpets. It seemed dry enough but there was a musty smell. Andrew handed me his candle then quickly dragged the rugs away to reveal a wooden trapdoor.

'There's more than one way into the catacombs,' he said, 'but this is the easiest and the least risky. You're not likely to get many folk nosing about down here.'

He lifted the trapdoor and I could see stone steps descending into the darkness. There was a smell of damp earth and rot. Andrew took the candle from me and went down first, telling me to wait for a moment. Then he called up, 'Down you come, but leave the trap open. We might have to get out of here in a hurry!'

I left the Spook's bag, with the cloaks, in the cellar and followed him, still clutching my master's staff. When I got down, to my surprise I found myself standing on cobbles rather than the mud I'd expected. The catacombs were as well paved as the streets above. Had these been made by the people who'd lived here before the town was built; those who'd worshipped the Bane? If so, the cobbled streets of Priestown had been copied from those of the catacombs.

Andrew set off without another word and I had a feeling he wanted to get the whole thing over with. I know I did.

At first the tunnel was wide enough for two people to walk side by side but the cobbled roof was low and Andrew was forced to walk with his head bowed forward. No wonder the Spook had called them the 'Little People'. The builders had certainly been a lot smaller than folk were now.

We'd not gone very far before the tunnel began to narrow; in places it was distorted, as if the weight of the cathedral and the buildings far above were squashing it out of shape. At times the cobbles that also lined the roof and walls had fallen away, allowing mud and slime to seep through and ooze down the walls. There was a sound of dripping water in the distance and the echo of our boots on the cobbles.

Soon the passage narrowed even further. I was forced to walk behind Andrew, and our path forked into two even smaller tunnels. After we'd taken the left-hand one, we came to a recess in the wall on our left. Andrew paused and held his candle up so that it lit part of the interior. I stared in horror at what I saw. There were rows of shelves and they were filled with bones: skulls with eyeless sockets, leg bones, arm bones, finger bones and bones I didn't recognize, all different sizes, all mixed up. And all human!

'The catacombs are full of crypts like this,' Andrew said. 'Wouldn't do to get lost down here in the dark.'

The bones were small too, like those of children. They were the remains of the Little People all right.

We moved on and soon I could hear fast-flowing water ahead. We turned a corner and there it was, more a small river than a stream.

'This flows under the main street in front of the cathedral,' Andrew said, pointing towards the dark water, 'and we cross there . . .'

Stepping stones, nine in all, broad, smooth and flat but each of them only just above the surface of the water.

Once again Andrew led the way, striding effortlessly from stone to stone. At the other side he paused and turned back to watch me complete my crossing.

'It's easy tonight,' he said, 'but after heavy rain the water level can be well above the stones. Then there's a real danger of being swept away.'

We walked on and the sound of rushing water began to recede into the distance.

Andrew halted suddenly and I could see over his shoulder that we'd come to a gate. But what a gate! I'd never seen one like it. From floor to ceiling, wall to wall, a grille of metal blocked the tunnel completely, metal that gleamed in the light of Andrew's candle. It seemed to be an alloy that contained a lot of silver and it had been fashioned by a blacksmith of great skill. Each bar was made up not of solid cylindrical metal, but of several much thinner bars, twisted around to form a spiral. The design was very complex: patterns and shapes were suggested, but the more I looked the more they seemed to change.

Andrew turned and put his hand on my shoulder. 'This is it, the Silver Gate. So listen,' he said, 'this is important. Is there anything near? Anything from the dark?'

'I don't think so,' I said.

'That's not good enough,' Andrew snapped, his voice harsh. 'You've got to be sure! If we let this creature escape it'll terrorize the whole County, not just the priests.'

Well, I didn't feel the cold, the usual warning that something from the dark was near. So that was one sign that everything was safe. But the Spook had always told me to trust my instincts, so to make doubly sure I took a deep breath and concentrated hard.

Nothing. I sensed nothing at all.

'It's all clear,' I told Andrew.

'You sure? You're really sure?'

'I'm sure.'

Andrew suddenly dropped to his knees and reached into the pocket of his breeches. There was a small curved door in the grille but its tiny lock was very close to the ground and that was why Andrew was bent so low. Very carefully he was easing the tiniest of keys into the lock. I remembered the huge key displayed on the wall of his workshop. You would

have thought that the bigger the key, the more important it was, but here the opposite was true. What could
be more important than the minute key that Andrew
now held in his hand? One that had kept the whole
County safe from the Bane.

He seemed to struggle and kept positioning and
repositioning the key. At last it turned and Andrew
opened the gate and stood up.

'Still want to do this?' he asked.

I nodded, then knelt down, pushed the staff through
the open gate and followed it, crawling on all fours.
Immediately Andrew locked the gate behind me and
poked the key through the grille. I put it inside my left
breeches pocket, pushing it down into the iron filings.

'Good luck,' Andrew said. 'I'll go back to the cellar
and wait for an hour in case you come back this way
for some reason. If you don't appear, I'll head home.
Wish I could do more to help. You're a brave lad, Tom.
I truly wish I'd the courage to go with you.'

I thanked him, turned and, carrying the staff in my
left hand and the candle in my right, set off into the

darkness alone. Within moments the full horror of what I was undertaking descended upon me. Was I mad? I was now in the Bane's lair and it could appear at any moment. What had I been thinking? It might already know that I was here!

But I took a deep breath and reassured myself with the thought that as it hadn't rushed to the Silver Gate when Andrew unlocked it, it couldn't be all-knowing. And if the catacombs were as extensive as people claimed, then at that very moment the Bane might be miles away. Anyway, what else could I do but keep walking forward? The lives of the Spook and Alice both depended on what I did.

I walked for about a minute before I came to two branching tunnels. Remembering what Brother Peter had told me, I chose the left one. The air around me grew colder and I sensed that I was no longer alone. In the distance, beyond the light of the candle, there were small, faint, luminous shapes flitting like bats, in and out of crypts along the tunnel walls. As I approached them, they disappeared. They didn't get too near but I felt certain that they were the ghosts of some of the Little People. The ghosts didn't bother me much; it was the Bane that I couldn't get out of my mind.

I came to the corner and, as I turned, following it to the left, I felt something underfoot and almost tripped. I'd stepped on something soft and sticky.

I moved back and lifted my candle to get a better look. What I saw started my knees shaking and the candle dancing in my trembling hand. It was a dead cat. But it wasn't the fact that it was dead that bothered me; it was the way it had died.

No doubt it had found its way down into the catacombs in search of rats or mice but it had met with a terrible end. It was lying on its belly, its eyes bulging. The poor animal had been squashed so flat that at no point was its body any thicker than an inch. It had been smeared into the cobbles but its protruding tongue was still glistening so it couldn't have been dead very long. I shuddered with horror. It had been 'pressed' all right. If the Bane found me, that would surely be my fate too.

I moved on quickly, glad to leave that terrible sight behind, and at last I came to the foot of a flight of stone steps that led up to a wooden door. If Brother Peter was right, behind that was the wine cellar of the priests' house.

I climbed to the top of the steps and used the Spook's key. A moment later I was easing the door open. Once inside the cellar, I closed it behind me but didn't lock it.

The cellar was very large, with huge barrels of ale and row upon row of dusty wine racks filled with bottles, some of which had clearly been there a long time – they were covered with spiders' webs. It was deadly silent down here, and unless somebody was hiding and watching me, it seemed completely deserted. Of course, the candle only illuminated the small area around me and beyond the nearest barrels was a darkness that could have hidden anything.

Before he'd left Andrew's house Brother Peter had told me that the priests only came down into the cellar once a week to collect the wine they needed, and that most of them wouldn't dream of going down into the catacombs because of the Bane. But he couldn't promise the same for the Quisitor's men: they weren't local and didn't know enough to be fearful. Not only that; they'd help themselves to the ale and probably wouldn't be content with just one barrel.

I crossed the length of the cellar cautiously, pausing every ten strides or so to listen. At last I could see the door that led to the corridor and there, in the ceiling to the left, right up against the wall, was a large wooden hatch. We had a similar hatch back home. Our farm had once been called 'Brewer's Farm' because it had supplied ale to neighbouring taverns and farms. As Brother Peter had explained, this trapdoor was used to get barrels and crates in and out of the cellar without the bother of going through the presbytery. And he was right in saying that it would be the easiest way of escaping. If I did use it I'd certainly run the risk of being spotted, but going back towards the Silver Gate would mean possibly facing the Bane, and after being locked up the Spook wouldn't be strong enough to deal with it. Not only that, there was the Spook's curse to think about. Whether he believed in it or not, it wasn't worth tempting fate.

There were big barrels of ale standing on end directly under the hatch. Resting the candle on one and setting the staff to one side, I climbed up onto another and was able to reach the lock, which was set into the wooden hatch so that it could be locked or unlocked from either side. It was simple enough and the Spook's key worked again, but I left the hatch closed for now in case someone spotted it from above.

I unfastened the door to the corridor just as easily, turning the key very slowly so as not to make any noise. It made me realize how lucky the Spook was to have a locksmith for a brother.

Next I eased open the door and stepped through into a long, narrow, flagged corridor. It was deserted, but about twenty steps ahead, on the right, I could see a flickering torch in a wall bracket above a closed door. It had to be the guardroom that Brother Peter had warned me about. Further down the corridor was a second door, and beyond it stone steps that must lead up to the rooms above.

I walked slowly down the corridor towards the first door, almost on tiptoe and keeping to the shadows. Once close to the guardroom, I could hear sounds coming from within. Somebody coughed, somebody laughed and there was the murmur of voices.

Suddenly my heart was set racing. I'd heard a deep voice very close to the door but before I could hide, the door was flung open with some force. It almost hit me but I stepped back behind it quickly and flattened myself against the rough stones of the wall. Heavy boots stepped out into the corridor.

'I must get back to my work,' said a voice that I recognized. It was the Quisitor and he was talking to someone who was standing just inside the doorway!

'Send someone to collect Brother Peter,' he continued, 'and have him brought to me when I've finished with the other. Father Cairns may have lost us a prisoner but he knew who was to blame, I'll say that for him. And at least he had the good sense to report it to me. Bind our good brother's hands tightly behind his back, and don't be gentle. Make the cord cut into his flesh so that he knows exactly what he's facing! It'll be more than a few harsh words, you can be sure of that. Hot irons'll soon loosen his tongue!'

By way of answer there came a burst of loud, cruel laughter from the guards. Then the Quisitor's long black cloak billowed out behind him in the draught as he closed the door and walked quickly towards the steps at the far end of the corridor.

If he turned round he'd see me right away! For a moment I thought he was going to stop outside the prisoners' cell, but to my relief he continued up the steps and out of sight.

Poor Brother Peter. He was going to be questioned but there was no way I could warn him. And I'd been the prisoner the Quisitor had referred to. They were going to torture him because he'd let me go free! And not only that – Father Cairns had told the Quisitor about me. Now that he had the Spook, the Quisitor would probably come looking for me too.

I had to rescue my master before it was too late for both of us.

I almost made a big mistake then and moved down the corridor towards the cell; however, just in time I realized that the Quisitor's order would be carried out immediately. Sure enough, the guardroom door opened again and two men came out brandishing clubs and strode away towards the steps.

When the door was again closed from within, I was in full view but my luck held once more and the guards didn't turn round. After they'd climbed up the steps and out of sight, I waited for a few moments until the echo of their distant boots had faded away and my heart had stopped pounding so loudly. It was then that I heard other voices from the cell ahead. Someone was crying; another chanted in prayer. I rushed towards the sound until I reached a heavy metal door, its top third formed of vertical metal bars.

I held the candle right up close to the bars and peered inside. In the flickering light the cell looked really bad but smelled even worse. There were about twenty people cramped into that small space. Some were lying on the floor and seemed to be asleep. Others were sitting with their backs against the wall. A woman was standing close to the door and it was her voice that I'd heard. I'd assumed she was praying but she was chanting gibberish and her eyes were rolling in her head as if what she'd gone through had driven her insane.

I couldn't see the Spook and I couldn't see Alice but that didn't mean they weren't inside. These were the prisoners all right. The prisoners of the Quisitor, ready for burning.

Wasting no time, I laid down the staff, unlocked the door and opened it slowly. I wanted to go in and look for the Spook and Alice, but even before the door was fully open the woman who'd been chanting moved forward and blocked my way.

She shouted something out, spitting her words into my face. I couldn't understand what she said but it was so loud it made me glance back towards the guard-room. Within seconds, others were at her back, pushing her forwards and out into the corridor. There was a girl to her left, no more than a year older than Alice. She had big brown eyes and a kind face, so I appealed to her.

'I'm looking for someone,' I said, my voice hardly more than a whisper.

Before I could say anything else, she opened her lips wide as if to speak, revealing two rows of teeth, some broken, others black with decay. Instead of words, loud wild laughter erupted from her throat and she immediately set off an uproar from the others around her. These people had been tortured and had spent days or even weeks under the threat of death. It was no good appealing to reason or asking for calm. Fingers jabbed at me and a big, gangling man with long limbs and wild eyes grabbed my left hand hard and began to pump it up and down in gratitude.

'Thank you! Thank you!' he cried, and his grip became so tight that I thought he would crunch my bones.

I managed to snatch my hand free, picked up the

staff and retreated a few steps. Any moment now the guards would hear the commotion and come out into the corridor to investigate. What if the Spook and Alice weren't in that cell? What if they were being held somewhere else?

It was too late now because, pushed roughly from behind, I was already retreating past the guardroom, and a few seconds more brought me to the door of the wine cellar. I glanced back and saw a line of people following me. At least nobody was shouting now but there was still too much noise for my liking. I just hoped that the guards had been drinking heavily. They'd probably be used to noise from the prisoners; they wouldn't be expecting a breakout.

Once inside the wine cellar, I climbed up onto a barrel and balanced there, while I quickly pushed the hatch upwards. Through the open hatch I glimpsed a stone buttress of the cathedral's outer wall and there was a rush of cool air and dampness on my face. It was raining hard.

Other people were clambering up onto the barrels.

The man who'd thanked me elbowed me aside roughly and started to pull himself up through the hatch. Moments later he was out, holding a hand down towards me, offering to pull me up.

'Come on!' he hissed.

I hesitated. I wanted to see if the Spook and Alice had got out of the cell. Then it was too late because a woman had clambered up onto the barrel beside me and was raising her arms towards the man who, without a moment's hesitation, gripped her wrists and pulled her up through the open hatch.

After that I'd missed my chance. There were others, some almost fighting amongst themselves in their desperation to get out. Not everyone was like that though. Another man pushed a barrel onto its side and rolled it against the upright one to form a step that made it easier to climb. He helped an old woman up and steadied her legs while the man above gripped her wrists and drew her slowly upwards.

Prisoners were getting out through the hatch, but others were still coming through the door into the wine cellar and I kept glancing towards them, hoping that one would be the Spook or Alice.

A thought suddenly struck me. What if one of them was too ill or weak to move and hadn't been able to leave the cell?

I had no choice. I had to go back and see. I jumped down from the barrel, but it was too late: a shout, then angry voices. Boots thundering along the corridor. A big burly guard pushed into the cellar brandishing a cudgel. He looked around and, with a bellow of anger, rushed directly towards me.

CHAPTER 10
GIRL SPIT

Without a second's hesitation I grabbed the staff and blew out the candle, plunging the cellar into darkness, and moved quickly in the direction of the door that led down into the catacombs.

There was a terrible commotion behind: shouts, screams and the sounds of a struggle. Glancing back, I saw another of the guards carrying a torch into the cellar, so I slipped behind the wine racks, keeping them between me and the light as I headed for the door in the far wall.

I felt terrible leaving the Spook and Alice behind. To have come this far and still be unable to rescue them left me feeling wretched. I only hoped that somehow in the confusion they'd managed to get out. They could both see well in the dark and if *I* could manage to find the door to the catacombs, so could they. I sensed some of the prisoners moving with me, away from the guards into the dark recesses of the cellar. A few seemed to be in front of me. Perhaps amongst them were my master and Alice but I couldn't risk calling out and alerting the guards. As I picked my way through the wine racks, ahead of me I thought I saw the door to the catacombs open and close quickly, but it was too dark to be sure.

A few moments later and I was through the door. The instant I closed it behind me I was plunged into a darkness so intense that, for a few seconds, I couldn't see my hand before my face. I stood there at the top of the steps, waiting desperately for my eyes to adjust.

As soon as I could make out the steps, I went down carefully and moved along the tunnel as quickly as I could, aware that, eventually, someone would probably check the door: I hadn't locked it behind me just in case Alice or the Spook were close behind.

I'm usually good at seeing in the dark but in those catacombs it seemed to be getting darker and darker so I came to a halt and tugged the tinderbox out of my jacket pocket. I knelt down and shook a small pile of tinder out onto the stones. Quickly I used the stone and metal to create a spark and a few seconds later I'd managed to light my candle.

With candlelight to guide me I made better progress but the air around me grew colder with every step, and not far ahead I could see sinister flickerings on the wall. Again, white luminous shapes were moving in and out of the shadows but there were now far more than last time. The dead were gathering. My previous walk along the tunnels had disturbed them.

I stopped. What was that? Somewhere in the distance I'd heard the howl of a dog. I came to a halt, my heart pounding. Was it a real dog or could it be the Bane? Andrew had mentioned a huge black dog with ferocious teeth. A huge dog that was really the Bane. I tried to tell myself it was a real dog I was hearing, one that had somehow found its way down into the catacombs. After all, if a cat could do it, why not a dog?

The howl came again, and it hung in the air for a long time, echoing and reverberating down the long tunnels. Was it ahead of me or behind? In this tunnel or another one? It was impossible to say. But with the Quisitor and his men behind me I had no choice but to keep moving towards the gate.

So I walked quickly, shivering with cold, skirting the pressed cat, till I reached the point where the forked tunnels merged. At last I rounded a corner and saw the Silver Gate. There I halted, my knees beginning to shake, my mind afraid to go on. For ahead, in the darkness beyond the candle flame, someone was waiting for me. A shadowy figure was sitting on the floor near the gate, its back against the wall, its head bowed forward. Could it be an escaped prisoner? Someone who'd got through the door before me?

I couldn't go back, so I took a few steps towards the gate and held the candle higher. A bearded face turned to me.

'What kept you?' called out a voice I recognized. 'I've been waiting here five minutes already!'

It was the Spook, alive and well! I rushed forward, filled with relief that he'd managed to escape. There was an ugly bruise over his left eye and his mouth was swollen. He'd clearly been beaten.

'Are you all right?' I asked anxiously.

'Aye, lad. Give me a few more moments to get my breath back and I'll be right as rain. Just get that gate open and we'll soon be on our way.'

'Was Alice with you?' I asked. 'Were you in the same cell?'

'No, lad. Best forget all about her. She's no good. Nowt but trouble and there's nothing we can do to help her now.' His voice sounded cruel and hard. 'She deserves what's coming to her.'

'Burning?' I asked. 'You've never held with burning a witch, let alone a young girl, and you told Andrew yourself that she's innocent.'

I was shocked. He'd never trusted Alice but it hurt me to hear him talk that way, especially as he'd faced such a terrible fate himself. And what about Meg? He hadn't always been so cold and heartless . . .

'For goodness' sake, lad, are you dreaming or awake?' the Spook demanded, his voice full of annoyance and impatience. 'Come on, snap out of it! Get the key and open that gate.'

When I hesitated, he held out his hand towards me. 'Give me my staff, lad. I've been in that damp cell far too long and my old bones are aching tonight . . .'

I reached out to hand it to him, but as his fingers began to close around it, I suddenly backed away in horror.

It wasn't just the sudden shock of his hot, foul-smelling breath searing up into my face. It was because he was holding out his right hand towards me! His right hand, not his left!

It wasn't the Spook! This wasn't my master!

As I watched, frozen to the spot, his hand dropped back to his side then, like a snake, began to writhe towards me over the cobbles. Before I could move, his arm slithered and stretched to twice its normal length and his hand closed upon my ankle, holding it in a tight, painful grip. My immediate reaction was to try and drag it away from his dreadful grasp, but I knew that wasn't the way. I kept perfectly still.

I tried to concentrate. I gripped the staff and tried to curb my fear, remembered to breathe. I was terrified, but although my body wasn't moving, my mind was. There was only one explanation and it made me shudder with terror: I was facing the Bane!

Forcing myself to focus, I studied the thing before me carefully, looking hard for anything that might help me in the slightest way. It looked just like the Spook and sounded like him too. It was impossible to tell the difference, but for the snaking hand.

After watching for a few seconds I felt a little better. It was a trick the Spook had taught me: when face to face with our greatest fears we should concentrate hard and leave our feelings behind.

'Gets them every time, lad!' he'd once told me. 'The dark feeds on fear, and with a calm mind and an empty belly the battle's half won before you even start.'

And it was working. My body had stopped shaking and I felt calmer, almost relaxed.

The Bane released my ankle and the hand slithered back to its side. The creature stood up and took a step towards me. As it did so I heard a curious noise: not the sound of boots I was expecting, more like the scratching of huge claws against the cobbles. The Bane's movement disturbed the air too, so that the candle flame flickered, distorting the shadow of the Spook cast against the Silver Gate.

Quickly I knelt and placed the candle and the staff on the floor between us. An instant later I was on my feet, my hands in each of my breeches pockets, grabbing a fistful of salt and one of iron.

'*Wasting your time, you are,*' said the Bane, its voice suddenly nothing like the Spook's at all. Harsh and deep, it reverberated through the very rocks of the catacombs, vibrating up through my boots and setting my teeth on edge. '*Old tricks like that won't get me. Been around too long, I have, to be hurt by that! Your master, Old Bones, tried it once but it did him no good. No good at all.*'

I hesitated, but only for a moment. It might just be lying – anything was worth a try. But then, amongst the iron filings, my left hand closed upon something hard. It was the small key to the Silver Gate. I couldn't risk losing that.

'*Ahhh . . . got what I need, you have,*' said the Bane with a sly smile.

Had it read my mind? Or perhaps just read the expression on my face, or maybe guessed? Either way, it knew too much.

'*Look,*' it said, a crafty look on its face, '*if Old Bones couldn't fix me then what chance have you? No chance at all! Down here they'll come, and be searching for you soon. Can't you hear the guards now? Burn, you will! Burn with the rest! There's no way out from here but through this gate. No way at all, see. So use the key now before it's too late!*'

The Bane stood to one side so that its back was against the tunnel wall. I knew exactly what it wanted: to follow me through the gate, to be free, able to work its mischief anywhere in the County. I knew what the Spook would say; what he'd expect from me. It was

183

my duty to make sure the Bane stayed trapped in the catacombs. That was more important than my own life.

'*Don't be a fool!*' the Bane hissed, its voice again far louder and harsher than I'd ever heard the Spook's. '*Listen to me and free you'll be! And rewarded as well. A big reward. The same as I offered Old Bones many years ago, but he wouldn't listen. And where has it got him, see? Tell me that! Tomorrow he'll be tried and found guilty. The day after that he'll burn.*'

'No!' I said. 'I can't do it.'

With that the Bane's face filled with anger. It still resembled the Spook but the features I knew so well were distorted and twisted with evil. It took another step towards me, raising a fist. It might only have been a trick of the candlelight but the creature seemed to be growing. And I could feel an invisible weight starting to press down on my head and shoulders. As I was forced to my knees, I thought of the cat smeared into the cobbles and realized that the same fate was awaiting me. I tried to suck in a breath but I couldn't and began to panic. I couldn't breathe! This was it!

The light of the candle was lost in the sudden darkness that covered my eyes. I tried desperately to speak, to beg for mercy, but I knew there would be no mercy unless I unlocked the Silver Gate. What had I been thinking? What a fool I'd been to believe that with a few months' training I could fend off a creature as evil and powerful as the Bane! I was dying – I felt sure of it. Alone in the catacombs. And the worst of it was that I'd failed miserably. I hadn't managed to rescue my master or Alice.

Then I heard something in the distance: the sound of a shoe scuffing against the cobbles. They say that, as you die, the last sense to go is your hearing. And for a moment I thought that the scuffing of that shoe was the last experience I'd have of this life. But then the invisible weight crushing my body slowly eased. My vision cleared and suddenly I could breathe again. I watched the Bane turn its head and look back towards the bend in the tunnel. The Bane had heard it too!

The sound came again. This time there was no doubt. Footsteps! Someone was coming!

I looked back towards the Bane and saw that it was changing. I hadn't imagined it before. It *was* growing. By now its head had almost reached the top of the tunnel, the body curving forward, the face shifting until it was no longer that of the Spook. The chin was elongating, jutting outwards and upwards to form the beginning of a hook, and the nose was curving downwards to meet it. Was it changing into its true form – that of the stone gargoyle above the main door of the cathedral? Had it gained its full strength?

I listened to the approaching footsteps. I would have blown the candle out, only that would have left me in the dark with the Bane. At least it sounded like there was only one person coming rather than a troop of the Quisitor's men. I didn't care who it was. They'd saved me for now.

I saw the feet first, as someone stepped round the corner and into the candlelight. Pointy shoes, then a slim girl in a black dress and the swing of her hips as she came round the corner.

It was Alice!

She halted, glanced towards me quickly, and her eyes widened. When she looked up at the Bane, her face was angry rather than afraid.

I looked back, and for a moment the Bane's eyes met mine. As well as the anger blazing in them, I could see something else, but before I could work it out Alice ran towards the Bane, hissing like a cat. Then, to my astonishment, she spat up into its face.

What happened next was too quick to see. There was a sudden wind and the Bane was gone.

We stood motionless for what seemed like a long time. Then Alice turned to face me.

'Didn't like girl spit much, did it?' she said with a faint smile. 'Good job I came along when I did.'

I didn't reply. I couldn't believe that the Bane had fled so easily, but I was already on my knees, struggling to fit the key into the lock of the Silver Gate. My hands were shaking and it was just as difficult as it had looked when Andrew did it.

At last I managed to get the key into the right position and it turned. I pushed the gate open, seized the key and the staff and crawled through.

'Bring the candle!' I shouted back to Alice, and as soon as she was safely through, I slid the key into the other side of the lock and struggled to turn it. This time it seemed to take an age; at any moment I expected the Bane to come back.

'Can't you go any quicker?' Alice asked.

'It's not as easy as it looks,' I told her.

Eventually I managed to lock it and let out a sigh of relief. Then I remembered the Spook . . .

'Was Mr Gregory in the cell with you?' I asked.

Alice shook her head. 'Not when you let us out. They took him away for questioning about an hour before you came.'

I'd been lucky in managing to avoid capture. Lucky in getting the prisoners out of the cell. But luck has a way of balancing itself out. I'd been just an hour too late. Alice was free but the Spook was still a prisoner, and unless I could do something about it, he was going to burn.

Wasting no more time, I led Alice along the tunnel until we came to the fast-flowing river.

I crossed quickly but when I turned back, Alice was still on the far bank, staring down at the water.

'It's deep, Tom,' she cried. 'It's too deep and the stones are slippery!'

I crossed back to where she was standing. Then, gripping her hand, I led her back across the nine flat stones. We soon reached the open hatch that led up into the empty house and, once inside the cellar, I closed the hatch behind us. To my disappointment, Andrew had already gone. I needed to talk to him: to tell him that the Spook hadn't been in the cell; warn him that Brother Peter was in danger and that the rumours really were true – the Bane's strength was back!

'We'd better stay down here for a while. The Quisitor will start searching the town once he realizes so many of you have escaped. This house is haunted –

the last place anybody will want to look is down here in the cellar.'

Alice nodded, and for the first time since the spring I looked at her properly. She was as tall as me, which meant that she'd grown at least an inch too, but she was still dressed as I'd last seen her when I'd taken her to her aunt in Staumin. If it wasn't the same black dress, it was its twin.

Her face was as pretty as ever but thinner, and older, as though it had seen things that had forced it to grow up quickly; things that nobody should have to see. Her black hair was matted and filthy and there were smears of dirt on her face. Alice looked like she hadn't had a wash for at least a month.

'It's good to see you again,' I said. 'When I saw you in the Quisitor's cart, I thought that would be it.'

She didn't reply. Just grabbed my hand and squeezed it. 'I'm half-starved, Tom. Ain't got anything to eat, have you?'

I shook my head.

'Not even a piece of that mouldy old cheese?'

'Sorry,' I said. 'I've none left.'

Alice turned away and seized one edge of the old carpet that was at the top of the heap.

'Help me, Tom,' she said. 'Need to sit down and I don't fancy the cold stones much.'

I put the candle and staff down and together we pulled the carpet onto the flags. The musty smell was stronger than ever and I watched the beetles and woodlice that we'd uncovered scurrying away across the cellar floor.

Unconcerned, Alice sat down on the carpet and drew her knees up so that she could rest her chin. 'One day I'm going to get even,' she said. 'Nobody deserves to be treated like that.'

I sat down next to her and put my hand on hers. 'What happened?' I asked.

She was silent for a while, and just as I'd decided she wasn't going to answer me, she suddenly spoke. 'Once she got to know me, my old aunt was good to me. Worked me hard, she did, but always fed me well. I was just getting used to living there at Staumin when the Quisitor came. Took us by surprise and broke down the door. But my aunt weren't no Bony Lizzie. She weren't no witch.

'They swam her down at the pond at midnight while a big crowd watched, all laughing and jeering. Real scared I was, expecting it was my turn next. Tied her feet to her hands and threw her in. Sank like a stone, she did. But it was dark and windy and a big gust came the moment she hit the water; blew a lot of the torches out. Took a long time to find her and drag her out.'

Alice buried her face into her hands and gave a sob. I waited quietly until she was able to go on. When she uncovered her face, her eyes were dry but her lips were trembling.

'When they pulled her out she was dead. It ain't fair, Tom. She didn't float, she sank, so she must have been innocent but they'd killed her anyway! After that they left me alone and just put me up in the cart with the rest.'

'My mam told me that swimming witches doesn't work anyway,' I said. 'Only fools use it.'

'No, Tom, the Quisitor's no fool. There's a reason for everything he does, you can be sure of that. He's greedy. Greedy for money. He sold my old aunt's cottage and kept the money. We watched him counting it. That's what he does. Calls people witches, gets them out of the way and takes their houses, land and money. What's more, he enjoys his work. There's darkness in him. He says he's doing it to rid the County of witches, but he's more cruel than any witch I've ever known – and that's saying something.

'There was a girl called Maggie. Not much older than me, she was. Didn't bother with swimming her. Used a different test and we all had to watch. Quisitor used a long sharp pin. He kept sticking it into her body over and over again. You should have heard her shriek. Poor girl almost went mad with the pain. She kept fainting and they had a bucket of water by the side of the table to bring her round. But at last they found what they were looking for. The Devil's mark! Know what that is, Tom?'

I nodded. The Spook had told me that it was one of

the things witchfinders used. But it was another lie, he'd said. There was no such thing as the Devil's mark. Anyone with true knowledge of the dark knew that.

'It's cruel and it ain't just,' Alice continued. 'After a bit the pain gets too much and your body goes numb, so eventually when the needle goes in you don't feel it. Then they say that's the spot where the Devil touched you, so you're guilty and have to burn. Worst thing was the look on the Quisitor's face. So pleased with himself, he was. I'll get even all right. I'll pay him back for that. Maggie don't deserve to burn.'

'The Spook doesn't deserve to burn either!' I said bitterly. 'All his life he's worked hard fighting the dark.'

'He's a man and he'll get an easier death than some,' said Alice. 'The Quisitor gives women a much harder time. Makes sure they take a long time to burn. Says it's harder to save a woman's soul than a man's. That they need a lot of pain to make them feel sorry for their sins.'

That brought to mind what the Spook had said

about the Bane not being able to abide women. The fact that they made it nervous.

'The creature you spat at was the Bane,' I told her. 'Have you heard of it? How did you manage to scare it away so easily?'

Alice shrugged. 'Ain't too difficult to tell when something ain't comfortable having you around. Some men are like that – I always know when I'm not welcome. I get that feeling near Old Gregory and it was the same down there. And spit sends most things on their way. Spit three times at a toad and nothing with cold damp skin will bother you for a month or more. Lizzie used to swear by it. Don't think it'll work that way on the Bane though. Yes, I've heard about that creature. And if it's now able to shape-shift then we're all in for some serious bother. I took it by surprise, that's all. It'll be ready next time so I ain't going down there again.'

For a while neither of us spoke. I just stared down at the musty old carpet, until suddenly I heard Alice's breathing deepen. When I looked back her eyes were closed and she'd fallen asleep in the same position, her chin resting on her knees.

I didn't really want to blow the candle out, but I didn't know how long we'd have to stay down in the cellar and it was better to save some light until later.

Once it was out I tried to get to sleep myself but it was difficult. For one thing I was cold and kept shivering. For another, I couldn't get the Spook out of my mind. We'd failed to rescue him, and the Quisitor would be really angry at what had happened. It wouldn't be long before he started burning people.

Finally I must have drifted off because I was suddenly woken by the sound of Alice's voice very close to my left ear.

'Tom,' she said, her voice hardly more than a whisper, 'there's something over there in the corner of the cellar with us. It's staring at me and I don't like it much.'

Alice was right. I could sense something in the corner and I felt cold. The hair on the back of my neck was beginning to rise. It was probably just Matty Barnes, the strangler, again.

'Don't worry, Alice,' I told her. 'It's just a ghost. Try and forget about it. As long as you're not afraid, it can't harm you.'

'I ain't afraid. At least not now.' She paused, then said, 'But I was scared in that cell. Didn't sleep a wink, what with all that shouting and screaming. I'll soon be off to sleep again. It's just that I want it to go away. It ain't right, it staring like that.'

'I don't know what to do next,' I said, thinking about the Spook again.

Alice didn't reply but her breathing deepened once more. She was asleep. And I must have gone back to sleep myself because a noise woke me up suddenly.

It was the sound of heavy boots. Someone was in the kitchen above us.

CHAPTER 11
THE SPOOK'S TRIAL

The door creaked open and candlelight filled the room. To my relief it was Andrew.

'Thought I'd find you down here,' he said. He was carrying a small parcel. As he put it down and placed the candle next to mine, he nodded towards Alice, who was still sleeping deeply but now lying on her side with her back to us, her face resting on her hands.

'So who's this then?' he asked.

'She used to live near Chipenden,' I told him. 'Her name's Alice. Mr Gregory wasn't there. They'd taken him upstairs for questioning.'

Andrew shook his head sadly. 'Brother Peter said as much. You couldn't have been more unlucky. Half an hour later and John would've been back in the cell with the others. As it was, eleven got away, but five were caught again soon afterwards. But there's more bad news. The Quisitor's men arrested Brother Peter in the street just after he'd left my shop. I saw it from the upstairs window. So that's me finished in this town. They'll probably come for me next but I'm not sticking around to answer any questions. I've locked the shop up already. My tools are on the cart and I'm heading south, back towards Adlington, where I used to work.'

'I'm sorry, Andrew.'

'Well don't be. Who wouldn't try to help his own brother? Besides, it's not that bad for me. The shop premises were only rented and I've got a trade at my fingertips. I'll always find work. Here,' he said, opening the parcel, 'I've brought you some food.'

'What time is it?' I asked.

'A couple of hours or so before dawn. I took a risk coming here. After all the commotion half the town's awake. A lot of people have gone to the big hall down Fishergate. After what happened last night the

Quisitor's holding a quick trial for all the prisoners he's still got.'

'Why doesn't he wait till daylight?' I asked.

'Even more people would attend then,' Andrew answered. 'Wants to get it over and done with before there's any real opposition. Some of the townsfolk are against what he's doing. As for the burning, it'll be tonight, after dark, on the beacon hill at Wortham, south of the river. The Quisitor will have a lot of armed men with him in case there's trouble, so if you've any sense, you'll stay here till nightfall then be on the road and away.'

Even before he managed to unwrap the parcel, Alice rolled towards us and sat up. Maybe she'd smelled the food or had been listening all the time, just pretending to be asleep. There were slices of ham, fresh bread and two big tomatoes. Without a word of thanks to Andrew, Alice set to work right away, and after just a moment's hesitation I joined her. I was really hungry and there didn't seem much point in fasting now.

'So I'll be off,' said Andrew. 'Poor John, but there's nothing we can do now.'

'Isn't it worth having one last try to save him?' I asked.

'No, you've done enough. It's too dangerous to go anywhere near the trial. And soon poor John'll be with the rest, under armed guard and on the way to Wortham to be burned alive with all those other poor wretches.'

'But what about the curse?' I said. 'You said yourself he's cursed to die alone underground, not up on a beacon.'

'Oh, the curse. I don't believe in that any more than John does. I was just desperate to stop him going after the Bane with the Quisitor in town. No, I'm afraid my brother's fate is sealed so you just get yourself away. John once told me that there's a spook operating some-where near Caster. He covers the County borders to the north. Mention John's name and he might just take you on. He was once one of John's apprentices.'

With a nod, Andrew turned to go. 'I'll leave you the

candle,' he said. 'Good luck on the road. And if you ever need a good locksmith, you'll know where to come.'

With that he was gone. I listened to him climb the cellar steps and close the back door. A few moments later Alice was licking tomato juice from her fingers. We'd eaten everything – not a crumb was left.

'Alice,' I said, 'I want to go to the trial. There might be a chance I can do something to help the Spook. Will you come with me?'

Alice's eyes widened. 'Do something? You heard what he said. Ain't nothing to be done, Tom! What can you do against armed men? No, be sensible. Ain't worth the risk, is it? Besides, why should I try to help? Old Gregory wouldn't do the same for me. Leave me to burn, he would, and that's a fact!'

I didn't know what to say to that. In a way it was true. I'd asked the Spook about helping Alice and he'd refused. So, with a sigh, I came to my feet.

'I'm going anyway,' I told her.

'No, Tom, don't leave me here. Not with the ghost . . .'

'I thought you weren't scared.'

'I ain't. But last time I fell asleep I felt it starting to squeeze my throat, I did. Might do worse if you're not here.'

'Come with me then. It won't be that dangerous because it'll still be dark. And the best place to hide is in a big crowd. Come on, please. What do you say?'

'Got a plan?' she asked. 'Something you ain't told me about?'

I shook my head.

'Thought as much,' she said.

'Look, Alice, I just want to go and see. If I can't help we'll come away. But I'd never forgive myself if I didn't at least try.'

Reluctantly, Alice stood up. 'I'll come and see what's what,' she said. 'But you've got to promise me that if it's too dangerous we'll turn back right away. I know the Quisitor better than you do. Trust me, we shouldn't be messing around near him.'

'I promise,' I told her.

I left the Spook's bag and staff in the cellar and we set off for Fishergate, where the trial was being held.

* * *

Andrew had said that half the town was awake. That was an exaggeration, but for so early in the morning there were a lot of candles flickering behind curtains and quite a few people seemed to be hastening through the dark streets in the same direction as we were.

I'd half expected that we wouldn't be able to get anywhere near the building, thinking guards would be lining the road outside, but to my surprise none of the Quisitor's men were anywhere to be seen. The big wooden doors were wide open and a crowd of people filled the doorway, spilling out onto the road outside, as if there wasn't room for them all to fit inside.

I led the way forward cautiously, glad of the darkness. When I reached the back of the crowd, I realized that it wasn't as densely packed as it had first seemed. Inside the hall the air was tainted with a sweet, sickly scent. It was just one big room with a flagged floor, across which sawdust was scattered unevenly. I couldn't see properly over the backs of the crowd because most of the people were taller than me, but there seemed to be a big space ahead that nobody wanted to move forward into. I grabbed Alice's hand and eased my way into the throng of people, tugging her along behind me.

It was dark towards the back of the hall but the front was lit by two huge torches at each corner of a wooden platform. The Quisitor was standing at the front of it, looking down. He was saying something but his voice sounded muffled.

I looked at those about me and saw the range of expressions on their faces: anger, sadness, bitterness and resignation. Some looked openly hostile. This crowd was probably mainly composed of those who opposed the work of the Quisitor. Some of them might even be relatives and friends of the accused. For a moment that thought gave me hope that some sort of rescue might be attempted.

But then my hopes were dashed: I saw why nobody had moved forward. Below the platform were five long benches of priests with their backs to us, but behind them and facing towards us was a double line of grim-faced armed men. Some had their arms folded; others had hands on the hilts of their swords as if they couldn't wait to draw them from their scabbards. Nobody wanted to get too close to them.

I glanced up towards the ceiling and saw that a high balcony ran along the sides of the hall; faces were peering down, pale white ovals that all looked the same from the ground. That would be the safest place to be and it would provide a much better view. There were steps to the left and I tugged Alice towards them. Moments later we were moving along the wide balcony.

It wasn't full and we soon found ourselves a place against the rail about halfway between the doors and the platform. There was still the same sweet stench in the air, much stronger now than it had been when we were standing on the flags below. I suddenly realized what it was. The hall was almost certainly used as a meat market. It was the smell of blood.

The Quisitor wasn't the only person on the platform.

Right at the back, in the shadows, a huddle of guards surrounded the prisoners awaiting trial, but immediately behind the Quisitor were two guards gripping a weeping prisoner by the arms. It was a tall girl with long dark hair. She was wearing a tattered dress and had no shoes.

'That's Maggie!' Alice hissed into my ear. 'The one they kept sticking pins into. Poor Maggie, it ain't fair. Thought she'd got away . . .'

Up here the sound was much better and I could hear every word the Quisitor spoke. 'By her own lips this woman is condemned!' he called out, his voice loud and arrogant. 'She has confessed all and the Devil's mark was found upon her flesh. I sentence her to be bound to the stake and burned alive. And may God have mercy upon her soul.'

Maggie began to sob even louder, but one of her captors seized her by the hair and she was dragged away towards a doorway at the back of the platform. No sooner had she disappeared through it than another prisoner wearing a black cassock and with his hands bound behind his back was pulled forward into the torchlight. For a moment I thought I was mistaken but there was no doubt.

It was Brother Peter. I knew him by the thin collar of white hair that fringed his bald head and by the curve of his back and shoulders. But his face was so badly beaten and streaked with blood that I hardly recognized it. His nose was broken, squashed back against his face, and one eye was closed to a swollen red slit.

Seeing him in that condition made me feel terrible. It was all because of me. To begin with he'd allowed me to escape; later he'd told me how I could get to the cell to rescue the Spook and Alice. Under torture, he must have told them everything. It was all my fault and I was racked with guilt.

'Once this was a brother, a faithful servant of the Church!' cried the Quisitor. 'But look at him now! Look at this traitor! One who has helped our enemies and allied himself with the forces of darkness. We have his confession, written with his own hand. Here it is!' he shouted, holding up a piece of paper high for all to see.

Nobody got a chance to read it – it could have said anything at all. Even if it was a confession, one look at poor Brother Peter's face told me that it had been beaten out of him. It wasn't fair. There was no justice here. This wasn't a trial at all. The Spook had once told me that when people were tried in the castle at Caster, at least they got a hearing – a judge, a prosecutor and someone to defend them. But here the Quisitor was doing it all himself!

'He is guilty. Guilty beyond all doubt,' he continued. 'I therefore sentence him to be taken down to the catacombs and left there. And may God have mercy on his soul!'

There was a sudden gasp of horror from the crowd but it was loudest of all from the priests seated at the front. They knew exactly what Brother Peter's fate would be. He would be pressed to death by the Bane.

Brother Peter tried to speak, but his lips were too swollen. One of the guards cuffed him about the head while the Quisitor gave a cruel smile. They pulled him away towards the door at the rear of the platform, and no sooner had he been led out of the building than another prisoner was brought forward from the gloom. My heart sank into my boots. It was the Spook.

At first glance, apart from a few bruises on his face, the Spook didn't seem to have had as hard a time as Brother Peter. But then I noticed something more chilling. He was squinting into the torchlight and looked bewildered, with a vacant expression in his green eyes. He seemed lost. It was as if his memory had gone and he didn't even know who he was. I began to wonder just how badly he'd been beaten.

'Before you is John Gregory!' cried the Quisitor, his voice echoing from wall to wall. 'A disciple of the Devil, no less, who for many years has plied his evil trade in this county, taking money from poor gullible folk. But does this man recant? Does he accept his sins and beg forgiveness? No, he is stubborn and will not confess. Now only through fire may he be purged and given hope of salvation. But furthermore, not content with the evil he can do, he has trained others and still continues to do so.

Father Cairns, I ask you to stand and give testimony!'

From the front row of benches a priest stepped forward into the torchlight closer to the platform. He had his back to me so I couldn't see his face, but I spotted his bandaged hand and when he spoke it was the same voice that I'd listened to in the confessional box.

'Lord Quisitor, John Gregory brought an apprentice with him on his visit to this town, one whom he has already corrupted. His name is Thomas Ward.'

I heard Alice let out a low gasp and my own knees began to tremble. I was suddenly sharply aware of how dangerous it was to be here in the hall, so close to the Quisitor and his armed men.

'By the grace of God the boy fell into my hands,' Father Cairns continued, 'and, but for the intervention of Brother Peter, who allowed him to escape justice, I would have delivered him to you for questioning. But I did question him myself, lord, and found him to be hardened beyond his years and far beyond persuasion by mere words. Despite my best efforts, he failed to see the error of his ways and for that we must blame John

Gregory, a man not content with practising his vile trade, one who actively corrupts the young. To my knowledge over a score of apprentices have passed through his hands and some, in turn, now follow that same trade and have taken on apprentices of their own. By such means does evil spread like a plague through the County.'

'Thank you, Father. You may be seated. Your testimony alone is enough to condemn John Gregory!'

As Father Cairns took his seat again, Alice gripped my elbow. 'Come on,' she whispered into my ear, 'it's too dangerous to stay!'

'No, please,' I whispered back. 'Just a bit longer.'

The mention of my name had scared me but I wanted to stay a few more minutes to see what happened to my master.

'John Gregory, for you there can be only one punishment!' roared the Quisitor. 'You will be bound to a stake and burned alive. I will pray for you. I will pray that pain teaches you the error of your ways. I will pray that you beg God's forgiveness so that, as your body burns, your soul is saved.'

The Quisitor stared at the Spook all the while he was ranting but he might as well have been shouting at a stone wall. There was no understanding behind the Spook's eyes. In a way it was a mercy because he didn't seem to know what was happening. But it made me realize that, even if I somehow did manage to rescue him, he might never be the same again.

A lump came to my throat. The Spook's house had become my new home and I remembered the lessons, the conversations with the Spook and even the scary times when we had to deal with the dark. I was going to miss all that, and the thought of my master being burned alive brought pricking tears to my eyes.

My mam had been right. At first I'd been doubtful about being the Spook's apprentice. I'd feared the loneliness. But she'd told me that I'd have the Spook to talk to; that although he was my teacher, eventually he'd become my friend. Well, I didn't know if that had happened yet, because he was still often stern and fierce, but I was certainly going to miss him.

As the guards dragged him towards the doorway, I nodded to Alice, and keeping my head down and not making eye contact with anybody, I led the way along the balcony and down the steps. Outside I could see that the sky was beginning to grow lighter. Soon we wouldn't have the cover of darkness and someone might recognize one of us. The streets were already busier and the crowd outside the hall had more than doubled since we'd been inside. I pushed through the throng so that I could look down the side of the building, towards the door the prisoners had been taken through.

One glance told me that the situation was hopeless. I couldn't see any prisoners, but that wasn't surprising because there must have been at least twenty guards near the doorway. What chance did we have against so many? With my heart in my boots I turned to Alice. 'Let's get back,' I said. 'There's nothing to be done here.'

I was anxious to reach the safety of the cellar so we walked quickly. Alice followed me without a word.

CHAPTER 12
THE SILVER GATE

Once back in the cellar, Alice turned to me, her eyes blazing with anger.

'It ain't fair, Tom! Poor Maggie. She doesn't deserve to burn. None of 'em do. Something's got to be done.'

I shrugged and just stared into space, my mind numb. After a while Alice lay back and fell asleep. I tried to do the same but I started thinking about the Spook again. Even though it seemed hopeless, should I still go to the burning and see if I could do anything to help? After turning it over in my mind for a while, I finally decided that, at nightfall, I would leave Priestown and go home to talk to my mam.

She'd know what I should do. I was out of my depth

here and I needed help. I'd be walking all night and would get no sleep then so it was best to grab what I could now. It took me a while to nod off, but when I did, almost immediately I started to dream and the next thing I knew I was back in the catacombs.

In most dreams you don't know that you're dreaming. But when you do, one of two things usually happens. Either you wake up right away or you stay in the dream and do what you want. That's the way it's always been with me, anyway.

But this dream was different. It was as if something was controlling my movements. I was walking down a dark tunnel with the stub of a candle in my left hand and I was approaching the dark doorway to one of the crypts that held the bones of the Little People. I didn't want to go anywhere near it but my feet just kept on walking.

I halted at the open doorway, the flickering light of the candle illuminating the bones. Most were on shelves at the rear of the crypt, but a few broken ones were scattered across the cobbled floor and lying in a heap in the corner. I didn't want to go in there, I really didn't, but I seemed to have no choice. I stepped into the crypt, hearing small fragments of bone crunching beneath my feet, when suddenly I felt very cold.

One winter when I was young, my brother James chased me and filled my ears with snow. I tried to fight back but he was only one year younger than my eldest brother Jack and just as big and strong, so much so that my dad had eventually got him apprenticed to a black-smith. He shared the same sense of humour as Jack too. Snow in the ears had been James's daft idea of a joke but it had really hurt and all my face had gone numb and ached for almost an hour afterwards. It was just like that in the dream. Extreme cold. It meant that something from the dark was approaching. The cold began inside my head until it felt frozen and numb, as though it didn't belong to me any more.

Something spoke from the darkness behind me. Something that was standing close to my back and between me and the doorway. The voice was harsh and deep and I didn't need to ask who was speaking.

Even though I wasn't facing towards it, I could smell its rank breath.

'*I'm got proper,*' said the Bane. '*I'm bound. This is all I have.*'

I said nothing and there was a long silence. It was a nightmare and I tried to wake up. I really struggled but it was useless.

'*A pleasant room, this,*' the Bane continued. '*One of my favourite places, it is. Full of old bones. But fresh blood is what I want and the blood of the young is best of all. But if I can't get blood then I'll make do with bones. New bones are the best. Give me new bones every time, fresh and sweet and filled with marrow. That's what I like. I love to split young bones and suck out the marrow. But old bones are better than nothing. Old bones like these. They're better than the hunger gnawing away at my insides. Hunger that hurts so much.*

'*There's no marrow inside old bones. But old bones still have memories, see. I stroke old bones, I do, slowly so that they give up all their secrets. I see the flesh that once covered them, the hopes and ambitions that ended in this dry, dead brittleness. That fills me up too. That eases the hunger.*'

The Bane was very close to my left ear, its voice now hardly more than a whisper. I had a sudden urge to turn round and look at it but it must have read my mind.

'*Don't turn round, boy,*' it warned. '*Or you won't like what you see. Just answer me this question . . .*'

There was a long pause and I could feel my heart hammering in my chest. At last the Bane asked its question.

'*After death, what happens?*'

I didn't know the answer. The Spook never spoke about such things. All I knew was that there were ghosts who could still think and talk. And fragments called ghasts that had been left behind when the soul had moved on. But moved on to what? I didn't know. Only God knew. If there was a God.

I shook my head. I didn't speak and I was too scared to turn round. Behind me I had a sense of something huge and terrifying.

'*There's nothing after death! Nothing! Nothing at all!*' bellowed the Bane close to my ear. '*There's just blackness and emptiness. No thinking. No feeling. Just oblivion. That's all that waits for you on the other side of death. But do my bidding, boy, and I can give you a long, long life! Three score years and ten is the best that most feeble humans can hope for. But ten or twenty times that I could give you! And all you have to do is open the gate and let me go free! Just open the gate and I'll do the rest. Your master could go free too. I know that's what you want. Go back, you could, to the life you once had.'*

A part of me longed to say yes. I faced the Spook being burned and a lonely journey north to Caster with no certainty that I'd be able to continue my apprenticeship. If only things could return to the way they'd been! But although I was tempted to say yes, I knew that it just wasn't possible. Even if the Bane kept its word, I couldn't allow it to roam loose in the County, able to work its evil at will. I knew the Spook would rather die than let that happen.

I opened my mouth to say no, but even before I could get the word out the Bane spoke again.

'The girl would be easy!' it said. *'All she wants is a warm*

fire. A home to live in. Clean clothes. But think what I offer you! And all I want is your blood. Not a lot, see. And it won't hurt that much. Just enough is all I ask. And then a pact we'll make together. Just let me suck your blood so I can be strong again. Just let me through the gate and give me my freedom. Three times after, I'll do your bidding and you'll live a long, long life. The girl's blood is better than nothing but you're what I really need. A seven times seven, you are. Only once before have I tasted sweet blood like yours. And I still remember it well, I do. The sweet blood of a seven times seven. How strong that would make me! How great would be your reward! Isn't that better than the nothingness of death?

'Ah, death will come to you one day. It will surely come despite all that I do, creeping towards you like the mist on a riverbank on a cold damp night. But I can delay that moment. Delay it for years and years. It would be a long time before you'd have to face that darkness. That blackness. That nothingness! So what do you say, boy? I'm got proper. I'm bound. But you can help!'

I was scared and tried again to wake up. But

suddenly words tumbled out of my mouth, almost as if they'd been spoken by somebody else:

'I don't believe there's nothing after death,' I said. 'I've a soul and if I live my life right, I'll live on in some way. There'll be something. I don't believe in nothingness. I don't believe in that!'

'*No! No!*' roared the Bane. '*You don't know what I know! You can't see what I see! I see beyond death. I see the emptiness. The nothingness. I know! I see the horrible state of being nothing. Nothing at all, there is! Nothing at all!*'

My heart began to slow and I suddenly felt very calm. The Bane was still behind me but the crypt was starting to get warmer. Now I understood. I knew the Bane's pain. I knew why it needed to feed upon people, upon their blood, upon their hopes and dreams . . .

'I've a soul and I'll live on,' I told the Bane, keeping my voice very calm. 'And that's the difference. I have a soul and you don't! For you there *is* nothing after death! Nothing at all!'

My head was pushed hard against the near wall of

the crypt and there was a hiss of anger behind me. A hiss that changed to a bellow of rage.

'*Fool!*' shouted the Bane, its voice booming to fill the crypt and echo beyond it down the long, dark tunnels of the catacombs. Violently, it swatted my head sideways, scraping my forehead against the hard, cold stones. Out of the corner of my left eye I could see the size of the huge hand that was gripping my head. Instead of nails, its fingers ended in huge yellow talons.

'*You had your chance but now it's gone for ever!*' bellowed the Bane. '*But there's someone else who can help me. So if I can't have you, I'll make do with her!*'

I was pushed downwards into the heap of bones in the corner. I felt myself falling through them. Down and down I went, deep into a bottomless pit filled with bones. The candle was out but the bones seemed to glow in the darkness: grinning skulls, ribcages, leg bones and arm bones, fragments of hands, fingers and thumbs, and all the while the dry dust of death covered my face, went up my nose into my mouth and down my throat, until I was choking and could hardly breathe.

'*This is what death tastes like!*' cried the Bane. '*And this is what death looks like!*'

The bones faded from view and I could see nothing. Nothing at all. I was just falling through blackness. Falling into the dark. I was terrified that the Bane had somehow killed me in my sleep, but I struggled and struggled to wake up. Somehow the Bane had been talking to me while I slept and I knew who it would now be persuading to do what I'd refused.

Alice!

At last I managed to wake myself up, but it was already too late. A candle was burning close beside me but it was just a stub. I'd been asleep for hours! The other one had gone and so had Alice!

I felt in my pocket but only confirmed what I'd guessed already. Alice had taken the key to the Silver Gate . . .

When I staggered to my feet I felt dizzy and my head

hurt. I touched the back of my hand to my forehead and it came away wet with blood. Somehow the Bane had done that to me in a dream. It could read minds too. How could you defeat a creature when it knew what you intended before you had a chance to move or even speak? The Spook was right – this creature was the most dangerous thing we'd ever faced.

Alice had left the hatch open and, snatching up the candle, I wasted no time in climbing down the steps into the catacombs. A few minutes later I reached the river, which seemed a bit deeper than before. The water, swirling downstream, was actually covering three of the nine stepping stones, the ones right in the middle, and I could feel the current tugging at my boots.

I crossed quickly, hoping against hope that I wouldn't be too late. But when I turned the corner, I saw Alice sitting with her back against the wall. Her left hand was resting on the cobbles, her fingers covered in blood.

And the Silver Gate was wide open!

CHAPTER 13
THE BURNING

'Alice!' I cried, staring in disbelief at the open gate. 'What have you done?'

She looked up at me, her eyes glistening with tears.

The key was still in the lock. Angrily, I seized it and pushed it back into my breeches pocket, burying it deep within the iron filings.

'Come on!' I snapped, almost too furious to speak. 'We've got to get out of here.'

I held out my left hand but she didn't take it. Instead she held her own, the one covered in blood, against her body and looked down at it, wincing with pain.

'What happened to your hand?' I asked.

'Ain't nothing much,' she replied. 'Soon be right as rain. Everything's going to be all right now.'

'No, Alice,' I replied, 'it's not. The whole County's in danger now, thanks to you.'

I pulled gently at her good hand and led her down the tunnel until we came to the river. At the edge of the water she tugged her hand free of mine and I didn't think anything of it. I simply crossed quickly. It was only when I got to the other side that I looked back to see Alice still standing there staring down at the water.

'Come on!' I shouted. 'Hurry up!'

'I can't, Tom!' Alice shouted back. 'I can't cross!'

I put the candle down and went back for her. She flinched away but I grabbed hold of her. If she'd struggled I'd have had no chance at all, but the moment my hands touched her, Alice's body became limp and she fell against me. Wasting no time, I bent my knees and lifted her over my shoulder, the way I'd seen the Spook carry a witch.

You see, I had no doubt. If she couldn't cross running water, then Alice had become what the Spook had always feared she would. Her dealings with the Bane had finally made her cross to the dark.

One part of me wanted to leave her there. I knew that's what the Spook would have done. But I couldn't. I was going against him but I had to do it. She was still Alice and we'd been through a lot together.

Light as she was, it was still quite difficult to cross the river with her over my shoulder and I struggled to keep my balance on the stepping stones. What made it worse was the fact that as soon as I started across, Alice began to wail as if she were in torment.

When we finally reached the other side, I lowered her back onto her feet and picked up the candle.

'Come on!' I said, but she just stood there trembling and I had to seize her hand and drag her along until we reached the steps that led up to the cellar.

Once back there, I put the candle down and sat on the edge of the old carpet. This time Alice didn't sit. She just folded her arms and leaned back against the wall. Neither of us spoke. There was nothing to say and I was too busy thinking.

I'd slept for a long time, both before the dream and after it. I went to peer out of the door at the top of the cellar steps and saw that the sun was just going down. I'd leave it another half-hour and then I'd be on my way. I desperately wanted to help the Spook but I felt utterly powerless. It hurt me even to think about what was going to happen to him, but what could I possibly do against dozens of armed men? And I wasn't going to the beacon hill just to watch the burning. I couldn't bear that. No, I was going home to see Mam. She'd know what I should do next.

Maybe my life as a spook's apprentice was over. Or she might just suggest that I go to north of Caster and find myself a new master. It was difficult to know what she'd advise me to do.

When I judged it time, I pulled the silver chain from where I'd tied it under my shirt, and put it back inside the Spook's bag with his cloak. As my dad always says: 'Waste not, want not!' So I also put the salt and iron back into their compartments inside the bag – as much as I could manage to get out of my breeches pockets.

'Come on,' I said to Alice. 'I'll let you out.'

So, wearing my cloak and carrying the bag and the staff, I climbed the steps, then used my other key to unlock the back door. Once we were out in the yard I locked it behind us again.

'Goodbye, Alice,' I said, turning to walk away.

'What? Ain't you coming with me, Tom?' Alice demanded.

'Where?'

'To the burning, of course, to find the Quisitor. He's going to get what's coming to him. What he deserves. I'm going to pay him back for what he did to my poor old aunt and Maggie.'

'And how are you going to do that?' I asked.

'I gave the Bane my blood, you see,' Alice said, her eyes opening very wide. 'I put my fingers through the grille and it sucked it out from under my fingernails. It may not like girls, but it likes their blood. It took what it wanted so the pact's sealed and now it has to do what I say. It has to do my will.'

The fingernails of Alice's left hand were black with

dried blood. Sickened, I turned away and opened the yard gate, stepping out into the passageway.

'Where you going, Tom? You can't leave now!' Alice shouted.

'I'm going home to talk to Mam,' I said, not even turning back to look at her.

'Go home to your mam, then! You're just a mam's lad, a mammy's boy, and you always will be!'

I hadn't taken more than a dozen paces before she came running after me.

'Don't go, Tom! Please don't go!' she cried.

I kept walking. I didn't even turn round.

The next time Alice shouted after me there was real anger in her voice. But more than that, she sounded desperate.

'You can't leave, Tom! I won't let you. You're mine. You belong to me!'

As she ran towards me, I turned round and faced her. 'No, Alice,' I said. 'I don't belong to you. I belong to the light and now you belong to the dark!'

She reached forward and gripped my left forearm

very hard. I could feel her nails cutting into my flesh. I flinched with the pain of it but stared back directly into her eyes.

'You don't know what you've done!' I said.

'Oh yes I do, Tom. I know exactly what I've done and one day you're going to thank me for it. You're so worried about your precious Bane but believe me, he ain't no worse than the Quisitor,' said Alice, releasing my arm. 'What I've done, I've done for all our sakes, yours and mine, even Old Gregory's.'

'The Bane will kill him. That's the first thing it will do now it's free!'

'No, you're wrong, Tom! It ain't the Bane who wants to kill Old Gregory, it's the Quisitor. Right now the Bane's his only hope of survival. And that's all thanks to me.'

I felt confused.

'Look, Tom, come with me and I'll show you.'

I shook my head.

'Well, whether you come with me or not,' she continued, 'I'll do it anyway.'

'Do what?'

'I'm going to save the Quisitor's prisoners. All of 'em! And I'm going to show him what it's like to burn!'

I looked hard at Alice again but she didn't flinch away from my gaze. Anger blazed in her eyes, and at that moment I felt that she could even have looked the Spook in the eye, something she wasn't usually capable of. Alice meant it all right and it seemed to me that the Bane might just obey her and help. After all, they'd made some kind of pact.

If there was any chance of saving the Spook then I had to be there to help him to safety. I didn't feel at all comfortable about relying on something as evil as the Bane, yet what choice did I have? Alice turned in the direction of the beacon fell and, slowly, I began to follow.

The streets were deserted and we walked quickly, heading south.

'I'd better get rid of this staff,' I said to Alice. 'It might give us away.'

233

She nodded and pointed to an old broken-down shed. 'Leave it behind there,' she said. 'We can pick it up on our way back.'

There was still some light left in the sky to the west and it was reflected in the river, twisting below the heights of Wortham. My eyes were drawn upwards to the daunting beacon fell. Its lower slopes were covered in trees, now starting to lose their leaves, but above there was only grass and scrub.

We left the last of the houses behind us and joined a throng of people crossing the narrow stone bridge over the river, moving slowly through the damp, still air. There was a white mist on the riverbank but we soon rose above it as we climbed up through the trees, trudging through mounds of damp, mouldering leaves to emerge near the summit of the hill. A large crowd had already gathered, with more people arriving by the minute. There were three huge piles of branches and twigs ready for lighting, the largest one set between the other two. Rising from these pyres were the thick wooden stakes to which the victims would be tied.

High on the beacon fell, with the lights of the town spread out below us, the air was fresher. The area was lit by torches attached to tall, slender wooden poles, which were swaying gently in the light westerly breeze. But there were patches of darkness, where the faces of the crowd were in shadow, and I followed Alice into one of these, so that we could watch what was going on without being noticed ourselves.

On guard, with their backs to the pyres, were a dozen big men wearing black hoods, with just slits for eyes and mouths. In their hands they carried cudgels and looked eager to use them. These were the assistant executioners, who would help the Quisitor with the burning and, if necessary, keep back the crowd.

I wasn't sure how the crowd would behave. Was it worth hoping that they might do something? Any relatives and friends of the condemned would want to save them, but whether there were enough of them to attempt a rescue was uncertain. Of course, as Brother Peter had said, there were lots of people who loved a burning. Many were here to be entertained.

235

No sooner had that thought entered my head than, in the distance, I heard the steady beat of drums.

'*Burn! Burn! Burn, witches, burn!*' the drums seemed to thunder.

At that sound the crowd began to murmur, their voices swelling to a roar that finally erupted into loud catcalls and hisses. The Quisitor was approaching, riding tall on his big white horse, and behind him trundled the open cart containing the prisoners. Other men on horseback were riding alongside and to the rear of the cart, and they had swords at their hips. Behind them, on foot, were a dozen drummers walking with a swagger, their arms rising and falling theatrically to the beat they were pounding out.

'*Burn! Burn! Burn, witches, burn!*'

Suddenly the whole situation seemed hopeless. Some in the front rank of the crowd started to shy rotten fruit at the prisoners but the guards on the flanks, probably worried about being hit by mistake, drew their swords and rode directly at them, driving them back into the throng, causing the whole mass of people to sway backwards.

The cart came nearer and halted, and for the first time I could see the Spook. Some of the prisoners were on their knees, praying. Others were wailing or tearing at their hair, but my master was standing straight and tall, staring ahead. His face looked haggard and tired, and there was the same vague expression in his eyes, as if he still didn't understand what was happening to him. There was a new dark bruise on his forehead above his left eye, and his bottom lip was split and swollen – he'd evidently been given another beating.

A priest stepped forward, a scroll in his right hand, and the rhythm of the drums changed. It became a deep roll which built to a crescendo then halted suddenly, as the priest began to read from the parchment.

'People of Priestown, hear this! We are gathered here to witness the lawful execution by fire of twelve witches and one warlock, the sinful wretches whom you see before you now. Pray for their souls! Pray that through pain they may come to know the error of their ways. Pray that they may beg God's forgiveness and thus redeem their immortal souls.'

There was another roll of drums. The priest hadn't finished yet and in the succeeding silence he continued to read.

'Our Lord Protector, the High Quisitor, wishes this to be a lesson to others who might choose the path of darkness. Watch these sinners burn! Watch their bones crack and their fat melt like candle tallow. Listen to their screams and all the while remember that this is nothing! This is nothing at all compared to the flames of Hell! Nothing compared to the eternity of torment that awaits those who do not seek forgiveness!'

The crowd had fallen silent at these words. Perhaps it was the fear of Hell that the priest had mentioned, but more likely, I thought, it was something else. It was what I now feared. To stand and watch the horror of what was about to happen. The realization that living flesh and blood was to be put into the flames to endure unspeakable agony.

Two of the hooded men came forward and roughly pulled the first prisoner from the cart – a woman with long grey hair that hung down thickly over her shoulders, almost as far as her waist. As they dragged her towards the nearest pyre, she began to spit and curse, fighting desperately to tear herself free. Some of the crowd laughed and jeered, calling her names, but unexpectedly she managed to break away and began running off into the darkness.

Before the guards could take even a step to follow, the Quisitor galloped his horse past them, its hooves throwing up mud from the soft ground. He seized the woman by the hair, twisting his fingers into her locks before bunching his fist. Then he tugged her upwards so violently that her back arched and she was almost lifted from her feet. She gave a high, thin wail as the Quisitor dragged her back towards the guards, who seized her again and quickly tied her to one of the stakes on the edge of the largest pyre. Her fate was sealed.

My heart sank as I saw that the Spook was the next

239

prisoner pulled down from the cart. They walked him towards the largest pyre and bound him to the central stake but not once did he struggle. He still just looked bewildered. I remembered once more how he'd told me that burning was one of the most painful deaths imaginable and he didn't hold with doing that to a witch. To watch him bound there, awaiting his fate, was unbearable. Some of the Quisitor's men were carrying torches and I imagined them lighting the pyres, the flames leaping upwards towards the Spook. It was too horrible to think about and tears began streaming down my face.

I tried to recall what my master had said about something or someone watching what we do. If you lived your life right, he'd told me, in your hour of need it would stand at your side and lend you its strength. Well, he'd lived his life right and had done everything for what he thought was the best. So he deserved something. Surely?

If I'd been part of a family that went to church and prayed more, I'd have prayed then. The habit wasn't in me and I didn't know how, but without realizing it I whispered something to myself. I didn't mean it to be a prayer but I suppose it was one really.

'Help him, please,' I whispered. 'Please help him.'

Suddenly the hair on the back of my neck began to move and I instantly felt cold, very cold. Something from the dark was approaching. Something strong and very dangerous. I heard Alice give a sudden gasp and a deep groan, and immediately my vision darkened so that, when I turned and reached towards her, I couldn't even see my hand before my face. The murmur of the crowd receded into the distance and everything grew still and quiet. I felt cut off from the rest of the world, alone in darkness.

I knew that the Bane had arrived. I couldn't see anything but I could sense it nearby, a vast dark spirit, a great weight that threatened to crush the life from me. I was terrified, for myself and for all the innocent people gathered there, but could do nothing but wait in the darkness for it to end.

When my eyes cleared, I saw Alice start forward.

Before I could stop her, she walked out of the shadows and headed directly towards the Spook and the two executioners at the central pyre. The Quisitor was close by, watching. As she approached, I saw him turn his horse towards her and spur it into a canter. For a moment I thought he intended to ride her down but he brought the animal to a halt, so close that Alice could have reached up and patted its nose.

A cruel smile split his face and I knew that he recognized her as one of the escaped prisoners. What Alice did next, I'll always remember.

In the sudden silence that had fallen she lifted her hands towards the Quisitor, pointing at him with both forefingers. Then she laughed long and loud and the sound echoed right across the hill, making the hair stand up on the back of my neck again. It was a laugh of triumph and defiance and I thought how strange it was that the Quisitor was preparing to burn those people, all of them falsely accused, all of them innocents, while free and facing him was a real witch, with real power.

Next, Alice turned on her heels and began to spin, holding her arms stretched out horizontally. As I watched, dark spots began to appear on the nose and head of the Quisitor's white stallion. At first I was puzzled and didn't understand what was happening. But then the horse whinnied in fear and reared up on its hind legs and I saw that droplets of blood were flying from Alice's left hand. Blood from where the Bane had just fed.

There was a sudden overpowering wind, a blinding flash of lightning and a clap of thunder so loud that it hurt my ears. I found myself on my knees and could hear people screaming and shouting. I looked back towards Alice and saw that she was still spinning, whirling faster and faster. The white horse reared up again, this time unseating the Quisitor, who fell off backwards onto the pyre.

Another flash of lightning and suddenly the edge of the pyre was alight, the flames crackling upwards and the Quisitor on his knees with flames all around him. I saw some of the guards rush forward to help him but the crowd was also moving forwards and one of the guards was dragged from his horse. Within moments a full-scale riot had begun. On all sides people were struggling and fighting. Others were running to escape and the air was full of shouts and screams.

I dropped the bag and ran to my master, for the flames were travelling fast, threatening to engulf him. Without thinking, I charged straight across the pyre, feeling the heat of the flames, which were already starting to take hold on the larger pieces of wood.

I struggled to untie him, my fingers fumbling at the knots. To my left a man was trying to free the grey-haired woman they'd bound first. I panicked because I was getting nowhere. There were too many knots! They were too tight and the heat was building!

Suddenly there was a shout of triumph to my left. The man had freed the woman and one look told me how: he was holding a knife and had cut through the ropes with ease. He was starting to lead her away from the stake when he glanced towards me. The air was filled with shouts and screams and the crackle of the flames. Even if I'd shouted, he wouldn't have heard me so I simply held out my left hand towards him. For a moment he seemed to hesitate, staring at my hand, but then he tossed the knife in my direction.

It fell short, into the flames. Without even thinking, I plunged my hand deep into the burning wood and retrieved it. It took just seconds to slash through the ropes.

To have freed the Spook when he had been so close to burning gave me a great feeling of relief. But my happiness was short-lived. We were still far from being safe. The Quisitor's men were all around us and there was a strong possibility that we'd be spotted and caught. This time we'd both burn!

I had to get him away from the burning pyre to the darkness beyond; to somewhere we couldn't be seen. It seemed to take an age. He leaned on me heavily and took small, unsteady steps. I remembered his bag, so we made for the spot where I'd dropped it. It was only by good fortune that we avoided the Quisitor's men. Of their leader there was no sign, but in the distance I could see mounted men cutting down with their swords anyone within range. At any moment I expected one of them to charge at us. It was getting harder and harder to make progress; the burden of the Spook seemed to increase against my shoulder and I still had the weight of his bag in my right hand. But then someone else was holding his other arm and we were moving towards the darkness of the trees and safety.

It was Alice.

'I did it, Tom! I did it!' she shouted excitedly.

I wasn't sure how to reply. Of course I was pleased but I couldn't approve of her method. 'Where's the Bane now?' I asked.

'Don't you worry about that, Tom. I can tell when it's near and I don't feel it anywhere now. Must have taken a lot of power to do what it just did so I reckon it's gone back to the dark for a while to build up its strength.'

I didn't like the sound of that. 'What about the Quisitor?' I asked. 'I didn't see what happened to him. Is he dead?'

Alice shook her head. 'Burned his hands when he fell, that's all. But now he knows what it's like to burn!'

As she said that, I became aware of the pain in my own hand, the left one that was supporting the Spook. I looked down and saw that the back of it was raw and blistered. With each step I took the pain seemed to increase.

We crossed the bridge with a jostling crowd of frightened people, all hastening north, eager to be away from the riot and what would follow. Soon the Quisitor's men would regroup, eager to recapture the prisoners and punish anyone who'd played a part in their escape. Anyone in their path would suffer.

Long before dawn we were clear of Priestown and spent the first few hours of daylight in the shelter of a dilapidated cattle shed, afraid that the Quisitor's men might be nearby searching for escaped prisoners.

The Spook hadn't said a single word when I'd spoken to him, not even after I'd collected his staff and handed it to him. His eyes were still vacant and staring, as though his mind was in an entirely different place. I began to worry that the blow to his head was serious, which gave me little choice.

'We need to get him back to our farm,' I told Alice. 'My mam will be able to help him.'

'Won't take too kindly to seeing me though, will she?' said Alice. 'Not when she finds out what I've done. Neither will that brother of yours.'

I nodded, wincing at the pain in my hand. What Alice said was true. It would be better if she didn't come with me but I needed her to help with the Spook, who was far from steady on his feet.

'What's wrong, Tom?' she asked. She'd noticed my hand and came across to take a look at it. 'Soon fix that,' she said, 'I won't be long . . .'

'No, Alice, it's too dangerous!'

But before I could stop her she slipped out of the shed. Ten minutes later she was back with some small pieces of bark and the leaves of a plant I didn't recognize. She chewed the bark with her teeth until it was in small fibrous pieces.

'Hold out your hand!' she commanded.

'What's that?' I asked doubtfully, but my hand was really hurting so I did as I was told.

Gently, she placed the small pieces of bark on the burn and wrapped my hand in the leaves. Then she teased a black thread from her dress and used that to bind them in position.

'Lizzie taught me this,' she said. 'It'll soon take away the pain.'

I was about to protest, but almost immediately the pain began to fade. It was a remedy taught to Alice by a witch. A remedy that worked. The ways of the world were strange. Out of evil good could come. And it wasn't just my hand. Because of Alice and her pact with the Bane, the Spook had been saved.

CHAPTER 14
DAD'S TALE

We came in sight of the farm about an hour before sunset. I knew that Dad and Jack would just be starting the milking so it was a good time to arrive. I needed a chance to speak to Mam on my own.

I hadn't been back home since the spring, when the old witch, Mother Malkin, had paid my family a visit. Thanks to Alice's bravery on that occasion we'd destroyed her, but the incident had upset Jack and his wife Ellie, and I knew they wouldn't be keen on me staying after dark. Spooks' business scared them and they were worried that something might happen to their child. So I just wanted to help the Spook and then get back on the road as quickly as possible.

I was also aware that I was risking everyone's lives by bringing the Spook and Alice to the farm. If the Quisitor's men followed us here they would have no mercy on those harbouring a witch and a spook. I didn't want to put my family in any more danger than I had to, so I decided to leave Alice and the Spook just outside the farm boundary. There was an old shepherd's hut belonging to the nearest farm to us. They'd gone over to cattle so it hadn't been used for years. I helped Alice get the Spook inside and told her to wait there. That done, I crossed the field, heading directly towards the fence that bordered our farmyard.

When I opened the door to the kitchen, Mam was in her usual place in the corner next to the fire, sitting in her rocking chair. The chair was very still and she just stared at me as I went in. The curtains were already closed, and in the brass candlestick the beeswax candle was alight.

'Sit down, son,' she invited, her voice low and soft. 'Pull up a chair and tell me all about it.' She didn't seem in the least bit surprised to see me.

It was what I was used to. Mam was often in demand when midwives encountered problems with a difficult birth, and eerily she always knew when someone wanted her help long before the message arrived at the farm. She sensed these things, just as she'd sensed my approach. There was something special about my mam. She had gifts that someone like the Quisitor would want to destroy.

'Something bad's happened, hasn't it?' Mam said. 'And what's wrong with your hand?'

'It's nothing, Mam. Just a burn. Alice fixed it. It doesn't hurt at all now.'

Mam raised her eyebrows at the mention of Alice. 'Tell me all about it, son.'

I nodded, feeling a lump come into my throat. I tried three times before I was able to get my first sentence out. When I did manage to speak, it all came out in a rush.

'They almost burned Mr Gregory, Mam. The Quisitor caught him in Priestown. We've escaped but they'll be after us, and the Spook's not well. He needs help. We all do.'

The tears started to run down my face as I admitted to myself what was now bothering me most of all. The main reason I hadn't wanted to go to the beacon fell was because I'd been scared. I'd been afraid that they'd catch me and that I would burn as well.

'What on earth were you doing in Priestown?' Mam asked.

'Mr Gregory's brother died and his funeral was there. We had to go.'

'You're not telling me everything,' Mam said. 'How did you escape from the Quisitor?'

I didn't want Mam to know what Alice had done. You see, Mam had once tried to help Alice and I didn't want her to know how she'd finally ended up, turning to the dark as the Spook had always feared.

But I had no choice. I told her the full story. When I'd finished, Mam sighed deeply. 'It's bad, really bad,' she said. 'The Bane on the loose doesn't bode well for any-one in the County – and a young witch bound to its will – well, I fear for us all. But we'll just have to make the best of it. That's all we can do. I'll get my

253

bag and go and see what I can do for poor Mr Gregory.'

'Thanks, Mam,' I told her, suddenly realizing that all I'd talked about had been my own troubles. 'But how are things here? How's Ellie's baby doing?' I asked.

Mam smiled but I detected a hint of sadness in her eyes. 'Oh, the baby's doing fine and Ellie and Jack are happier than they've ever been. But son,' she said, touching my arm gently, 'I've got some bad news for you too. It's about your dad. He's been very ill.'

I stood up, hardly able to believe what she was saying. The look on her face told me that it was serious.

'Sit down, son,' she said, 'and listen carefully before you start getting all upset. It's bad but it could have been a lot worse. It started as a heavy cold but then it got on his chest and turned to pneumonia and we nearly lost him. He's on the mend now, I hope, but he'll need to wrap up well this winter. I'm afraid he won't be able to do much on the farm any more. Jack will just have to cope without him.'

'I could help out, Mam.'

'No, son, you've got your own job to do. With the

Bane free and your master weakened the County needs you more than ever. Look, let me just go up first and tell your dad that you're here. And I wouldn't say anything about the trouble you've had. We don't want to give him any bad news or nasty shocks. We'll just keep that to ourselves.'

I waited in the kitchen but a couple of minutes later Mam came back downstairs, carrying her bag.

'Well, you go up and see your dad while I go and help your master. He's glad that you're back but don't keep him talking too long. He's still very weak.'

Dad was sitting propped up in bed on several pillows. He smiled weakly when I came into the room. His face was gaunt and tired and there was a grey stubble on his chin that made him look much older.

'What a nice surprise, Tom. Sit down,' he said, nodding towards the chair at the side of the bed.

'I'm sorry,' I said. 'If I'd known you were ill I'd have come home sooner to see you.'

Dad held up his hand as if to say it didn't matter.

255

Then he began to cough violently. He was supposed to be getting better so I wouldn't like to have heard him when he was really ill. The room had a smell of illness. The hint of something you never smelled outdoors. Something that only lingers in sick rooms.

'How's the job going?' he asked, when he'd finally stopped choking.

'Not bad. I'm getting used to it now and I prefer it to farming,' I said, pushing all that had happened to the very back of my mind.

'Farming too dull for you, eh?' he asked with a faint smile. 'Mind you, I wasn't always a farmer.'

I nodded. In his younger days Dad had been a seaman. He'd told lots of tales of the places he'd visited. They'd been rich stories, full of colour and excitement. His eyes always shone with a faraway look when he remembered those times. I wanted to see that spark of life return to them.

'Aye, Dad,' I said, 'tell me one of your stories. The one about that huge whale.'

He paused for a moment, then grabbed my hand,

pulling me closer. 'Reckon there's one story I needs be telling you, son, before it's too late.'

'Don't talk daft,' I said, shocked by this turn in the conversation.

'Nay, Tom, I'm hoping to see another spring and summer but I don't think I'm long for this world. I've been thinking a lot lately and I reckon it's time I told you what I know. I wasn't expecting to see you for a while but you're here now and who knows when I'll see you next?' He paused and then said, 'It's about your mother – how we met and the like.'

'You'll see lots of springs, Dad,' I said, but I was surprised. For all my father's wonderful stories, there was one he'd never told properly: how he'd met Mam. We could always tell that he never really wanted to talk about it. He either changed the subject or told us to go and ask her. We never did. When you're a child there are things you don't understand but just don't ask about. You know that your dad and mam don't want to tell you. But today was different.

He shook his head wearily, then bowed it low, as if a

great burden was pressing down on his shoulders. When he straightened up again, the faint smile was back on his face.

'I'm not sure she'll thank me for telling you, mind, so let's keep this between ourselves. I'll not be telling your brothers either, and I'd ask you to do the same, son. But I think in your line of work, and you being a seventh son of a seventh son and all, well . . .'

He paused again and shut his eyes. I stared at him and felt a wave of sadness as I realized how old and ill he was looking. He opened his eyes again and began to talk.

'We sailed into a little harbour to take on water,' he said, beginning his tale as if he needed to get going quickly before he changed his mind. 'It was a lonely place overhung with high, rocky hills, with just the harbour master's house and a few small fishermen's cottages built of white stone. We'd been at sea for weeks and the captain, being a good man, said that we deserved a break. So he gave us all shore leave. We took it in two shifts and I got the second one, which started well after dark.

'There were a dozen of us and when we finally made it to the nearest tavern, which was on the edge of a village almost halfway up a mountain, it was almost ready to close. So we drank fast, throwing strong spirits down our throats like there was no tomorrow, and then bought a flagon of red wine each to drink on the way back to the ship.

'I must have drunk too much because I woke up alone at the side of the steep track that led down to the harbour. The sun was just about to come up but I wasn't too bothered because we weren't sailing till noon. I climbed to my feet and dusted myself off. It was then that I heard the sound of distant sobbing.

'I listened for almost a minute before I made up my mind. I mean, it sounded just like a woman but how could I be sure? There are all sorts of strange tales from those parts about creatures that prey on travellers. I was alone and I don't mind telling you I was scared, but if I hadn't gone to see who was crying I'd never have met your mam and you wouldn't be here now.

'I climbed the steep hill at the side of the track and

scrambled down the other side until it brought me right to the edge of a cliff. It was a high cliff, with the waves crashing on the rocks below, and I could see the ship at anchor in the bay and it was so small that it seemed as if it could fit into the palm of my hand.

'A narrow rock jutted up from the cliff like a rat's tooth and a young woman was sitting with her back to it, facing out to sea. She'd been bound to that rock with a chain. Not only that, but she was as naked as the day she was born.'

With those words, Dad blushed so deeply that his face turned almost County-red.

'She started to try and tell me something then. Something that she feared. Something far worse than just being fastened to that rock. But she was speaking in her own language and I didn't understand a word of it – I still don't but she taught you well enough and, do you know, you were the only one that she bothered with in that way? She's a good mother but none of your brothers heard even a word of Greek.'

I nodded. Some of my brothers hadn't been best

pleased by that, particularly Jack, and it had sometimes made life difficult for me.

'No, she couldn't explain in words what it was but there was something out to sea that was terrifying her. I couldn't think what it could be, but then the tip of the sun came up above the horizon and she screamed.

'I stared at her but I couldn't believe what I was seeing: tiny blisters began to erupt on her skin until, within less than a minute, she was a mass of sores. It was the sun she feared. To this day, as you've probably noticed, she finds it difficult to be out even in a County sun, but the sunlight in that land was fierce and without help she'd have died.

He paused to catch his breath, and I thought about Mam. I'd always known that she avoided sunlight – but it was something I'd just taken for granted.

'What could I do?' Dad continued. 'I had to think fast so I took off my shirt and covered her with it. It wasn't big enough so there was nothing else for it and I had to use my trousers as well. Then I crouched there with my back to the sun, so that my shadow fell over her, protecting her from its fierce light.

'I stayed that way until long after noon, when the sun finally moved out of sight behind the hill. By then my ship had sailed without me and my back was raw with sunburn, but your mam was alive and the blisters had already faded away. I struggled to get her free of the chain, but whoever had tied it knew even more about knots than I did and I was a seaman. It was only when I finally got it off her that I noticed something so cruel that I could hardly believe it. I mean, she's a good woman, your mam – how could someone have done such a thing, and to a woman too?'

Dad fell silent and stared down at his hands and I could see that they were trembling with the memory of what he'd seen. I waited almost a minute and then I prompted him gently.

'What was it, Dad?' I asked. 'What had they done?'

When he looked up, his eyes were full of tears. 'They'd nailed her left hand to the rock,' he said. 'It was a thick nail with a broad head and I couldn't begin to think how I was going to get her hand free without hurting her even more. But she just smiled and tore her hand free, leaving the nail still in the rock. There was blood dripping onto the ground at her feet but she stood up and walked towards me as if it were nothing.

'I took a step backwards and almost fell over the cliff but she put her right hand on my shoulder to steady me and then we kissed. Being a seaman who visited dozens of ports each year, I'd kissed a few women before but usually it was after I'd had a skinful of ale and was numb, sometimes even close to passing out. I'd never kissed a woman when sober and certainly never in broad daylight. I can't explain it but I knew right away that she was the one for me. The woman I'd spend the rest of my life with.'

He started coughing then and it went on for a long time. When he'd finished it left him breathless and it was another couple of minutes before I spoke again. I should have let him rest but I knew I might not get another chance. My mind was racing. Some things in Dad's tale reminded me of what the Spook had written

263

about Meg. She'd also been bound with a chain. When released she'd kissed the Spook just as Mam had kissed Dad. I wondered if the chain was silver but I couldn't ask. Part of me didn't want to know the answer. If Dad had wanted me to know, he'd have told me.

'What happened next, Dad? How did you manage to get back home?'

'Your mother had money, son. She lived alone in a big house set in a garden surrounded by a high wall. It wasn't more than a mile or so from where I'd found her so we went back there and I stayed. Her hand healed quickly, leaving not even the faintest of scars, and I taught her our language. Or, to be honest, she taught me how to teach her. I pointed at objects and said their names aloud. When she'd repeated what I'd said I'd just nod to say it sounded right. Once was enough for each word. Your mam's sharp, son. Really sharp. She's a clever woman and never forgets a thing.

'Anyway, I stayed at that house for weeks and I was happy enough but for the odd night or so when her sisters came to visit. There were two of them, tall, fierce-looking women, and they used to build a fire out back behind the house and stay there till dawn talking to your mam. Sometimes all three of them would dance around the fire; other nights they played dice. But each time they came there were arguments and they gradually got worse.

'I knew it was something to do with me because her sisters would glare at me through the window with anger in their eyes and your mam would wave at me to go back into the room. No, they didn't like me much and that was the main reason, I think, that we left that house and came back to the County.

'I'd set sail as a hired hand, an ordinary seaman, but I came back like a gentleman. Your mam paid for our passage home and we had a cabin all to ourselves. Then she bought this farm and we were married in the little church at Mellor, where my own mam and dad are buried. Your mother doesn't believe what we believe but she did it for me so that the neighbours wouldn't talk, and before the end of the year your brother Jack was born. I've had a good life, son, and the best part of it started the day I met your mam. But I'm telling you this because I want you to understand. You do realize, don't you, that one day when I'm gone, she'll go back home, back to where she belongs?'

My mouth opened in amazement when Dad said that. 'What about her family?' I asked. 'Surely she wouldn't leave her grandchildren?'

Dad shook his head sadly. 'I don't think she's any choice, son. She once told me she's what she calls "unfinished business" back there. I don't know what it is and she never did tell me why she'd been fastened to the rock to die. She has her own world and her own life, and when the time comes, she'll go back to it, so don't make it hard for her. Look at me, lad. What do you see?'

I didn't know what to say.

'What you see is an old man who's not long for this life. I see the truth of it every time I look in a mirror, so don't try to tell me I'm wrong. As for your mam, she's still in the prime of life. She may not be the girl she once was but she's still got years of good living left in her. But for what I did that day, your mam wouldn't have looked at me twice. She deserves her freedom, so let her go with a smile. Will you do that, son?'

I nodded and then stayed with him until he calmed down and drifted off to sleep.

CHAPTER 15
THE SILVER CHAIN

When I went downstairs, Mam was already back. I was anxious to ask how the Spook was and what she'd done for him but I didn't get the chance. Through the kitchen window I'd spied Jack crossing the yard with Ellie, their baby cradled in her arms.

'I've done what I can for your master, son,' Mam whispered just before Jack opened the door. 'We'll talk after supper.'

For a moment Jack froze in the doorway looking at me, a mixture of expressions flickering across his face. At last he smiled and walked forward to rest his arm across my shoulders.

'Good to see you, Tom,' he said.

'I was just passing on my way back to Chipenden,' I told him. 'Thought I'd call in and see how you all were. I'd have visited earlier if I'd known that Dad had been so ill . . .'

'He's on the mend now,' Jack said. 'That's the important thing.'

'Oh, yes, Tom, he's much better now,' Ellie agreed. 'He'll be right as rain in a few weeks.'

I could see that the sad expression on Mam's face said otherwise. The truth of it was that Dad would be lucky to make it till spring. She knew it and so did I.

At supper everybody seemed subdued, even Mam. I couldn't work out whether it was my being there or Dad's illness making everyone so quiet, but during the meal Jack could barely more than nod at me, and when he did speak it was to say something sarcastic.

'You're looking pale, Tom,' he said. 'Must be all that skulking about in the dark. Can't be good for you.'

'Don't be cruel, Jack!' Ellie scolded. 'Anyway, what

do you think about our Mary? Had her christened last month. Grown up quite a bit since you last saw her, hasn't she?'

I smiled and nodded. I was astonished to see how much the baby had grown. Instead of being a tiny thing with a red, wrinkled-up face, she was plump and round with sturdy limbs and a watchful, alert expression. She looked ready to leave Ellie's knee and start crawling round the kitchen floor.

I hadn't felt very hungry but the moment Mam heaped a large portion of steaming hotpot onto my plate, I tucked in right away.

No sooner had we finished than she smiled at Jack and Ellie. 'I've something to discuss with Tom,' she said. 'So why don't you two go up and get an early night for once? And don't worry about the washing-up, Ellie. I'll see to it.'

There was still some hotpot left in the dish and I saw Jack's eyes flicker towards it then back to Mam. But Ellie stood up and Jack followed slowly. I could see he wasn't best pleased.

'I think I'll just take the dogs and walk the boundary fence first,' he said. 'There was a fox about last night.'

As soon as they'd left the room I blurted out the question I'd been dying to ask.

'How is he, Mam? Is Mr Gregory going to be all right?'

'I've done what I can for him,' Mam said. 'But injuries to the head usually sort themselves out one way or the other. Only time will tell. I think the sooner you get him back to Chipenden the better. He'd be welcome here but I've got to respect Jack and Ellie's wishes.'

I nodded and stared down at the table sadly.

'Can you manage a second helping, Tom?' Mam asked.

I didn't need to be asked twice and Mam smiled as I tucked in. 'I'll just go up and see how your dad is,' she said.

She soon came back downstairs. 'He's fine,' she said. 'He's just nodded off to sleep again.'

She sat down opposite and watched me eat, her face serious. 'The wounds I saw on Alice's fingers – is that where the Bane took blood from her?'

I nodded.

'Do you trust her now after all that's happened?' she asked suddenly.

I shrugged. 'I don't know what to do. She's crossed to the dark, but without her the Spook and lots of other innocent people would have died.'

Mam sighed. 'It's a nasty business and I'm not sure the answer's clear yet. I wish I could go with you and help you get your master back to Chipenden, because it won't be an easy journey, but I can't leave your dad. Without careful nursing he could suffer a relapse and I can't risk that happening.'

I cleaned my plate with a piece of bread then pushed back my chair.

'I think I'd better get going, Mam. The longer I'm here, the more danger I'm putting you all in. There's no way the Quisitor will let us go without a chase. And now the Bane's free and has fed on Alice's blood I can't risk leading him here.'

'Don't rush off just yet,' Mam said. 'I'll slice you some ham and bread to eat on the road.'

'Thanks, Mam.'

She set to work slicing the bread while I watched, wishing I could stay longer. It would be good to be home again, even if only for one night.

'Tom, in your lessons about witches, did Mr Gregory tell you about those who use familiars?'

I nodded. Different types of witches gained their power in different ways. Some used bone magic, others blood magic; recently he'd told me about a third and even more dangerous type. They used what was called 'familiar magic'. They gave their blood to some creature – it could be a cat, a toad or even a bat. In return it became their eyes and ears and did their will. Sometimes it grew so powerful that they fell completely under its power and had little or no will of their own.

'Well, that's what Alice thinks she's doing now, Tom – using familiar magic. She's made a pact with that creature, and is using it to get what she wants. But she's playing a dangerous game, son. If she's not careful she'll end up belonging to it and you'll never really be able to trust her again. At least, not while the Bane still lives.'

'Mr Gregory said that it was getting stronger, Mam. That soon it would be able to take on the flesh of its original shape. I saw it down in the catacombs – it had shape-shifted into the Spook and tried to trick me. So it's obviously been getting stronger down there.'

'That's true enough but what's just happened will have set it back a bit. You see, the Bane will have used up a lot of energy in flying free of a place it's been bound to for so long. So for now it will be confused and lost, probably a spirit again, not strong enough to clothe itself in flesh at all. It probably won't be able to regain its full strength until the blood pact with Alice is completed.'

'Can it see through Alice's eyes?' I asked.

The thought was terrifying. I was about to go off with Alice through the darkness. I remembered the feel of the Bane's weight on my head and shoulders, the expectation that I was about to be pressed and that my last moment had come. Maybe it was safer to wait until daylight . . .

'No, not yet, son. She gave it her blood and its freedom. In return it will have promised to obey her three times, but each time it'll want more of her blood. After feeding it again at the Wortham burning, she'll be weakened and finding it harder and harder to resist. If she feeds it once more, it will be able to see out of her eyes. Finally, on the last feeding, she'll belong to it and it will have the strength to return to its true form. And there'll be nothing anyone can do to save Alice then,' Mam said.

'So wherever it is it'll be looking for Alice?'

'It will, son, but for a short while, unless she calls it to her, the chances of it finding her will be very slight. Especially when she's on the move. If she stays in one place for any length of time the Bane will have more chance of finding her. Each night it'll get a little stronger though, especially if it chances upon some other victim. Any sort of blood would help it, animal or human. Someone alone in the dark would be easy to terrorize. Easy to bend to its will. In a while it'll find Alice, and after that it'll always be somewhere near to her except during daylight hours, when it'll probably stay underground. Creatures of the dark rarely venture abroad when it's light. But with the Bane on the loose, gaining in strength, everyone in the County should be afraid when night falls.'

'How did it all start, Mam? Mr Gregory told me that King Heys of the Little People had to sacrifice his sons to the Bane and that somehow the last son managed to bind it.'

'It's a sad and terrible story,' Mam said. 'What happened to the king's sons doesn't bear thinking about. But I think it's better that you know so you understand just what you're up against. The Bane lived in the long barrows at Heysham, amongst the bones of the dead. First it took the eldest son there to use him as a plaything, picking the thoughts and dreams from his mind until little remained but misery and darkest despair. And so it went on with son after son. Think how their father must have felt! He was a king and yet he could do nothing to help.'

Mam sighed sadly. 'Not one of Heys's sons survived much more than a month of such torment. Three threw themselves from the cliffs nearby to smash themselves to pieces on the rocks below. Two refused to eat and wasted away. The sixth swam out to sea until his strength failed and he drowned – his body was brought back to shore by the spring tides. All six are buried in the stone graves carved from the rock. A further grave holds the body of their father, who died soon after his six sons, of a broken heart. So only Naze, the last of his children, his seventh son, outlived him.

'The king was a seventh son too, so Naze was like you and had the gift. He was small, even by the standards of his own people, and the old blood ran strongly through his veins. He managed to bind the Bane somehow but nobody knows how, not even your master. Afterwards the creature slew Naze on the spot, pressing him flat against the stones. Then, years later, because they reminded the Bane of how it had been tricked, it broke his bones into tiny pieces and pushed them through the Silver Gate so that at last Naze's people were able to give him a proper burial. His remains are with the others in the stone graves at Heysham, which is named after the ancient king.'

We didn't say anything for a few moments. It was a terrible tale.

'Then how can we stop it now it's loose again, Mam?' I asked, breaking the silence. 'How can we kill it?'

'Leave that to Mr Gregory, Tom. Just help him get back to Chipenden and grow fit and well again. He'll work out what to do next. The easiest way would be to bind it again, but even then it would still be able to work its evil as it has more and more in recent years. If it was able to clothe itself in flesh before, down there in the catacombs, then it would do it again, and before long, as its strength grew, it would revert to its natural form, corrupting Priestown and the County beyond. So although we'd be safer with it bound, it's not a final solution. Your master needs to learn how to kill it, for all our sakes.'

'But what if he doesn't recover?'

'Let's just hope that he does, for there is more to be done than perhaps you are ready to cope with yet. You see, son, wherever Alice goes, it will use her to hurt others so your master may have no choice but to put her into a pit.'

Mam looked troubled, then suddenly paused and put her hand to her forehead, squeezing her eyes shut as if she had a sudden painful headache.

'Are you all right, Mam?' I asked anxiously.

She nodded and smiled weakly. 'Look, son, you sit yourself down for a while. I need to write a letter for you to take.'

'A letter? Who for?'

'We'll talk more when I've finished.'

I sat in a chair by the fire, staring into the embers while Mam wrote at the table. I kept wondering what she was writing. When she'd finished, she sat down in her rocking chair and handed me the envelope. It was sealed and on it was written:

To my youngest son, Thomas J. Ward

279

I was surprised. I'd imagined it must be a letter for the Spook to read when he got better.

'Why are you writing to me, Mam? Why not just tell me what you have to say now?'

'Because every little thing we do changes things, son,' Mam said, putting her hand gently on my left forearm. 'To see the future is dangerous and to communicate what you see doubly so. Your master must follow his own path. He must find his own way. We each have free will. But there's a darkening ahead and I have to do everything in my powers to avert the worst that might happen. Only open the letter in a time of great need when the future looks hopeless. Trust your instincts. You'll know when this moment comes – though I pray for all your sakes that it never does. Till then, keep it safe.'

Obediently, I slipped it inside my jacket.

'Now follow me,' Mam said. 'I've something else for you.'

From the tone of her voice and strange manner I guessed where we were heading. And I was right.

Carrying the brass candlestick, she led me upstairs to her private storeroom, the locked room just below the attic. Nowadays nobody ever went in that room but Mam. Not even Dad. I'd been in with her a couple of times as a small child, although I could hardly remember it now.

Taking a key from her pocket, she unlocked the door and I followed her inside. The room was full of boxes and chests. I knew she came in here once a month. What she did I couldn't guess.

Mam walked into the room and halted before the large trunk closest to the window. Then she stared at me hard until I felt a bit uneasy. She was my mam and I loved her but I certainly wouldn't have liked to be her enemy.

'You've been Mr Gregory's apprentice for nearly six months, so you've had long enough to see things for yourself,' she said. 'And by now the dark has noticed you, and will be trying to hunt you down. So you're in danger, son, and for a while that danger will keep on growing. But remember this. You're growing too.

You're growing up fast. Each breath, each beat of your heart makes you stronger, braver, better. John Gregory's been struggling against the dark for years preparing the way for you. Because, son, when you're a man then it'll be the dark's turn to be afraid, because then you'll be the hunter, not the hunted. That's why I gave you life.'

She smiled at me for the first time since I'd gone into the room, but it was a sad smile. Then, lifting the lid of the box, she held the candle up so I could see what lay inside.

A long silver chain with fine links gleamed brightly in the candlelight. 'Lift it out,' Mam said. 'I can't touch it.'

I shivered at her words because something told me that this was the same chain that had bound Mam to the rock. Dad hadn't mentioned it being silver, a vital omission because a silver chain was used to bind a witch. It was an important tool of a spook's trade. Could this mean that Mam was a witch? Perhaps a lamia witch like Meg? The silver chain, the way she'd kissed my dad – it all sounded very familiar.

I lifted out the chain and balanced it in my hands. It was fine and light, of better quality than the Spook's chain, with much more silver in the alloy.

As if she guessed what I'd been thinking, Mam said, 'I know your dad told you how we met. But always remember this, son. None of us is either all good or all bad – we're all somewhere in between – but there comes a moment in each life when we take an important step, either towards the light or towards the dark. Sometimes it's a decision we make inside our head. Or maybe it's because of a special person we meet. Because of what your dad did for me I stepped in the right direction and that's why I'm here today. That chain now belongs to you. So put it away and keep it safe until you need it.'

I coiled the chain around my wrist, then slipped it into my inside pocket, next to the letter. That done, Mam closed the lid and I followed her out of the room, waiting while she locked the door.

Downstairs I picked up the packet of sandwiches and prepared to leave.

'Let's have a look at that hand before you go!'

I held it out and Mam carefully untied the threads and pulled away the leaves. The burn seemed to be healing already.

'That girl knows her stuff,' she said. 'I'll give her that. Let the air get to it now and it'll be right as rain in a few days.'

Mam hugged me and, after thanking her once more, I opened the back door and stepped out into the night. I was halfway across the field, heading for the boundary fence, when I heard a dog bark and saw a figure heading towards me through the darkness.

It was Jack, and when he got close, I saw by the starlight that his face was twisted with anger.

'Do you think I'm stupid?' he shouted. 'Do you? It didn't take five minutes for the dogs to find them!'

I looked at the dogs, which were both cowering behind Jack's legs. They were working dogs and weren't soft, but they knew me and I'd have expected some sort of greeting. Something had scared them badly.

'You might well look,' said Jack. 'That girl hissed and spat at them and they ran off as if the Devil himself were twisting their tails. When I told her to clear off, she had the cheek to tell me that she was on somebody else's land and it was nothing at all to do with me.'

'Mr Gregory's ill, Jack. I had no choice but to call in and get Mam's help. I kept him and Alice outside the farm boundary. I know how you feel so I did the best I could.'

'I'll bet you did. I'm a grown man but Mam ordered me to bed like a child. How do you think that makes me feel? And in front of my own wife too. Sometimes I wonder if the farm will ever really belong to me.'

I was angry myself by then and I felt like telling him that it probably would and a lot sooner than he thought. It would all be his once Dad was dead and Mam had gone back home to her own land. But I bit my lip and said nothing about it.

'I'm sorry, Jack, but I've got to be off,' I told him, setting off towards the hut where I'd left Alice and the Spook. After a dozen or so steps I turned but Jack already had his back to me and was on his way home.

We set off without saying a word. I had a lot to think about and I think Alice knew that. The Spook just stared into space but he did seem to be walking better and no longer needed to lean on us.

About an hour before the sun came up, I was the first to break the silence.

'Are you hungry?' I asked. 'Mam's made us some breakfast.'

Alice nodded and we sat down on a grassy bank and started on the food. I offered some to the Spook but he pushed my arm away roughly. After a few moments he walked a little way off and sat down on a stile as if he didn't want to be anywhere near us. Or Alice at least.

'He seems stronger. What did Mam do?' I asked.

'She bathed his forehead and kept looking at his

eyes. Then she gave him a potion to drink. I kept my distance and she didn't even glance in my direction.'

'That's because she knows what you've done. I had to tell her. I can't lie to Mam.'

'I did what I did for the best. Paid him back, I did, and saved all those people. I did it for you too, Tom. So you could get Old Gregory back and carry on with your studies. That's what you want, ain't it? Ain't I done the right thing?'

I didn't reply. Alice had stopped the Quisitor burning innocent people. She'd saved a lot of lives, including the Spook's. She'd done all those things and they were all good things. No, it wasn't what she'd done, it was how she'd gone about it. I wanted to help her but I didn't know how.

Alice belonged to the dark now, and once the Spook was strong enough he'd want to put her in a pit. She knew that and so did I.

CHAPTER 16

A PIT FOR ALICE

At last, with the sun once more sinking into the west, the fells were directly ahead and soon we were climbing up through the trees towards the Spook's house, taking the path that avoided Chipenden village.

I halted just short of the front gate. The Spook was about twenty paces further back, staring up at the house as if he were seeing it for the first time.

I turned to face Alice. 'You'd better go,' I said.

Alice nodded. There was the Spook's pet boggart to worry about. It guarded the house and grounds. One step inside the gate and she'd be in great danger.

'Where will you stay?' I asked.

'Don't you worry about me none. And don't go thinking I belong to the Bane either. I ain't stupid. Have to summon him twice more before that happens, don't I? The weather's not that cold yet, so I'll stay close by for a few days. Maybe in what's left of Lizzie's house. Then I'll most likely go east to Pendle. What else can I do?'

Alice still had family in Pendle but they were witches. Despite what she said, Alice belonged to the dark now. That's where she'd feel most comfortable.

Without another word she turned and walked away into the gloom. Sadly, I watched her until she'd disappeared from sight, then I turned and opened the gate.

I unlocked the front door and the Spook followed me inside. I led the way to the kitchen, where a fire was blazing in the grate and the table was set for two. The boggart had been expecting us. It was a light supper, just two bowls of pea soup and thick slices of bread. I was hungry after our long walk so I tucked in straight away.

For a while the Spook just sat there staring at his bowl of steaming hot soup but then he picked up a slice of bread and dunked it in.

'It's been hard, lad. And it's good to be home,' he said.

I was so surprised that he was speaking again that I almost fell off my chair.

'Are you feeling better?' I asked.

'Aye, lad, better than I did. A good night's sleep and I'll be right as rain. Your mam's a good woman. Nobody in the County knows their potions better.'

'I didn't think you'd remember anything,' I said. 'You seemed distant. Almost like you were sleepwalking.'

'That's what it was like, lad. I could see and hear everything but it didn't seem real. It was just like I was in a nightmare. And I couldn't speak. I couldn't seem to find the words. It was only when I was outside, standing there looking up at this house, that I found myself again. Have you still got the key to the Silver Gate?'

Surprised, I reached into my left breeches pocket and pulled out the key. I held it out to the Spook.

'Caused a lot of trouble, this,' he said, turning it over in his hand. 'But you did well, all things considered.'

I smiled, feeling happier than I had in days, but when my master spoke again, his voice was harsh.

'Where's the girl?' he snapped.

'Probably not too far away,' I admitted.

'Well, we'll deal with her later.'

All through supper I thought of Alice. What would she find to eat? Well, she was good at catching rabbits so she wouldn't starve – that was one thing sorted out. However, in the spring, after Bony Lizzie had kidnapped a child, the men from the village had set fire to her house and the ruin wouldn't provide much shelter on an autumn night. Still, as Alice had said, the weather still hadn't turned cold. No, her biggest threat was from the Spook.

As it turned out, it was the last mild night of the year: the following morning there *was* a distinct chill in the air. The Spook and I sat on the bench staring towards the fells, the wind getting stronger. The leaves were falling in earnest. The summer was well and truly over.

I'd already got my notebook out but the Spook seemed in no hurry to start the lesson. He wasn't recovered from his ordeal with the Quisitor. During breakfast he'd said little and spent most of the time staring into space, as if deep in thought.

I was the one who finally broke the silence. 'What does the Bane want now that it's free? What will it do to the County?'

'That's easily answered,' said the Spook. 'Above all it wants to grow bigger and more powerful. Then there will be no limit to the terror it will cause. It will cast a shadow of evil over the County. And no living thing will be able to hide from it. It will take blood and read minds until its powers are complete. It will see through the eyes of people who can walk in daylight while it's forced to hide in the dark somewhere underground. Whereas before it just controlled the priests in the cathedral and extended its influence into Priestown, now nowhere in the County will be safe.

'Caster could well be the next to suffer. But first the Bane might just pick on some small hamlet and press everyone to death as a warning, just to show what it can do! That was the way it controlled Heys and the kings who ruled before him. Disobedience meant a whole community would be pressed.'

'Mam told me that it'll be looking for Alice,' I said miserably.

'That's right, lad! Your foolish friend Alice. It needs her to regain its strength. She's twice given it her blood, so while she remains free she's fast on her way to becoming totally under its control. If nothing happens to stop it, she'll become part of the Bane and have hardly any will left of her own. It could move her, use her just as easily as I can bend my little finger. The Bane knows this – it'll be doing all it can to feed from her again. It'll be searching for her now.'

'But she's strong,' I protested. 'And anyway, I thought the Bane was afraid of women. We both met it in the catacombs when I was trying to rescue you. It had shape-shifted into you in order to trick me.'

'So the rumours were true – it had learned to take on a physical form down there.'

'Yes, but when Alice spat at it, it ran off. Perhaps she could just keep doing that.'

'Yes, the Bane does find it harder to control a woman than a man. Women make it nervous because they're wilful creatures and often unpredictable. But once it's drunk the blood of a female all that changes. It'll be after Alice now and give her no peace. It'll worm its way into her dreams and show her the things she can have – the things that can be hers just for the asking – until finally she'll think there's a need to summon it again. No doubt that cousin of mine was under the Bane's control. Otherwise he'd never have betrayed me like that.'

The Spook scratched at his beard. 'Aye, the Bane will grow and grow and there'll be little to stop it working its evil through others until everything becomes rotten in the County. That's what happened to the Little

People until, finally, desperate measures were called for. We need to find out exactly how the Bane was bound; even better, how it can be killed. That's why we need to go to Heysham. There's a big barrow there, a burial mound, and the bodies of Heys and his sons are in stone graves nearby.

'As soon as I'm strong enough, that's where we're going. As you know, those who suffer violent deaths sometimes have trouble moving on from this world. So we'll visit those graves. If we're lucky, a ghost or two might still linger there. Maybe even the ghost of Naze, who did the binding. That might well be our only hope because, to be honest, lad, at the moment I haven't a clue how we're going to bring this to an end.'

With those words the Spook hung his head and looked really sad and worried. I'd never seen him so low.

'Have you been there before?' I asked, wondering why the ghosts hadn't been given a talking to and asked to move on.

'Aye, lad, just once. I went there as an apprentice.

My master was there to deal with a troublesome sea wraith that had been haunting the shore. That done, on the hill above the cliffs we passed the graves and I knew there was something there because what had been a warm summer's night suddenly became very cold. When my master kept on walking, I asked him why he wasn't stopping to do something.

' "Leave well enough alone," he told me. "It's a bother to nobody. Besides, some ghosts stay on this earth because they've a task to perform. So it's best to leave 'em to it." I didn't know what he meant at the time, but as usual he was right.'

I tried to imagine the Spook as an apprentice. He'd have been a lot older than me because he'd trained as a priest first. I wondered what his own master had been like, a man who would take on an apprentice so old.

'Anyway,' said the Spook, 'we'll be going to Heysham very soon, but before that happens there's something else that has to be done. Know what it is?'

I shivered. I knew what he was going to say.

'We have to deal with the girl, so we need to know where she's hiding. My guess would be in the ruin of Lizzie's house. What do you think?' the Spook demanded.

I was going to tell him that I disagreed but he stared at me hard until I was forced to drop my gaze to the ground. I couldn't lie to him.

'That's where she'd probably stay,' I admitted.

'Well, lad, she can't stay there for much longer. She's a danger to everyone. She'll have to go into a pit. And the sooner the better. So you'd better start digging . . .'

I looked at him, hardly able to believe what I was hearing.

'Look, lad, it's hard but it's got to be done. It's our duty to make the County safe for others and that girl will always be a threat.'

'But that's not fair!' I said. 'She saved your life! Back in the spring she saved my life too. Everything she's done has turned out all right in the end. She means well.'

The Spook held up his hand to silence me. 'Don't waste your breath!' he commanded, his expression very stern. 'I know that she stopped the burning. I know that she saved lives, including my own. But she released the Bane and I'd rather be dead than have that foul thing loose and free to do its mischief. So follow me and let's get it over with!'

'But if we killed the Bane Alice would be free! She'd have another chance!'

The Spook's face reddened with anger, and when he spoke there was a sharp edge of menace to his voice. 'A witch who uses familiar magic is always dangerous. In time, in her maturity, far more deadly than those who use blood or bone. But usually it's just a bat or a toad – something small and weak that gradually grows in power. But think what that girl's done! The Bane of all things! And she thinks the Bane is bound to *her* will!

'She's clever and reckless and there's nothing that she wouldn't dare. And yes, arrogant too! But even with the Bane dead, it wouldn't be over. If she's allowed to grow into a woman, unchecked, she'll be the most dangerous witch the County has ever seen! We have to deal with her now before it's too late. I'm the master; you're the apprentice. Follow me and do as you're told!'

With that he turned his back and set off at a furious pace. With my heart down in my boots I followed him back to the house to collect the spade and measuring rod. We went directly to the eastern garden and there, less than fifty paces from the dark pit that held Bony Lizzie, I started to dig a new deep pit, eight feet deep and four feet by four square.

It was after sunset before I'd finished it to the Spook's satisfaction. I climbed out of the pit feeling uneasy, knowing that Bony Lizzie was in her own pit not far away.

'That'll do for now,' the Spook said. 'Tomorrow morning go down to the village and fetch the local mason to measure up.'

The mason would cement a border of stones around the pit into which thirteen strong iron bars would eventually be set to prevent any chance of escape. The Spook would have to be on watch while he worked to keep him safe from the pet boggart.

As I trudged back towards the house, my master briefly rested his hand on my shoulder. 'You've done your duty, lad. That's all that anybody can ask and I'd just like to tell you that so far you've more than lived up to what your mam promised . . .'

I looked up at him in astonishment. My mam had once written him a letter saying that I'd be the best apprentice he'd ever had, but he hadn't liked her telling him that.

'Carry on like this,' the Spook continued, 'and when the day comes for me to retire, I'll be sure I'm leaving the County in very good hands. I hope that makes you feel a little better.'

The Spook was always grudging with his praise and to hear him say that was something really special. I suppose he was just trying to cheer me up but I couldn't get the pit and Alice out of my mind and I'm afraid his praise didn't help at all.

* * *

That night I found it hard to sleep, so I was wide awake when it happened.

At first I thought it was a sudden storm. There was a roar and a whoosh and the whole house seemed to shake and tremble as if buffeted by a great wind. Something struck my window with terrible force and I clearly heard glass crack. Alarmed, I knelt up on the bed and pulled back the curtains.

The large sash window was divided into eight thick, uneven panes so you couldn't see that much through them at the best of times, but there was a half moon and I could just make out the tops of the trees, bowing and writhing as if their trunks were being shaken by an army of angry giants. And three of my thick windowpanes were cracked. For a moment I was tempted to use the sash cord to raise the bottom half of the window so I could see what was happening. But then I thought better of it. The moon was shining so it was unlikely to be a natural storm. Something was attacking us. Could it be the Bane? Had it found us?

Next came a loud pounding and ripping noise from somewhere directly above my head. It sounded as if something was beating hard on the roof, thumping it with heavy fists. I heard the slates begin to fly off and crash down onto the flags that bordered the western lawn.

I dressed quickly and rushed downstairs two steps at a time. The back door was wide open and I ran out onto the lawn, straight into the teeth of a wind so powerful that it was hardly possible to breathe, never mind take a step forward. But I did force myself on, one slow step at a time, battling to keep my eyes open as the wind pounded my face.

By the light of the moon I could see the Spook standing halfway between the trees and the house, his black cloak flapping in the fierce wind. He had his staff held high before him as if ready to ward off a blow. It seemed to take an age to reach him.

'What is it? What is it?' I shouted, as I finally made it to his side.

My answer came almost immediately, but not from

the Spook. A terrible, menacing sound filled the air; a mixture of an angry scream and a throbbing growl that could have been heard for miles. It was the Spook's boggart. I'd heard that sound before, in the spring, when it had prevented Bony Lizzie from chasing me into the western garden. So I knew that down there in the darkness amongst the trees, it was face to face with something that was threatening the house and gardens.

What else could it be but the Bane?

I stood there shivering with fear and cold, my teeth chattering and my body aching from the battering the gale was giving it. But after a few moments the wind subsided and very gradually everything became very still and quiet.

'Back to the house,' said the Spook. 'There's nothing to be done here until morning.'

When we reached the back door I stood looking at the fragments of tiles that littered the flags.

'Was it the Bane?' I asked.

The Spook nodded. 'Didn't take long to find us, did

it?' he said, shaking his head. 'No doubt the girl's to blame for that. It must have found her first. Either that or she called it.'

'She wouldn't do that again,' I said, trying to defend Alice. 'Did the boggart save us?' I asked, changing the subject.

'Aye, it did for now and at what cost we'll find out in the morning. But I wouldn't bet on it succeeding a second time. I'll stay on watch here,' said the Spook. 'Go up to your room and get some sleep. Anything could happen tomorrow so you'll need all your wits about you.'

CHAPTER
17
THE QUISITOR ARRIVES

I came downstairs again just before dawn. The clear sky of the night was now overcast, the air perfectly still and the lawns dusted white with the first real frost of the autumn.

The Spook was near the back door, still standing in almost the same position as when I'd last seen him. He looked tired and his face was as bleak and grey as the sky.

'Well, lad,' he said wearily, 'let's go and inspect the damage.'

I thought he meant the house but instead he set off towards the trees in the western garden. Damage there was, certainly, but not as bad as it had sounded last night. There were some big branches down, twigs scattered across the grass and the bench had been over-turned. The Spook gestured and I helped him to lift the bench and position it again.

'It's not that bad,' I said, trying to cheer him up for he looked really glum and down in the mouth.

'It's bad enough,' he said grimly. 'The Bane was always going to get stronger but this is much faster than I expected. Much faster. It shouldn't have been able to do this so soon. We haven't much time left!'

The Spook led the way back towards the house. We could see slates missing from the roof and one of the chimneypots had been toppled from the stack.

'It'll have to wait until we've time to get it fixed,' he said.

Just then there came the sound of a bell from the kitchen. For the first time that morning the Spook gave a faint smile. He looked relieved.

'I wasn't sure we'd be having breakfast this morning,' he said. 'Perhaps it's not quite as bad as I thought . . .'

As we entered the kitchen the first thing I noticed was that the flags between the table and the hearth were spotted with bloodstains. And the kitchen was really chilly. Then I saw why. I'd been the Spook's apprentice for almost six months, but this was the first morning there'd been no fire burning in the grate. And on the table there were no eggs, no bacon, just one thin slice of toast each.

The Spook touched my shoulder in warning. 'Say nothing, lad. Eat it up and be grateful for what we've received.'

I did as I was told but when I'd swallowed my last mouthful of toast my belly was still rumbling.

The Spook came to his feet. 'That was an excellent breakfast. The bread was toasted to perfection,' he said to the empty air. 'And thank you for everything you did last night. We're both very grateful.'

Mostly, the boggart didn't show itself, but now once again it took the form of the big ginger cat. There was just the faintest of purrs and it appeared briefly close to the hearth. However, I'd never seen it looking as it did then. Its left ear was torn and bleeding and the fur on its neck was matted with blood. But the worst thing of all was what had been done to its face. It had been blinded in one eye. Where its left eye used to be there was now a raw vertical wound.

'It'll never be quite the same again,' said the Spook sadly when we were outside the back door. 'We should be grateful that the Bane's still not regained its full strength or we'd have died last night. That boggart's bought us a little time. Now we've got to use it before it's too late . . .'

Even as he spoke the bell began to ring down at the crossroads. Business for the Spook. With all that had happened and the danger from the Bane, I thought he'd ignore it but I was wrong.

'Well, lad,' he said. 'Off you go and find out what's wanted.'

The bell stopped ringing just before I got there but the rope was still swaying. Down amongst the withy trees it was gloomy as usual but it only took me a second to realize that it wasn't a summons to spook's business. A girl in a black dress was waiting there.

Alice.

'You're taking a big risk!' I told her, shaking my head. 'You're lucky that Mr Gregory didn't come down here with me.'

Alice smiled. 'Old Gregory couldn't catch me the way he is now. Ain't half the man he was.'

'Don't be too sure about that!' I said angrily. 'He made me dig a pit. A pit for you. And that's where you'll end up if you're not careful.'

'Old Gregory's strength has gone. No wonder he got you to dig it!' Alice jibed, her voice full of mockery.

'No,' I said, 'he made me dig it so that I'd accept what has to be done. That it's my duty to put you in there.'

Alice's tone suddenly became sad. 'Would you really do that to me, Tom?' she asked. 'After all we've been through together? I saved you from a pit. Don't you remember that, when Bony Lizzie wanted your bones? When Lizzie was sharpening her knife?'

I remembered it well. But for Alice's help I would have died that night.

'Look, Alice, go to Pendle now before it's too late,' I told her. 'Get as far away from here as possible!'

'Bane don't agree. Thinks I should stay nearby a while longer, he does.'

'The Bane's an *it*, not a *he*!' I said, irritated by what Alice was saying.

'No, Tom, he ain't,' said Alice. 'Sniffed him out, I did, and he's a man-thing for certain!'

'The Bane attacked the Spook's house last night. It could have killed us. Did you send it?'

Alice shook her head in a firm denial. 'That ain't nothing to do with me, Tom. I swear it. We talked, that's all, and he told me things.'

'I thought you weren't going to have any more dealings with it!' I said, hardly able to believe what she was saying.

'I've tried hard, Tom, I really have. But he comes and whispers things to me. Comes to me in the dark, he does, when I'm trying to sleep. He even talks to me in my dreams. He promises me things.'

'What sort of things?'

'It ain't easy, Tom. It's getting colder at nights. The weather's drawing in. Bane said I could have a house with a big fireplace and lots of coal and wood and that I'd never want for anything. He said I could have nice clothes too, so that people wouldn't look down their noses at me like they do now, thinking I'm something that's just crawled out of a hedge.'

'Don't listen to it, Alice. You've got to try harder!'

'Good job I do listen to him sometimes,' Alice said, a strange half-smile on her face, 'otherwise you'd be really sorry. I know something, see. Something that might save Old Gregory's life as well as yours.'

'Tell me,' I urged.

'Not sure why I should, seeing as you're plotting for me to spend the rest of my days in a pit!'

'That's not fair, Alice.'

'I'll help you again, I will. But I wonder if you'd do the same for me . . . ?'

She paused and gave me a sad smile. 'You see, the Quisitor's on his way up here to Chipenden. Burned his hands in that fire, that's all, and now he wants revenge. He knows Old Gregory lives somewhere nearby and he's coming with armed men and dogs. Big bloodhounds, they are, with big teeth. He'll be here by noon at the latest. So go and tell Old Gregory what I said. Don't expect he'll say thanks though.'

'I'll go and tell him,' I said, and set off right away, running up the hill towards the house. As I ran, I realized that I hadn't thanked Alice, but how could I thank her for using the dark to help us?

The Spook was waiting just inside the back door. 'Well, lad,' he said, 'get your breath back first. I can tell from your face you're bringing bad news.'

'The Quisitor's on his way here,' I said. 'He's found out that we live near Chipenden!'

'And who told you this?' asked the Spook, scratching at his beard.

'Alice. She said he'll be here by noon. The Bane told her . . .'

The Spook sighed deeply. 'Well, we'd better get away as soon as possible. First of all, you go down to the village and let the butcher know we're heading north over the fells to Caster and won't be back for some time. Go into the grocer's and tell him the same and say that we won't need any provisions next week.'

I ran down into the village and did exactly what he'd told me. When I got back the Spook was already waiting at the door, ready to set off. He handed me his bag.

'Are we going south?' I asked.

The Spook shook his head. 'No, lad, we're heading north as I said. We need to get to Heysham and, if we're lucky, speak to the ghost of Naze.'

'But we've told everyone the way we're going. Why didn't I pretend we were heading south?'

'Because I'm hoping the Quisitor will pay a visit to the village on his way up here. Then, instead of searching for this house, he'll head north and the hounds will pick up our trail. We've got to draw them away from the house. Some of the books in my library are irreplaceable. If he comes here, his men might loot this place and maybe burn it to the ground. No, I can't risk anything happening to my books.'

'But what about the boggart? Won't it guard the house and gardens? How can they even get in without the risk of being torn to pieces? Or is it too weak now?'

The Spook sighed and stared down at his boots. 'No, it's still got strength enough to deal with the Quisitor and his men but I don't want unnecessary deaths on my conscience. And even if it killed those who entered, some might get away. What more proof would they need then that I deserve to burn? They'd come back with an army. There'd be no end to it. No peace until the end of my days. I'd have to flee the County.'

'But won't they catch us anyway?'

'No, lad. Not if we take the route over the fells. They won't be able to use their horses and we'll have a good few hours' start. We have the advantage. We know the County well, but the Quisitor's men are outsiders. Anyway, let's get started. We've wasted enough time already!'

Heading for the fells, the Spook set off at a very fast pace. I followed as best I could, carrying his heavy bag as usual.

'Won't some of his men just ride ahead and wait for us at Caster?' I said.

'No doubt they will, lad, and if we were going to Caster, that could just be a problem. No, we're going to pass the town to the east. Then we're going south-west, as I just told you, to Heysham, to visit the stone graves. There's the Bane still to be dealt with and time is running out. Talking to the ghost of Naze is our last chance to find out how to do it.'

'And after that? Where will we go? Will we ever be able to come back here?'

'I see no reason why we couldn't in time. Eventually we'll throw the Quisitor off our trail. There are ways to do that. Oh, he'll search for a bit and make a nuisance of himself, no doubt. But before long he'll go back to where he came from. To where he can keep himself warm during the coming winter.'

I nodded but I wasn't entirely happy. I could see all sorts of flaws in the Spook's plan. For one thing he might have set off strongly, but he still wasn't fully fit and crossing the fells would be hard work. And they might just catch us before we reached Heysham. Then again, they might search for the Spook's house anyway and burn it out of spite, especially if they lost our trail. And there was next year to worry about. In the spring the Quisitor was bound to come north again. He seemed like a man who'd never give up. I couldn't see any way that life would ever return to normal. And another thought struck me . . .

What if they caught me? The Quisitor tortured people to make them answer questions. What if they forced me to tell them where I used to live? They confiscated or burned the homes of witches and warlocks. I thought of Dad, Jack and Ellie with nowhere to live. And what would they do when they saw Mam? She couldn't go out in sunlight. And she often helped the local midwives with difficult deliveries and had a big collection of herbs and other plants. Mam would be in real danger!

I didn't say any of this to the Spook because I could see that he was already weary of my questions.

* * *

We were high on the fells within the hour. The weather was calm and it looked like we'd have a fine day ahead.

If only I could have got out of my mind the reason we were up there, I'd have enjoyed myself because it was good walking weather. We'd only curlews and rabbits for company, and far to the north-west the distant sea was sparkling in the sunshine.

At first the Spook strode out energetically, leading the way. But long before noon he began to flag, and when we stopped and sat ourselves down close to a cairn of stones, he looked utterly weary. As he unwrapped the cheese, I noticed that his hands were trembling.

'Here, lad,' he said, handing me a small piece. 'Don't eat it all at once.'

Doing as he advised, I nibbled on it slowly.

'You do know the girl's following us?' the Spook asked.

I looked at him in astonishment and shook my head.

'She's about a mile or so back there,' he told me,

gesturing south. 'Now we've stopped, she's stopped. What do you suppose she wants?'

'I suppose she's nowhere else to go, apart from east to Pendle and she doesn't really want to go there. And she'd no choice but to leave Chipenden. It wouldn't be safe when the Quisitor and his men arrived.'

'Aye, and maybe it's because she's taken a shine to you and just wants to go where you go. I wish I'd had time to deal with her before we left Chipenden. She's a threat because wherever she is, the Bane won't be too far away. It'll be hiding underground for now, but once it's dark she'll draw it to her like a moth to a candle flame and it'll be hovering about for sure. If she feeds it again, it'll grow stronger and start seeing through her eyes. Before then it may chance upon other victims – people or animals, the effect will be the same. After bloating itself with blood, it'll grow stronger and soon be able to clothe itself in flesh and bones again. Last night was just the start.'

'If it hadn't been for Alice we'd never have left

Chipenden,' I pointed out. 'We'd be prisoners of the Quisitor.'

But the Spook chose to ignore me. 'Well,' he said, 'we'd best get on. I'm not getting any younger while I'm sitting here.'

But after another hour we rested again. This time the Spook stayed down longer before finally forcing himself to his feet. It went on like that throughout the day, with the periods of rest getting longer and the time we were on our feet getting shorter. Towards sunset the weather began to change. The smell of rain was strong in the air and soon it began to drizzle.

As darkness fell we began to descend towards a patchwork of drystone wall enclosures. The fell side was steep and the grass was slippery and we both kept losing our footing. What's more, the rain was getting heavier and the wind starting to build from the west.

'We'll rest while I get my breath back,' the Spook said.

He led the way to the nearest section of wall and we

clambered over and hunkered down on its eastern edge, to shelter from the worst of the rain.

'The damp gets deep into your bones when you're my age,' said the Spook. 'That's what a lifetime of County weather does to you. It gets us all eventually. Either your bones or your lungs suffer.'

We crouched against the wall miserably. I was tired and weary, and even though we were outside on such a night it was a struggle to keep awake. Before long I fell into a deep sleep and began to dream. It was one of those long dreams that seem to go on all night. And towards the end it became a nightmare . . .

CHAPTER 18
NIGHTMARE ON THE HILL

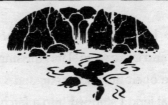

It was quite definitely the worst nightmare I'd ever had. And in a job like mine I'd had a lot. I was lost and trying to find my way home. I should have been able to manage it easily enough because everything was bathed in the light of the full moon, but every time I turned a corner and thought I recognized some landmark, I was soon proved wrong. At last I came over the top of Hangman's Hill and saw our farm below.

As I walked down the hill, I began to feel very uneasy. Even though it was night time everything was too still and too quiet and nothing was moving below. The fences were in a poor state of repair, something that Dad and Jack would never have allowed to happen, and the barn doors were hanging half off their hinges.

The house looked deserted: some of the windows were broken and there were slates missing from the roof. I struggled to open the back door, and when it yielded with the usual jerk, I stepped into a kitchen that looked as though it hadn't been lived in for years. There was dust everywhere and cobwebs hung from the ceiling. Mam's rocking chair was right at the centre of the room and on it was a piece of folded paper, which I picked up and carried outside to read by the light of the moon.

Your dad's, Jack's, Ellie's and Mary's graves are up on Hangman's Hill. You'll find your mother in the barn.

My heart aching to bursting point, I ran out into the yard. Then I halted outside the barn, listening carefully. Everything was silent. There wasn't even a breath of wind. I stepped nervously into the gloom, hardly knowing what to expect. Would there be a grave there? Mam's grave?

There was a hole in the roof almost directly above, and within a shaft of moonlight I could see Mam's head. She was looking straight at me. Her body was in darkness, but from the position of her face she seemed to be kneeling on the ground.

Why would she do that? And why did she look so unhappy? Wasn't she pleased to see me?

Suddenly Mam let out a scream of anguish. 'Don't look at me, Tom! Don't look at me! Turn away now!' she cried as if in torment.

The moment I looked away Mam rose up from the floor, and out of the corner of my eye I glimpsed something that turned my bones to jelly. From the neck down Mam was different. I saw wings and scales and a glint of sharp claws as she flew straight up into the air and smashed her way out through the barn roof, taking half of it with her. I looked up, shielding my face from the pieces of wood and debris that were falling towards me, and saw Mam, a black silhouette against the disc of the full moon as she flew upwards from the wreckage of the barn roof.

'No! No!' I shouted. 'This isn't true, This isn't happening!'

In reply, a voice spoke inside my head. It was the low hiss of the Bane.

'The moon shows the truth of things, boy. You know that already. All you have seen is true or will come to pass. All it takes is time.'

Someone began to shake my shoulder and I woke up in a cold sweat. The Spook was bending over me.

'Wake up, lad! Wake up!' he called. 'It's just a nightmare. It's the Bane trying to get into your mind, trying to weaken us.'

I nodded but didn't tell the Spook what had happened in the dream. It was too painful to talk about. I glanced up at the sky. Rain was still falling but the cloud was patchy and a few stars were visible. It was still dark, but dawn was not far off.

'Have we slept all night?'

'We have that,' replied the Spook, 'but I didn't plan it that way.'

He rose stiffly. 'Better move on while we still can,' he said anxiously. 'Can't you hear 'em?'

I listened and finally, above the noise of the wind and rain, I heard the distant baying of hounds.

'Aye, they're not too far behind,' the Spook said. 'Our only hope is to throw them off our scent. We need water to do that but it needs to be shallow enough for us to walk in. Of course, we'll have to get back on dry land sometime but the dogs will have to be taken up and down the bank to pick up the scent again. And if there's another stream close by it makes the job a lot easier.'

We scrambled over another wall and walked down a steep slope, moving as fast as we dared across the damp, slippery grass. There was a shepherd's cottage below us, a faint silhouette against the sky, and next to it an ancient blackthorn tree, bent over towards it by the prevailing winds, its bare branches like claws clutching at the eaves. We kept walking towards the cottage for a few moments but then came to a sudden halt.

There was a wooden pen ahead and to our left. And there was just enough light to see that it contained a small flock of sheep, about twenty or so. And all of them were dead.

'I don't like the look of this one little bit, lad.'

I didn't like the look of it either. But then I realized that he didn't mean the dead sheep. He was looking at the cottage beyond.

'We're probably too late,' he said, his voice hardly more than a whisper. 'But it's our duty to go in and see . . .'

With that he set off towards the cottage, gripping his staff. I followed carrying his bag. As I passed the pen, I glanced sideways at the nearest of the dead sheep. The white wool of its coat was streaked with blood. If that was the work of the Bane it had fed well. How much stronger would it be now?

The front door was wide open so without ceremony we went in, the Spook leading the way. He'd just taken one step over the threshold when he halted and sucked in his breath. He was staring to the left. There was a candle somewhere deeper in the room and by its flickering light I could see what, at first glance, I took to be a shadow of the shepherd. But it was too solid to be just a shadow. He had his back to the wall and the crook of his staff was raised above his head as if to threaten us. It took a while for me to understand what I was looking at, but something set my knees a-trembling and my heart fluttering up into my mouth.

On his face was a mixture of anger and terror. His teeth were showing but some of them were broken and blood was smeared across his mouth. He was upright but he wasn't standing. He'd been flattened. Pressed back against the wall. Smeared into the stones. It was the work of the Bane.

The Spook took another step into the room. And another. I followed close behind until I could see the whole of the nightmare within. There'd been a baby's cot in the corner but it had been smashed against the wall and amongst the debris were blankets and a small sheet streaked with blood. Of the child there was no sign. My master approached the blankets and raised them cautiously. What he saw clearly distressed him and he motioned at me not to look before replacing the blankets with a sigh.

By now I had spotted the infant's mother. A woman's body was on the floor, partly hidden by a rocking chair. I was grateful that I couldn't see her face. In her right hand she gripped a knitting needle, and a ball of wool had rolled into the hearth close to the embers, which were fading to grey.

The door to the kitchen was open and I had a sudden sense of dread. I felt certain something was lurking there. No sooner had that thought entered my head than the temperature in the room dropped. The Bane was still here. I could feel it in my bones. In terror I almost fled from that cottage but the Spook stood his ground and while he remained how could I leave him?

At that moment the candle was suddenly extinguished, as if snuffed out by unseen fingers, plunging us into gloom, and a deep voice spoke out of the utter blackness of the kitchen doorway. A voice that resounded through the air and vibrated along the flagged floor of the cottage so that I could feel it in my feet.

'Hello, Old Bones. At last we meet again. Been looking for you. Knew you were somewhere nearby.'

'Aye and now you've found me,' said the Spook wearily, resting his staff on the flags and leaning his weight against it.

'Always were a meddler, weren't you, Old Bones? But you've meddled once too often now. I'll kill the boy first, while you stand and watch. Then it'll be your turn.'

An invisible hand picked me up and slammed me back against the wall so hard that all the breath was driven from my body. Then the pressure began, a steady force so strong that my ribs felt about to snap. Worst of all was the terrible weight against my forehead and I remembered the face of the shepherd flattened and smeared into the stones. I was terrified, unable to move or even breathe. A darkness came over my eyes and the last thing I knew was a sense that the

Spook had rushed towards the kitchen doorway raising his staff.

Someone was shaking me gently.

I opened my eyes and saw the Spook bending over me. I was lying on the floor of the cottage. 'Are you all right, lad?' he asked anxiously.

I nodded. My ribs felt sore. With every breath I took they hurt. But I was breathing. I was still alive.

'Come on, let's see if we can get you to your feet . . .'

With the Spook supporting me, I managed to stand.

'Can you walk?'

I nodded and took a step forward. I didn't feel too steady on my feet but I could walk.

'Good lad.'

'Thanks for saving me,' I said.

The Spook shook his head. 'I did nothing, lad. The Bane just disappeared suddenly, as if it had been called. I saw it moving up the hill. It looked just like a black cloud blotting out the last of the stars. A terrible thing's been done here,' he said, glancing at the horror within the cottage. 'But we've got to get away just as fast as we can. First we must save ourselves. We might be able to escape the Quisitor, but with that girl following us the Bane will always be near and growing more powerful all the time. We need to get to Heysham and find out how we can deal with that foul thing once and for all!'

With the Spook leading the way, we left the cottage and continued down the hill. We crossed two more sections of wall until I could hear the sound of rushing water. My master was moving a lot quicker now, almost as fast as when we'd set out from Chipenden, so I suppose the sleep had done him some good. Whereas I was sore all over and struggling to keep up, his bag heavy in my hand.

We came out onto a steep, narrow path beside a beck, a wide torrent of water rushing headlong downwards over rocks.

'About a mile further down this empties out into a tarn,' said the Spook, striding down the path. 'The land levels and two streams flow out of it. It's just what we're looking for.'

I followed as best I could. It seemed to be raining harder than ever and the ground was treacherous underfoot. One slip and you'd end up in the water. I wondered if Alice was nearby and if she could walk down a path like this so close to fast-flowing water. Alice would be in danger too. The dogs might pick up her scent.

Even above the noise of the beck and the rain I could hear the bloodhounds; they seemed to be getting closer and closer. Suddenly I heard something that made me catch my breath.

It was a scream!

Alice! I turned and looked back up the path but the Spook grabbed my arm and pulled me forward. 'There's nothing we can do, lad!' he shouted. 'Nothing at all! So just keep moving.'

I did as I was told, trying to ignore the sounds that were coming from the fell side behind us. There were shouts and yells and more horrifying screams until gradually everything grew quiet and all I could hear was the water rushing by. The sky was much lighter now and below us, in the first dawn light, I could see the pale waters of the tarn spread out amongst the trees.

My heart ached at the thought of what could have happened to Alice. She didn't deserve this.

'Keep moving, lad,' the Spook repeated.

And then we heard something on the path behind us – but moving closer and closer. It sounded like an animal bounding down towards us. A big dog.

It didn't seem fair. We were so close to the tarn and its two streams. Just another ten minutes and we'd have been able to throw the hounds off our scent. But to my surprise the Spook wasn't moving any faster. He even seemed to be slowing down. Finally he stopped altogether and pulled me to the side of the path; I wondered if he'd come to the end of his strength. If so, then it was all over for both of us.

I looked to the Spook, hoping he'd produce something from his bag to save us. But he didn't. The dog was now running towards us at full pelt. Yet as it got closer I noticed something strange about it. For one thing it was yelping rather than baying like a hound in full cry. And its eyes were fixed ahead rather than upon us. It passed so close that I could have reached out and touched it.

'If I'm not mistaken, it's terrified,' said the Spook. 'Watch out! Here comes another one!'

The next one passed, yelping like the first, its tail between its legs. Quickly, two more came by. Then, close behind, a fifth hound. All taking no notice of us but running headlong down the muddy path towards the tarn.

'What's happened?' I asked.

'No doubt we'll find out soon enough,' said the Spook. 'Let's just keep going.'

Soon the rain stopped and we reached the tarn. It was big and, for the most part, calm. But near us the beck entered it in a fury of white water, hurtling down a steep slope to agitate the surface. We stood staring at the falling water, where twigs, leaves and even the occasional log were being swept down into the tarn.

Suddenly something larger hit the water with a

tremendous splash. It was thrust deep under the surface but reappeared about thirty or so paces further on and began to drift towards the western shore of the tarn. It looked like a human body.

I rushed forward to the water's edge. What if it was Alice? But before I could plunge in, the Spook put his hand on my shoulder and gripped it hard.

'It's not Alice,' he said softly. 'That body's too big. Besides, I think she called the Bane. Why else would it have left so suddenly? With the Bane on her side she'll have won any argument going on back there. We'd best walk round to the far shore and take a closer look.'

We followed the curved shore until, after a few minutes, we were standing on the western bank under the branches of a large sycamore tree, inches deep in fallen leaves. The thing in the water was some distance away but getting closer. I hoped the Spook was right, that the body was too big to be Alice's, but it was still too dark to be sure. And if it wasn't her, whose body was it?

I began to feel afraid but there was nothing I could

do but wait as the sky grew lighter and the body drifted closer towards us.

Slowly the clouds broke up and soon the sky was light enough for us to identify the body beyond all doubt.

It was the Quisitor.

I looked at the floating body. It was on its back and only the face was clear of the water. The mouth was open and so were the eyes. There was terror on the pale dead face. It was as if there wasn't a drop of blood left in his body.

'He's swum a lot of innocents in his time,' said the Spook. 'The poor, the old and the lonely. Many who'd worked hard all their lives and just deserved a bit of peace and quiet in their old age, and a bit of respect too. And now it's his turn. He's got exactly what he deserves.'

I knew that swimming a witch was just superstitious nonsense, but I couldn't get out of my head the fact that he was floating. The innocent sank; the guilty floated. Innocents like Alice's aunt, who'd died of shock.

'Alice did this, didn't she?' I said.

The Spook nodded. 'Aye, lad. Some would say she did. But it was the Bane really. Twice she's called him now. Its power over her will be growing and what she sees it can see also.'

'Shouldn't we be on our way?' I asked nervously, looking back across the lake to where the tarn rushed headlong into it. Beside it was the path. 'Won't his men come down here?'

'They might eventually, lad. That's if they've still got breath in their bodies. But I've a feeling that they won't be in a fit state to do much for a while. No, I'm expecting somebody else, and if I'm not much mistaken, here she comes now . . .'

I followed the Spook's gaze towards the beck, where a small figure walked down the path and stood for a moment watching the falling water. Then Alice's gaze turned towards us and she began to walk along the bank in our direction.

'Remember,' the Spook warned, 'the Bane sees through her eyes now. It's building its strength and power, learning our weaknesses. Be very careful what you say or do.'

One part of me wanted to shout out and warn Alice to run away while she still could. There was no knowing what the Spook might do to her now. Another part of me was suddenly desperately afraid of her. But what could I do? Deep down, I knew that the Spook was her only hope. Who else could free her from the Bane now?

Alice walked up to stand at the edge of the water, keeping me between her and the Spook. She was staring towards the body of the Quisitor. There was a mixture of terror and triumph on her face.

'You might as well take a good look, girl,' said the Spook. 'Examine your handiwork close up. Was it worth it?'

Alice nodded. 'He got what was coming to him,' she said firmly.

'Aye, but at what cost?' asked the Spook. 'You belong more and more to the dark. Call the Bane once more and you'll be lost for ever.'

Alice didn't reply and we stood there for a long time in silence, just staring at the water.

'Well, lad,' said the Spook, 'we'd best be on our way. Someone else will have to deal with the body because we've got work to do. As for you, girl, you'll come with us if you know what's good for you. And now you'd better listen and you'd better listen carefully because what I'm proposing is your only hope. The only chance you'll ever have to break free of that creature.'

Alice looked up, her eyes very wide.

'You do know the danger you're in? You do want to be free?' he asked.

Alice nodded.

'Then come here!' he commanded sternly.

Alice walked obediently to his side.

'Wherever you are the Bane won't be far behind so for now you'd better come with me and the lad. I'd rather know roughly where that creature is than have it roaming anywhere it likes through the County, terrorizing decent folks. So listen to me and listen good. For now it's important that you see and hear nothing – that way the Bane will learn nothing from you. But you have to do it willingly, mind. If you cheat in the slightest way, it'll go hard with all of us.'

He opened his bag and began to rummage about inside it. 'This is a blindfold,' he said, holding up a strip of black cloth for Alice to see. 'Will you wear it?' he asked.

Alice nodded and the Spook held out the palm of his left hand towards her. 'See these?' he said. 'They're plugs of wax for your ears.'

Each plug had a small silver stud embedded in it to make it easy to get the wax out afterwards.

Alice looked at them doubtfully but then she tilted her head obediently while the Spook gently inserted the first plug. After pushing in the second plug he tied the blindfold firmly across her eyes.

We set off, heading north-east, the Spook guiding Alice by her elbow. I hoped we didn't pass anybody on the road. What would they think? We'd certainly attract a lot of unwelcome attention.

CHAPTER
19
THE STONE GRAVES

It was daylight, so there was no immediate threat from the Bane. Like most creatures of the dark it would be hiding underground. And with Alice blind-folded and her ears plugged, it could no longer look out through her eyes or listen to what we said. It wouldn't know where we were.

I had anticipated another day of hard walking and wondered if we'd get to Heysham before nightfall. But to my surprise the Spook led us up a track to a large farm and we waited at the gate, the dogs barking fit to wake the dead, while an old farmer limped towards us leaning on a stick. He had a worried expression on his face.

'I'm sorry,' he croaked. 'I'm really sorry, but nothing's changed. If I had it to give, it'd be yours.'

It seemed that five years earlier the Spook had rid this man's farm of a troublesome boggart and still hadn't been paid. My master wanted paying now but not in money.

Within half an hour we were riding in a cart pulled by one of the biggest shire horses I'd ever seen; driving the cart was the farmer's son. At first, before setting off, he'd stared at the blindfolded Alice, a puzzled look on his face.

'Stop gawping at the girl and concentrate on your own business!' the Spook had snapped and the lad had quickly averted his eyes. He seemed happy enough to take us, glad to be away from his chores for a few hours, and soon we were following the back lanes, passing east of Caster. The Spook made Alice lie down in the cart and covered her with straw so that she couldn't be seen by other travellers.

No doubt the horse was used to pulling a heavy load, and with just us three in the back was trotting ahead at a fair old lick. In the distance we could see the city of

Caster with its castle. Many a witch had died there after a long trial, but they didn't burn witches in Caster, they hanged them. So, to use one of my dad's sea-going expressions, we gave it 'a wide berth', and soon we were beyond it and crossing a bridge over the river Lune, before changing our direction to head south-west towards Heysham.

The farmer's lad was told to wait at the end of the lane on the outskirts of the village.

'We'll be back at dawn,' said the Spook. 'Don't worry. I'll make it well worth your while.'

We climbed a narrow track up a hill, with an old church and graveyard on our right. There, on that lee side of the hill, everything was still and quiet and tall ancient trees shrouded the gravestones. But on clambering over a gate onto the cliff top we were met by a stiff breeze and the tang of the sea. Before us was the ruin of a small stone chapel with just three of its walls standing. We were quite high up and I could see a bay below, with a sandy beach almost covered by the tide and the sea crashing against the rocks of a small headland in the distance.

'Mostly, shores to the west are flat,' said the Spook, 'and this is as high as County cliffs ever get. They say this is where the first men landed in the County. They came from a land far to the west and their boat ran aground on the rocks below. Their descendants built that chapel.'

He pointed and there, just beyond the ruin, I saw the stone graves. 'There's nothing like them anywhere else in the County,' said the Spook.

Carved into a huge slab of stone, right on the edge of a steep hill, there was a row of six coffins, each in the shape of a human body and with a stone lid fitting into a groove. They were different sizes and shapes but generally small, as if hewn for children, but these were the graves of six of the Little People. Six of King Heys's sons.

The Spook knelt down beside the nearest of the graves. Above the head of each was a square socket and he traced the shape of it with his finger. Then he extended the fingers of his left hand. The span of his hand just covered the socket.

'Now what could those have been used for?' he muttered to himself.

'How big were the Little People?' I asked. The graves were all different sizes and, now that I looked closely I saw that they weren't quite as small as I'd first thought.

By way of answer the Spook opened his bag and pulled out a folded measuring rod. He opened it out and measured the grave.

'This is about five foot five long,' he announced, 'and about thirteen and a half inches wide in the middle. But some belongings would have been buried with the Little People for use in the next world. Few were above five feet tall and a lot were much smaller. As the years went by, each generation got bigger because there were marriages between them and the invaders from the sea. So they didn't really die out. Their blood still runs through our veins.'

The Spook turned to Alice and, to my surprise, untied her blindfold. Next he removed her earplugs, putting everything safely back in his bag. Alice blinked and looked about her. She didn't look happy.

'Don't like it here,' she complained. 'Something ain't right. It feels bad.'

'Does it, girl?' the Spook said. 'Well, that's the most interesting thing you've said all day. It's odd because I find this spot quite pleasant. There's nothing like a bit of bracing sea air!'

It didn't seem bracing to me. The breeze had died away and now tendrils of mist were snaking in from the sea and it was starting to grow colder. Within an hour it would be dark. I knew what Alice meant. It was a place to be avoided after sunset. I could sense something and I didn't think it was too friendly.

'There's something lurking nearby,' I told the Spook.

'Let's sit over there and give it time to get used to us,' said the Spook. 'We wouldn't want to frighten it off . . .'

'Is it Naze's ghost?' I asked.

'I hope so, lad! I certainly hope so. But we'll find out soon enough. Just be patient.'

We sat on a grassy bank some distance away, while the light slowly failed. I was getting more and more worried.

'What about when it gets dark?' I asked the Spook. 'Won't the Bane appear? Now you've taken Alice's blindfold off it'll know where we are!'

'I think we're safe enough here, lad,' said the Spook. 'This is possibly the one place in the whole County where it has to keep its distance. Something was done here, and if I'm not mistaken, the Bane won't come within a mile of the place. It might know where we are but there's not much it can do about it. Am I right, girl?'

Alice shivered and nodded. 'Trying to speak to me, he is. But his voice is very faint and distant. He can't even get inside my head.'

'That's just what I hoped,' said the Spook. 'It means our journey here hasn't been wasted.'

'He wants me to get right away from here. Wants me to go to him . . .'

'And is that what *you* want?'

Alice shook her head and shivered.

'Glad to hear it, girl, because after the next time, as I told you, nobody will be able to help you. Where is it now?'

'He's deep under the earth. In a dark, damp cavern. He's found himself some bones but he's hungry and they aren't enough.'

'Right! Now it's time to get down to business,' said the Spook. 'You two settle yourselves down in the shelter of those walls.' He pointed towards the ruin of the chapel. 'Try to get some sleep while I keep watch here by the graves.'

We didn't argue and settled ourselves down on the grass within the ruins of the chapel. Because of the missing wall we could still see the Spook and the graves. I thought he might have sat down but he remained standing, his left hand resting on his staff.

I was tired out and it wasn't long before I fell asleep. But I awoke suddenly. Alice was shaking me by the shoulder.

'What's wrong?' I asked.

'Wasting his time there, he is,' Alice said, pointing to where the Spook was now crouched down by the graves. 'There's something nearby but it's back there, close to the hedge.'

'Are you sure?'

Alice nodded. 'But you go and tell him. Won't take it too kindly coming from me.'

I walked over to the Spook and called out, 'Mr Gregory!' He didn't move and I wondered if he'd gone to sleep crouching down. But slowly he stood up and turned his upper body towards me, keeping his feet in exactly the same position.

There were a few gaps in the cloud but those patches of starlight weren't enough to let me see the Spook's face. It was just a dark shadow under his hood.

'Alice says there's something back there close to the hedge,' I told him.

'Did she now,' muttered the Spook. 'Then we'd better go and have a look.'

We walked back towards the hedge. As we got nearer it seemed to get even colder so I knew Alice was right. There was some sort of spirit lurking nearby.

The Spook pointed downwards, then suddenly he was on his knees, pulling at the long grass. I knelt too and began to help him. We uncovered two more stone graves. One was about five foot long but the other was only half that size. It was the smallest grave of all.

'Someone with the old blood running pure in his veins was buried here,' said the Spook. 'With that would come strength. This is the one we're looking for. This'll be the ghost of Naze all right! Walk back a little way, lad. Keep your distance.'

'Can't I stay and listen?' I asked.

The Spook shook his head.

'Don't you trust me?' I asked.

'Do you trust yourself?' was his reply. 'Ask yourself that! For a start he's more likely to put in an appearance with only one of us here. Anyway, it's better that you don't hear this. The Bane can read minds, remember? Are you strong enough to stop it reading yours? We can't let it know that we're onto it; that we have a plan; that we know its weaknesses. When it's in your dreams, rummaging through your brain for clues and plans, do you trust yourself not to give anything away?'

I wasn't sure.

'You're a brave lad, the bravest that was ever apprenticed to me. But that's what you are, an apprentice, and we mustn't let ourselves lose sight of that. So get back there with you!' he said, waving me away.

I did as I was told and trudged my way back to the ruined chapel. Alice was asleep so I sat down next to her for a few moments but I couldn't settle. I was restless because I really wanted to know what the ghost of Naze would have to say for itself. As for the Spook's warning about the Bane rummaging through my mind while I was sleeping, it didn't worry me that much. We were safe from the Bane here, and if the Spook found out what he needed to know, it would all be over for the Bane by tomorrow night.

So I left the ruins again and crept along the wall nearer to the Spook. It wasn't the first time I'd disobeyed my master, but it was the first time so much had been at stake. I sat down with my back against the wall and waited. But not for long. Even at that distance I began to feel very cold and kept shivering. One of the dead was approaching, but was it the ghost of Naze?

A faint glimmer of light began to form above the smaller of the two graves. It wasn't particularly human in shape, just a luminous column hardly up to the Spook's knees. Immediately I heard him begin to question it. The air was very still, and even though the Spook was keeping his voice low, I could hear every word he said.

'Speak!' said the Spook. 'Speak, I command you!'

'Leave me be! Let me rest!' came the reply.

Although Naze had died when he was young and in the prime of life, the voice of the ghost sounded like that of a very old man. It croaked and rasped and was filled with utter weariness. But that didn't necessarily mean this wasn't his ghost. The Spook had told me that ghosts didn't speak as they had in life. They communicated directly to your mind and that was why you could understand one that had lived many ages ago; one that might have spoken a very different language.

'John Gregory's my name and I'm the seventh son of a seventh son,' said the Spook, raising his voice. 'I'm here to do what should have been done long ago; here to put an end to the evil of the Bane and give you peace at last. But there are things that I need to know. First, you must tell me your name!'

There was a long pause and I thought the ghost wasn't going to answer but at last it replied.

'*I am Naze, the seventh son of Heys. What do you wish to know?*'

'It is time to finish this once and for all,' said the Spook. 'The Bane is free and soon will grow to its full power and threaten the whole land. It must be destroyed. So I've come to you for knowledge. How did you bind it within the catacombs? How can it be slain? Can you tell me that?'

'*Are you strong?*' the voice of Naze rasped. '*Can you close your mind and prevent the Bane from reading your thoughts?*'

'Aye, I can do that,' said the Spook.

'*Then maybe there is hope. I will tell you what I did. How I bound the Bane. Firstly, I made a pact giving it my blood to drink. Three more times after could it drink, and in return*'

353

three times it must obey my commands. At the deepest point of the catacombs of Priestown is a burial chamber which contains the urns holding the dust of our ancient dead, the founding fathers of our people. It was to that chamber that I summoned the Bane and gave it my blood to drink. In return I proved myself to be a hard taskmaster.

'The first time I demanded that the Bane should never more return to the barrows and keep well clear of this area where my father and brothers are buried, because I wanted them to rest in peace. The Bane groaned in dismay because the barrows were its favourite dwelling place, where it lay through the daylight hours hugging the bones of the dead and sucking the last of the memories contained within them. But a pact was a pact and it had no option but to obey. When I summoned it for a second time, I sent it questing to the ends of the earth in search of knowledge, and it was away for a month and a day, giving me all the time that I needed.

'For then I set my people to work, making and fitting the Silver Gate. But even upon its return the Bane knew nothing of this because my mind was strong and I kept my thoughts hidden.

'*After giving it my blood for the final time, I told the Bane what I required, crying out in a loud voice the price that it must pay.*

' "*You are bound to this place!*" *I commanded. "Confined to the inner catacombs with no way out. But because I would wish no being, however foul, to endure without even a glimmer of hope, I have built a Silver Gate. If anyone is ever foolish enough to open that gate in your presence, you may pass through it to freedom. However, following that, if you ever return to this spot, you will be bound here for all eternity!*"

'*Thus the softness of my heart dictated to me and the binding was not as firm as it might have been. During my lifetime I was filled with compassion for others. Some considered it a weakness and on this occasion they were proved correct. For I could not doom even the Bane to an eternity of imprisonment without offering it a faint chance of escape.*'

'You did enough,' said the Spook. 'And now I'm going to finish the job. If we can only get it back there it will be bound for ever! That is a start. But how can it be slain? Can you tell me that? This creature is so evil now, binding it is no longer enough. I need to destroy it.'

'Firstly it must have taken on the mantle of flesh. Secondly it must be deep within the catacombs. Thirdly its heart must be pierced with silver. Only if all three conditions are met will it finally die. But there is a great risk for he who attempts this. In its death throes the Bane will release so much energy that its slayer will almost certainly die.'

The Spook gave a deep sigh. 'I thank you for that knowledge,' he said to the ghost. 'It will be hard but it must be done, whatever the cost. But your task is now complete. Go in peace. Pass over to the other side.'

In reply the ghost of Naze groaned so deeply that the hair began to move on the back of my neck. It was a groan filled with agony.

'There'll be no peace for me,' moaned the ghost wearily. *'No peace until the Bane is finally dead . . .'*

And with those words the small column of light faded away. Wasting no time, I moved back along the wall and into the ruins once more. A few moments later the Spook walked in, lay down on the grass and closed his eyes.

'I've some serious thinking to do,' he whispered.

I didn't say anything. Suddenly, I felt guilty for listening to his conversation with Naze's ghost. Now I knew too much. I was afraid that if I told him, he'd send me away and face the Bane alone.

'I'll explain at first light,' he whispered. 'But for now, get some sleep. It's not safe to leave this spot until the sun comes up!'

To my surprise, I slept quite well. Just before dawn I was awakened by a strange grating sound. It was the Spook, sharpening the retractable blade in his staff with a whetstone that he'd taken from his bag. He worked methodically, occasionally testing it with his finger. At last he was satisfied and there was a click as the blade snapped back into the staff.

I clambered to my feet and stretched my legs for a few moments, while the Spook reached down, unfastened his bag again and rummaged around inside it.

'I know exactly what to do now,' he said. 'We can defeat the Bane. It can be done but it'll be the most

357

difficult task I've ever had to undertake. If I fail, it will go hard with all of us.'

'What has to be done?' I asked, feeling bad because I knew already. He didn't answer and he walked right past me towards Alice, who was sitting up, hugging her knees.

He tied the blindfold in position and inserted the first of the wax earplugs. 'Now for the other one, but before it goes into place listen well to me, girl, because this is important,' he said. 'When I take this out tonight, I'll speak to you right away and you must do what I say immediately and without question. Do you understand?'

Alice nodded and he fitted the second plug. Once again, Alice couldn't see and she couldn't hear. And the Bane wouldn't know what we were up to or where we were going. Unless it somehow managed to read my mind. I began to feel very uneasy about what I'd done. I knew too much.

'Now,' said the Spook, turning towards me. 'I'll tell you one thing you won't like. We have to go back to Priestown. Back to the catacombs.'

Then he turned on his heels and, gripping Alice by her left elbow, walked her back to the horse and cart where the farmer's lad was still waiting.

'We need to get to Priestown as fast as this horse can manage,' said the Spook.

'Don't know about that,' said the lad. 'My old dad expects me back before noon. There's work to be done.'

The Spook held out a silver coin. 'Here, take this. Get us there before dark and there'll be another one. I don't think your dad'll mind too much. He likes to count his money.'

The Spook made Alice lie down at our feet and he covered her with straw again so that she wouldn't be visible to anybody we passed, and soon we were on our way. At first we skirted Caster but then, instead of moving back towards the fells, we headed for the main road which led directly to Priestown.

'Won't it be dangerous to go back in daylight?' I asked nervously. The road was very busy and we kept passing other carts and people on foot. 'What if the Quisitor's men spot us?'

'I won't say it's not without risk,' said the Spook. 'But those who were searching for us are now probably busy bringing the body down the fellside. No doubt they'll bring him to Priestown for burial but that won't take place till tomorrow; by then it'll all be over and we'll be on our way. Of course, then there's the storm to think about. People with any sense will be indoors, sheltering from the rain.'

I looked at the sky. To the south, clouds were building but didn't look that bad to me. When I said as much, the Spook smiled.

'You've still a lot to learn, lad,' he said. 'This will be one of the biggest storms you've ever seen.'

'After all that rain I'd have thought we were due a few days of good weather,' I complained.

'No doubt we are, lad. But this is far from natural. Unless I'm very much mistaken it's been called up by the Bane just as it called up the wind to batter my house. It's another sign of just how powerful it's become. It'll wield the storm to show its anger and frustration at not being able to use Alice as it wants.

Well, that's good for us: while it's concentrating on that, it's not bothering much about me and you. And it'll help us to get into the town without problems.'

'Why do we have to go to the catacombs to kill the Bane?' I asked, hoping that he'd tell me what I already knew. That way I wouldn't have to keep up the pretence any longer.

'It's in case I fail to destroy it, lad. At least once back there, with the Silver Gate locked, the Bane'll be trapped again. This time for ever. That's what the ghost of Naze told me. Then, even if I don't succeed in destroying it, at least I'll have returned things to the way they were. And now that's enough of your questions. I need some peace to prepare myself for what I'm going to do . . .'

We didn't speak again until we reached the outskirts of Priestown. By then the sky was as black as pitch, split with great zigzags of lightning as thunderclaps burst almost directly overhead. The rain was coming straight down and soaking into our clothes and I was wet and uncomfortable. I felt sorry for Alice because she was still lying on the floor of the cart, which now held almost an inch of water. It must have been really hard not being able to see or hear and not knowing where she was going or when the journey would end.

My own journey ended a lot sooner than I'd expected. On the outskirts of Priestown, when we came to the last crossroads, the Spook called out to the farmer's lad to stop the cart.

'This is where you get out,' he said, looking at me sternly.

I gazed at him in astonishment. The rain was dripping from the end of his nose and running into his beard but he didn't blink as he stared at me with a very fierce expression.

'I want you to go back to Chipenden,' he said, pointing towards the narrow road that went roughly north-east. 'Go into the kitchen and tell that boggart of mine that I might not be coming back. Tell him that if that's the case he's got to keep the house safe for when you're ready. Safe and secure until you complete your apprenticeship and are finally fit to take over.

'That done, go north of Caster and look for Bill Arkwright, the local Spook. He's a bit of a plodder but he's honest enough and he'll train you for the next four years or so. In the end you'll need to go back to Chipenden and do a lot more studying. You must get your head down in those books to make up for the fact that I've not been there to train you!'

'Why? What's wrong? Why won't you be coming back?' I asked. It was another question to which I already knew the answer.

The Spook shook his head sadly. 'Because there's only one certain way to deal with the Bane and it's probably going to cost me my life. The girl's too, if I'm not mistaken. It's hard, lad, but it has to be done. Maybe one day, years from now, you'll be faced with a task like this yourself. I hope not but it sometimes happens. My own master died doing something similar and now it's my turn. History can repeat itself, and if it does, we have to be ready to lay down our lives. It's just something that goes with the job so you'd better get used to it.'

I wondered if the Spook was thinking about the curse. Was he expecting to die because of that? If he died then there'd be no one to protect Alice down there at the mercy of the Bane.

'But what about Alice?' I protested. 'You didn't tell Alice what was going to happen! You tricked her!'

'It had to be done. The girl's probably too far gone to be saved anyway. It's for the best. At least her spirit will be free. It's better than being bound to that filthy creature.'

'Please,' I begged. 'Let me come with you. Let me help.'

'The best way you can help is to do what I say!' the Spook said impatiently, and seizing my arm he pushed me roughly from the cart. I landed awkwardly and fell onto my knees. When I scrambled to my feet, the cart was already moving away and the Spook wasn't looking back.

CHAPTER 20
MAM'S LETTER

I waited until the cart was almost out of sight before I began to follow it, my breath sobbing in my throat. I didn't know what I was going to do but I couldn't bear the thought of what lay ahead. The Spook seemed resigned to his death and poor Alice didn't even know what was going to happen to her.

There shouldn't have been too much risk of being seen – the rain was teeming straight down and the black clouds above made it almost as dark as midnight. But the Spook's senses were keen, and if I got too close, he'd know right away. So I ran and walked alternately, keeping my distance but still managing to get a glimpse of the cart from time to time. The streets of Priestown were deserted, and despite the rain, even when the cart was far ahead, I could still hear the distant *clip-clop* of hooves and the trundling of the cart's wheels over the cobbles.

Soon the white limestone spire began to loom up above the rooftops, confirming the Spook's direction and destination. As I'd expected, he was heading for the haunted house with the cellar that led down into the catacombs.

At that moment I felt something very strange. It wasn't the usual numbing sensation of cold that announced the approach of something from the dark. No, this was more like a sudden tiny splinter of ice right inside my head. I'd never experienced anything like it before but it was all the warning I needed. I guessed what it was and managed to clear my mind just before the Bane spoke.

'Found you at last, I have!'

Instinctively, I halted and closed my eyes. When I realized that it wouldn't be able to see out of them, I kept them closed anyway. The Spook had told me that the Bane didn't see the world as we saw it. Even though it might be able to find you, just like a spider linked to its prey by a silken thread, it still wouldn't know where you were. So I had to keep it that way. Anything my eyes saw would be filtered into my thoughts and soon the Bane would start trying to sift through them. It might be able to pick up clues that I was in Priestown.

'Where are you, boy? Might as well tell me. Sooner or later you'll do it. Easy or hard, it can be. You choose . . .'

The splinter of ice was growing and the whole of my head was becoming numb. It made me think again of my brother James and the farm. Of how he'd chased me that winter and filled my ears with snow.

'I'm on my way back home,' I lied. 'Back home for a rest.'

As I spoke, I imagined walking into the farmyard with Hangman's Hill just visible on the horizon, through the murk. The dogs were starting to bark and I was approaching the back door, splashing through puddles, the rain driving into my face.

'Where's Old Bones? Tell me that. Where's he going with the girl?'

'Back to Chipenden,' I said. 'He's going to put Alice in a pit. I tried to talk him out of it but he wouldn't listen. That's what he always does with a witch.'

I imagined myself jerking open the back door and entering the kitchen. The curtains were drawn and the beeswax candle was alight in the brass candlestick on the table. Mam was sitting in her rocking chair. As I came in, she looked up and smiled.

Instantly the Bane was gone and the cold began to fade. I hadn't stopped it from reading my mind but I'd deceived it. I'd done it! Seconds later my elation faded. Would it pay me another visit? Or worse still, would it pay my family one?

I opened my eyes and began to run as fast as I could towards the haunted house. After a few minutes I heard the sound of the cart again and went back to walking and running alternately.

At last the cart came to a halt, but almost immediately it set off again and I ducked into an alley as it rumbled back towards me. The farmer's lad sat hunched low and flicked the reins, sending the hooves of the big shire horse clattering across the wet cobbles. He was in a rush to get home and I couldn't say I blamed him.

I waited five minutes or so to let Alice and the Spook get into the house before I ran along the street and lifted the latch on the yard door. As I expected, the Spook had locked the back door but I still had Andrew's key, and a moment later I was standing in the kitchen. I took the candle stub from my pocket, lit it and after that it didn't take me long to get down into the catacombs.

I heard a scream somewhere ahead and guessed what it was. The Spook was carrying Alice over the river. Even with the blindfold and the earplugs she must have been able to sense the running water.

Soon I was crossing the steps over the river myself and I reached the Silver Gate just in time. Alice and the Spook were already on the other side and he was on his knees, just about to close it.

He looked up angrily as I ran towards him. 'I might have known it!' he shouted, his voice filled with fury. 'Didn't your mam teach you any obedience?'

Looking back, I can see now that the Spook was right, that he just wanted to keep me safe, but I rushed forward, gripped the gate and started to pull it open. The Spook resisted for a moment but then he simply let go and came through to my side, carrying his staff.

I didn't know what to say. I wasn't thinking clearly. I'd no idea what I hoped to achieve by going with them anyway. But suddenly I remembered the curse again.

'I want to help,' I said. 'Andrew told me about the curse. That you'll die alone in the dark without a friend at your side. Alice isn't your friend but I am. If I'm there it can't come true . . .'

He lifted the staff above his head as if he was going to hit me with it. He seemed to grow in size until he towered over me. I'd never seen him so angry. Next, to my surprise and dismay, he lowered his staff, took a step towards me and slapped me across the face. I stumbled backwards, hardly able to believe that it had happened.

It wasn't a hard blow but tears flooded into my eyes and ran down my cheeks. Dad had never slapped me like that. I couldn't believe the Spook had done it and I felt hurt inside. Hurt much more than by any physical pain.

He stared hard at me for a few moments and shook his head as if I'd been a big disappointment to him. Then he went back through the gate, closing and locking it behind him.

'Do as I say!' he commanded. 'You were born into this world for a reason. Don't throw it away for something you can't change. If you won't do it for me, do it for your mam's sake. Go back to Chipenden. Then go to Caster and do what I've asked. That's what she'd want. Make her proud of you.'

With those words the Spook turned on his heels and, guiding Alice by the left elbow, walked her along the tunnel. I watched until they turned the corner and were out of sight.

* * *

I must have waited there for half an hour or so, just staring at the locked gate, my mind numb.

At last, all hope gone, I turned and began to retrace my steps. I didn't know what I was going to do. Probably just obey the Spook, I suppose. Go back to Chipenden and then to Caster. What other choice did I have? But I couldn't get out of my mind the fact that the Spook had slapped me. That it was probably the last time we'd ever meet and we'd parted in anger and disappointment.

I crossed the river, followed the cobble path and climbed up into the cellar. Once there, I sat on the musty old carpet trying to decide what to do. Suddenly I remembered another way down into the catacombs that would bring me out beyond the Silver Gate. The hatch that led down to the wine cellar, the one that some of the prisoners had escaped through! Could I get to it without being seen? It was just possible if everybody was in the cathedral.

But even if I could get down into the catacombs, I

didn't know what I could do to help. Was it worth disobeying the Spook again and all for nothing? Was I just going to throw my life away when it was my duty to go to Caster and carry on learning my trade? Was the Spook right? Would Mam agree that it was the right thing to do? The thoughts just kept whirling around inside my head but led me to no clear answer.

It was hard to be sure of anything but the Spook had always told me to trust my instincts and they seemed to be telling me that I had to try and do something to help. Thinking of that, I suddenly remembered Mam's letter because that's exactly what she'd said.

'*Only open it in a time of great need. Trust your instincts.*'

It was a time of great need all right so, very nervously, I pulled the envelope from my jacket pocket. I stared at it for a few moments, then tore it open and pulled out the letter within. Holding it close to the candle, I began to read.

Dear Tom,

You face a moment of great danger. I had not expected such a crisis to come so soon and now all I can do is prepare you by telling you what you face and indicating the outcomes that depend upon the decision that you must make.

There is much that I cannot see but one thing is certain. Your master will descend to the burial chamber at the deepest point of the catacombs and there he will confront the Bane in a struggle to the death. Of necessity, he will use Alice to lure it to that spot.

He has no choice. But you do have a choice. You can go down to the burial chamber and try to help. But then, of the three who face the Bane, only two will leave the catacombs alive.

But if you turn back now, the two down there will surely die. And they'll die in vain.

Sometimes in this life it is necessary to sacrifice oneself for the good of others. I would like to offer you comfort but cannot. Be strong and do what your conscience tells you. Whatever you choose, I will always be proud of you.

Mam

I remembered what the Spook had once told me soon after he took me on as his apprentice. He'd spoken it with such conviction that I'd committed it to memory.

'Above all, we don't believe in prophecy. We don't believe that the future is fixed.'

I badly wanted to believe what the Spook said because, if Mam was right, one of us – the Spook, Alice or I – would die below in the dark. But the letter in my hand told me beyond a shadow of all doubt that prophecy was possible. How else could Mam have known that the Spook and Alice would be down in the burial chamber now about to face the Bane? And how had it happened that I'd read her letter at just the right time?

Instinct? Was that enough to explain it? I shivered and felt more afraid than at any time since I'd started working for the Spook. I felt as if I were walking in a nightmare where everything had been decided in advance and I could do nothing and had no choice at all. How could there be a choice, when to leave Alice and the Spook and walk away would result in their deaths?

And there was another reason why I had to go down into the catacombs again. The curse. Was that why the Spook had slapped me? Was he angry because he secretly believed in it and was afraid? All the more reason to help. Mam had once told me that he'd be my teacher and eventually become my friend. Whether that time had arrived or not it was hard to say but I was certainly more of a friend to him than Alice was and the Spook needed me!

When I left the yard and walked into the alley, it was still raining but the skies were quiet. I sensed that more thunder was to come and we were in what my dad calls 'the eye of the storm'. It was then that, in the relative silence, I heard the cathedral bell. It wasn't the mournful sound that I'd heard from Andrew's house, tolling for the priest who'd killed himself. It was a bright, hopeful bell summoning the congregation to the evening service.

So I waited in the alley, leaning back against a wall to avoid the worst of the rain. I don't know why I bothered because I was already soaked to the skin. At last the bell stopped ringing, which I hoped meant that everybody was now inside the cathedral and out of the way. So I began to head slowly towards it too.

I turned the corner and walked down towards the gate. The light was starting to fail, and the black clouds were still piled up overhead. Then the sky suddenly lit up with a sheet of lightning and I saw that the area in front of the cathedral was completely deserted. I could see the building's dark exterior with its big buttresses and its tall pointy windows. There was candlelight illuminating the stained glass, and in the window to the left of the door was the image of St George dressed in armour, holding a sword and a shield with a red cross. On the right was St Peter, standing in front of a fishing boat. And in the centre, over the door, was the malevolent carving of the Bane, the gargoyle head glaring towards me.

The saint I was named after wasn't there. Thomas

the Doubter. Thomas the Disbeliever. I didn't know whether it was my mam or my dad who'd chosen that name but they'd chosen it well. I didn't believe what the Church believed; one day I'd be buried outside a churchyard, not in it. Once I became a spook, my bones could never rest in holy ground. But it didn't bother me in the slightest. As the Spook often said, priests knew nothing.

I could hear singing from inside the cathedral. Probably the choir I'd heard practising after I visited Father Cairns in his confessional. For a moment I envied them their religion. They were lucky to have something they could all believe in together. It was easier to be inside the cathedral with all those people than to go down into the damp, cold catacombs alone.

I walked across the flags and onto the wide gravel path that ran parallel to the north wall of the church. Instantly, as I was about to turn the corner, my heart lurched up into my mouth. There was somebody sitting down opposite the hatch with his back against the wall, sheltering from the rain. At his side was a stout wooden club. It was one of the churchwardens.

I almost groaned aloud. I should have expected that. After all those prisoners had escaped they'd be worried about security – and their cellar full of wine and ale.

I was filled with despair and almost gave up there and then, but just as I turned, about to tiptoe away, I heard a sound and listened again until I was sure. But I hadn't been mistaken. It was the sound of snoring. The warden was asleep! How on earth could he have slept through all that thunder?

Hardly able to believe my luck, I walked towards the hatch very, very slowly, trying not to let my boots crunch on the gravel, worrying that the warden might wake up at any moment and I'd have to run for it.

I felt a lot better when I got closer. There were two empty bottles of wine nearby. He was probably drunk and unlikely to wake up for some time. However, I still couldn't take any chances. I knelt and inserted Andrew's key into the lock very carefully. A moment later I'd pulled the hatch open and lowered myself down onto the barrels below before easing it carefully back into place.

I still had my tinderbox and a stub of candle that I always carried about with me. It didn't take me long to light it. Now I could see – but I still didn't know how I was going to find the burial chamber.

A CHAPTER 21 SACRIFICE

I picked my way through the barrels and wine racks until I came to the door that led to the catacombs. By my reckoning it was less than fifteen minutes or so before nightfall so I didn't have long. I knew that as soon as the sun went down, my master would make Alice summon the Bane for the final time.

The Spook would try to stab the Bane through the heart with his blade but he would only get one chance. If he succeeded, the energy released would probably kill him. It was brave of him to be prepared to sacrifice his life, but if he missed, Alice would also suffer. Realizing it had been tricked, and was now trapped behind the Silver Gate for ever, the Bane would be furious; Alice and my master would certainly both pay with their lives if it wasn't destroyed quickly enough. It would press their bodies into the cobbles.

At the bottom of the steps I paused. Which way should I go? Immediately my question was answered: one of Dad's sayings came into my head.

'Always put your best foot forward!'

Well, my best foot was my left foot so, rather than taking the tunnel directly ahead, the one that led to the Silver Gate and the underground river beyond it, I followed the one to the left. This was narrow, just wide enough to allow one person through, and it curved and sloped steeply downwards so that I had a sense of descending a spiral.

The deeper I went, the colder it got and I knew that the dead were gathering. I kept glimpsing things out of the corner of my eye: the ghosts of the Little People, small shapes hardly more than glimmers of light that kept moving in and out of the tunnel walls. And I had a suspicion that there were more behind me than in front – a feeling that they were following me; that we were all moving down towards the burial chamber.

At last I saw a flicker of candlelight ahead and I emerged into the burial chamber. It was smaller than I'd expected, a circular room perhaps no more than twenty paces in diameter. There was a high shelf above, recessed into the rock, and on it were the large stone urns that held the remains of the ancient dead. At the centre of the ceiling was a roughly circular opening like a chimney, a dark hole into which the candlelight couldn't reach. From that hole dangled chains and a hook.

Water was dripping from the stone ceiling and the walls were covered in green slime. There was a strong stench too: a mixture of rot and stagnant water.

A stone bench curved around the wall; the Spook was sitting on it, both hands leaning on his staff, while to his right was Alice, still wearing the blindfold and earplugs.

As I approached, he stared at me but he didn't look angry any more, just very sad.

'You're even dafter than I thought,' he said quietly,

as I walked up and stood before him. 'Go back now while you still can. In a few moments it'll be too late.'

I shook my head. 'Please, let me stay. I want to help.'

The Spook let out a long sigh. 'You might make things even worse,' he said. 'If the Bane gets any warning at all, it'll stay well clear of this place. The girl doesn't know where she is and I can close my mind against it. Can you? What if it reads your mind?'

'The Bane tried to read my mind a while back. It wanted to know where you were. Where I was too. But I stood up to it and it failed,' I told him.

'How did you stop it?' he asked, his voice suddenly harsh.

'I lied to it. I pretended that I was on my way home and I told it you were on your way to Chipenden.'

'And did it believe you?'

'It seemed to,' I said, suddenly feeling less certain.

'Well, we'll find out soon enough when it's summoned. Go a little way back up the tunnel then,' said the Spook, his voice softer. 'You'll be able to watch from there. If things go badly you might even have half a chance of escaping. Go on, lad! Don't hesitate. It's nearly time!'

I did as I was told, moving back quite some distance into the tunnel. I knew that by now the sun would have dipped below the horizon and dusk would be drawing in. The Bane would leave its hiding place below ground. In its spirit form it could fly freely through the air and pass through solid rock. Once summoned it would fly straight to Alice, faster than a hawk with folded wings, dropping like a stone towards its prey. If the Spook's plan worked, it wouldn't realize where Alice was waiting. Once it was here, it would be too late. But we'd be here too, facing its anger when it realized it had been tricked and trapped.

I watched the Spook climb to his feet and stand facing Alice. He bowed his head and stayed perfectly still for a long time. Had he been a priest I'd have thought he was praying. Finally he reached towards Alice and I saw him draw the wax plug from her left ear.

'Summon the Bane!' he shouted, in a loud voice that

filled the chamber and echoed down the tunnel. 'Do it now, girl! Don't delay!'

Alice didn't speak. She didn't even move. She didn't need to because she called it from within her mind, willing its presence.

There was no warning of its arrival. One moment there was just silence, the next there was a blast of cold and the Bane appeared in the chamber. From the neck upwards it was the replica of the gargoyle over the main cathedral door: gaping teeth, lolling tongue, huge dog's ears and wicked horns. From the neck down, it was a vast, black, shapeless boiling cloud.

It had gained the strength to take on its original form! What chance had the Spook against it now?

For one short moment the Bane remained perfectly still while its eyes darted everywhere. Eyes with pupils that were dark green, vertical slits. Pupils shaped like those of a goat.

Then, upon realizing where it was, it let out a groan of anguish and dismay that boomed along the tunnel so that I could feel it vibrate through the very soles of my boots and shiver up into my bones.

'*Bound again, I am! Bound fast!*' it cried with harsh, hissing coldness that echoed in the chambers and penetrated me like ice.

'Aye,' said the Spook. 'You're here now and here you'll stay, bound for ever to this cursed place!'

'*Enjoy what you've done! Suck in your last breath, Old Bones. Tricked me, you have, but what for? What will you gain but the darkness of death? Nothing, you'll be, but I'll still have my way with the ones above. Still do my bidding, they will. Fresh blood they'll send me down! So all for nothing it was!*'

The head of the Bane grew larger, the face becoming even more hideous, the chin lengthening and curving upwards to meet the hooked nose. The dark cloud was boiling downwards, forming flesh so that now a neck was visible and the beginnings of broad, powerful, muscular shoulders. But instead of skin they were covered in rough green scales.

I knew what the Spook was waiting for. The moment

the chest was clearly defined he would strike straight for the heart within. Even as I watched, the boiling cloud descended further to form the body as far down as the waist.

But I was mistaken! The Spook didn't use his blade. As if appearing from nowhere, the silver chain was in his left hand and he raised his arm to hurl it at the Bane.

I'd seen him do it before. I'd watched him throw it at the witch, Bony Lizzie, so that it formed a perfect spiral and dropped upon her, binding her arms to her sides. She'd fallen to the ground and could do nothing but lie there snarling, the chain enclosing her body and tight against her teeth.

The same would have happened here, I'm sure of it, and it would have been the Bane's turn to lie there helplessly. But at the very moment when the Spook prepared to hurl the silver chain, Alice lurched to her feet and tore off her blindfold.

I know she didn't mean to do it, but somehow she got between the Spook and his target and spoiled his aim. Instead of landing over the Bane's head, the silver chain fell against its shoulder. At its touch, the creature screamed out in agony and the chain fell to the floor.

But it wasn't over yet and the Spook snatched up his staff. As he held it high, preparing to drive it into the Bane, there was a sudden click and the retractable blade, made from an alloy containing silver, was now bared, glinting in the candlelight. The blade that I'd watched him sharpening at Heysham. I'd seen him use it once before, when he'd faced Tusk, the son of the old witch, Mother Malkin.

Now the Spook stabbed his staff hard and fast, straight at the Bane, aiming for its heart. It tried to twist away but was too late to avoid the thrust completely. The blade pierced its left shoulder and it screamed out in agony. Alice backed away, a look of terror on her face, while the Spook pulled back his staff and readied it for a second thrust, his face grim and determined.

But suddenly, both candles were snuffed out, plunging the chamber and tunnel into darkness. Frantically,

I used my tinderbox to light my own candle again but it flickered into life to reveal that the Spook now stood alone in the chamber. The Bane had simply disappeared! And so had Alice!

'Where is she?' I cried, running towards the Spook, who just shook his head sadly.

'Don't move!' he commanded. 'It's not finished yet!'

He was staring up at where the chains disappeared into the dark hole in the ceiling. There was a loop, and beside it a second single length of chain. Affixed to the end of it, and almost touching the floor, was a large hook. It was a sort of block and tackle similar to the ones used by riggers to lower boggart stones into position.

The Spook seemed to be listening for something. 'It's somewhere up there,' he whispered.

'Is that a chimney?' I asked.

'Aye, lad. Something like that. At least, that was the purpose it sometimes served. Even long after it had been bound, and the Little People were dead and gone, weak and foolish men made sacrifices to the Bane on

391

this very spot. The chimney carried the smoke up into its lair above and they used the chain to send up the burnt offering. Some of them got pressed for their trouble!'

Something was beginning to happen. I felt a draught from the chimney and there was a sudden chill in the air. I looked up as what looked like smoke began to waft slowly downwards to fill the upper reaches of the chamber. It was as if all the burnt offerings that had ever been made on this spot were being returned!

But it was far denser than smoke; it looked like water, like a black whirlpool swirling above our heads. Within seconds it became calm and still, resembling the polished surface of a dark mirror. I could even see our reflections in it: me standing next to the Spook, his staff at the ready, blade pointing upwards, ready to jab.

What happened next was too swift to see properly. The surface of the smoke mirror bulged out towards us and something broke through fast and hard enough to send the Spook sprawling backwards. He fell heavily, the staff flying out of his hand and breaking into two unequal pieces with a sharp snapping sound.

At first I stood there stunned, hardly able to think, unable to move a muscle, but at last, my whole body trembling, I went across to see if the Spook was all right.

He was on his back, his eyes closed, a trickle of blood running from his nose down into his open mouth. He was breathing deeply and evenly so I shook him gently, trying to wake him up. He didn't respond. I walked across to the broken staff and picked up the smaller of the two pieces, the one with the blade attached. It was about the length of my forearm so I tucked it into my belt. I stood at the side of the chain looking upwards.

Somebody had to try to help Alice destroy this creature once and for all, and I was the only one who could. I couldn't leave her to the Bane. So firstly I tried to clear my mind. If it was empty, the Bane couldn't read my thoughts. The Spook had probably been practising that for days but I would just have to do my best.

I put the end of the candle in my mouth, biting into it with my teeth, then gripped the single chain carefully with both hands, trying to keep it as still as possible. Next I placed my feet above the hook and gripped the chain between my knees. I was good at climbing ropes and a chain couldn't be that different.

I began to move upwards quite fast, the chain cold and biting in my hand. At the bottom of the thick smoke I took a deep breath, held it, and pushed my head up into the darkness. I couldn't see a thing, and despite not breathing the smoke was getting up my nose and into my open mouth and there was a sharp acrid taste at the back of my throat that reminded me of burned sausages.

Suddenly, my head was out of the smoke and I pulled myself further up the chain until my shoulders and chest were clear of it. I was in a circular chamber almost identical to the one below except that, rather than a chimney above, there was a shaft below and the smoke filled the lower half of the chamber.

A tunnel led from the opposite wall into the darkness and there was another stone bench where Alice was sitting, the smoke almost up to her knees. She was holding out her left hand towards the Bane. That heinous creature was kneeling in the smoke bending over her, the naked arch of its back reminding me of a large green toad. Even as I watched, it drew her hand into its large mouth and I heard Alice cry out in pain as it began to suck the blood from beneath her nails. This was the third time the Bane had fed on Alice's blood since she released it. When it had finished, Alice would belong to it!

I was cold, as cold as ice, and my mind was blank. I was thinking about nothing at all. I pulled myself up further and stepped from the chain onto the stone floor of the upper chamber. The Bane was too preoccupied with what it was doing to be aware of my presence. No doubt in that respect it was like the Horshaw ripper: when it was feeding, hardly anything else mattered.

I stepped closer and pulled the piece of the Spook's staff from my belt. I raised it and held it above my head, the blade pointing at the Bane's scaly green back. All I had to do was bring it down hard and pierce its heart. It was clothed in flesh and that would be the end of it. It would be dead. But just as I was tensing my arm, I suddenly became afraid.

I knew what would happen to me. So much energy would be released that I would die too. I would be a ghost just like poor Billy Bradley, who'd died after having his fingers bitten off by a boggart. He'd been happy once as the Spook's apprentice but now was buried outside the churchyard at Layton. The thought of it was too much to bear.

I was terrified – terrified of death – and I began to tremble again. It started at my knees and travelled right up my body until the hand holding the blade began to shake.

The Bane must have sensed my fear because it suddenly turned its head, Alice's fingers still in its mouth, blood trickling down its big curved chin. But then, when it was almost too late, my fear simply evaporated away. All at once I realized why I was there facing the Bane. I remembered what Mam had said in her letter . . .

'Sometimes in this life it is necessary to sacrifice oneself for the good of others.'

She'd warned me that of the three who faced the Bane, only two would leave the catacombs alive. I'd somehow thought it was going to be the Spook or Alice who would die, but now I realized that it would be me! I was never going to complete my apprenticeship, never going to become a spook. But by sacrificing my life now I could save both of them. I was very calm. I simply accepted what had to be done.

I feel sure that at the very last moment the Bane realized what I was going to do, but instead of pressing me dead on the spot it turned its head back towards Alice, who gave it a strange, mysterious smile.

I struck quickly with all my strength, driving the blade towards its heart. I didn't feel the blade make contact but a shuddering darkness rose before my eyes; my body quivered from head to foot, so that I had no control over my muscles. The candle dropped out of my mouth and I felt myself falling. I'd missed it's heart!

For a moment I thought that I'd died. Everything was dark but for now the Bane seemed to have vanished. I fumbled around on the floor for my candle and lit it again. Listening carefully, I gestured to Alice to be silent, and heard a sound from the tunnel. The padding of a large dog.

I tucked the piece of staff with the blade back into my belt. Next I eased Mam's silver chain from my jacket pocket and coiled it round my left hand and wrist, ready for throwing. With my other hand I picked up the candle, and without further delay I set off after the Bane.

'No, Tom, no! Leave it be!' Alice called out from behind. 'It's over. You can go back to Chipenden!'

She ran towards me but I pushed her back hard. She staggered and almost fell. When she moved towards me again, I lifted my left hand so that she could see the silver chain.

'Keep back! You belong to the Bane now. Keep your distance or I'll bind you too!'

The Bane had fed for the final time and now nothing she said could be trusted. It would have to be dead before she'd be free.

I turned my back on her and moved away quickly. Ahead of me I could hear the Bane; behind me the *click-click* of Alice's pointy shoes as she followed me into the tunnel. Suddenly the padding ahead stopped.

Had the Bane simply vanished and gone to another part of the catacombs? I stopped and listened before moving forward more cautiously. It was then that I saw something ahead. Something on the floor of the tunnel. I halted close to it and my stomach heaved. I was almost sick on the spot.

Brother Peter lay on his back. He'd been pressed. His head was still intact; the wide-open, staring eyes showed the terror he had obviously felt at the time of his death. But from the neck downwards his body had been flattened against the stones.

The sight horrified me. During my first few months as an apprentice I'd seen many terrible things and been close to death and the dead more times than I cared to remember. But this was the first time I'd seen the death of someone I cared about – and such a horrible death.

I stood, distracted by the sight of Brother Peter, and the Bane chose that moment to come loping out of the darkness towards me. For a moment it halted and stared at me, the green slits of its eyes glowing in the gloom. Its heavy, muscular body was covered in coarse black hair and its jaws were wide revealing the rows of sharp yellow teeth. Something was dripping from that long tongue which lolled forwards, beyond the gaping jaws. Instead of saliva, it was blood!

Suddenly the Bane attacked, bounding towards me. I readied my chain and heard Alice scream behind me. Just in time I realized that it had changed its angle of attack. I wasn't the target! Alice was!

I was stunned. I was the threat to the Bane, not Alice. So why her rather than me?

Instinctively I adjusted my aim. Nine times out of ten I could hit the post in the Spook's garden but this was different. The Bane was moving fast, already beginning to leap. So I cracked the chain and cast it towards the creature, watching it open like a net and drop in the shape of a spiral. All my practice paid off and it fell over the Bane cleanly and tightened against its body. It rolled over and over, howling, struggling to escape.

In theory it couldn't get itself free and neither could it vanish or change shape. But I wasn't taking any chances. I had to pierce its heart quickly. I had to finish it now. So I ran forward, pulled the blade from my belt and prepared to stab downwards into its chest. Its eyes looked up at me as I readied the blade. They were filled with hatred. But there was fear there too: the absolute terror of death; terror of the nothingness it faced, and it spoke inside my head begging frantically for its life.

'Mercy! Mercy!' it cried. 'Nothing for us, there is! Just darkness. Is that what you want, boy? You'll die too!'

'No, Tom, no! Don't do it!' Alice shouted out behind me, adding her voice to the Bane's. But I didn't listen to either of them. No matter what the cost to myself it had to die. It was writhing within the coils of the chain and I stabbed it twice before I found its heart.

The third time I lunged downwards the Bane simply vanished, but I heard a loud scream. Whether it was the Bane, Alice or me who made that sound, I'll never know. Maybe it was all three of us.

I felt a tremendous blow to my chest, followed by a strange sinking feeling. Everything went very quiet and I felt myself falling into darkness.

The next thing I knew I was standing by a large expanse of water.

Despite its size, it was more like a lake than a sea for although a pleasant breeze was blowing towards the shore, the water remained calm, like a mirror, reflecting the perfect blue of the sky.

Small boats were being launched from a beach of golden sand, and beyond them I could see an island quite close to the shore. It was green with trees and rolling meadows and seemed to me more wonderful than anything I'd ever seen before in my whole life. Amongst the trees on a hilltop was a building like the castle we'd glimpsed from the low fells as we skirted

Caster. But instead of being constructed of cold grey stone it shimmered with light as if built from the beams of a rainbow and its rays warmed my forehead like a glorious sun.

I wasn't breathing but I was calm and happy and I remember thinking that if I was dead then it was nice to be dead and I just had to get to that castle, so I ran towards the nearest of the boats, desperate to get on board. As I drew closer, the people stopped trying to launch the boat and turned their faces towards me. At that moment I knew who they were. They were small, very small, and had dark hair and brown eyes. It was the Little People! The Segantii!

They smiled in welcome, rushed towards me and began to pull me towards the boat. I'd never felt so happy in my life, so welcomed, so wanted, so accepted. All my loneliness was over. But just as I was about to climb aboard, I felt a cold hand grip my left forearm.

When I turned, there was nobody there but the pressure on my arm increased until it began to hurt. I could feel fingernails cutting into my skin. I tried to pull away and get into the boat and the Little People tried to help me but the pressure on my arm was now a burning pain. I cried out and sucked in a huge, painful breath that sobbed in my throat and made my whole body tingle then grow hotter and hotter as if I were burning inside.

I was lying on my back in the dark. It was raining very hard and I could feel the raindrops drumming on my eyelids and forehead and even falling into my mouth, which was wide open. I was too weary to open my eyes but I heard the Spook's voice from some distance away.

'Leave him be!' he said. 'Give him peace, girl. That's all we can do for him now!'

I opened my eyes and looked up to see Alice bending over me. Behind her I could see the dark wall of the cathedral. She was gripping my left forearm, her nails very sharp against my skin. She leaned forwards and whispered into my ear.

'You don't get away that easily, Tom. You're back now. Back where you belong!'

I sucked in a deep breath and the Spook came forward, his eyes filled with amazement. As he knelt at my side, Alice stood up and drew back.

'How do you feel, lad?' he asked gently, helping me up into a sitting position. 'I thought you were dead. When I carried you out of the catacombs, I swear there was no breath left in your body!'

'The Bane?' I asked. 'Is it dead?'

'Aye, it is that, lad. You finished it off and nearly did for yourself in the process. But can you walk? We need to get away from here.'

Beyond the Spook I could see the guard with the empty bottles of wine by his side. He was still in a drunken sleep, but he could wake up at any moment.

With the Spook's help I managed to get to my feet and the three of us left the cathedral grounds and made our way through the deserted streets.

At first I was weak and shaky, but as we climbed away

from the rows of terraced houses and back up into the countryside, I started to feel stronger. After a while I turned and looked back towards Priestown, which was spread out below us. The clouds had lifted and the moon was out. The cathedral spire seemed to be gleaming.

'It looks better already,' I said, stopping to take in the view.

The Spook halted beside me and followed the direction of my gaze. 'Most things look better from a distance,' he said. 'And as a matter of fact, so do most people.'

He seemed to be joking so I smiled.

'Well,' he sighed, 'it should be a far better place from now on. But, that said, we won't be coming back in a hurry.'

After an hour or so on the road we found an old abandoned barn to shelter in. It was draughty but at least it was dry and there was a bit of the yellow cheese to nibble on. Alice dropped off to sleep right away but I sat up a long time thinking about what had happened. The Spook didn't seem tired either but just sat in silence, hugging his knees. Eventually he spoke.

'How did you know how to kill the Bane?' he asked.

'I watched you,' I answered. 'I saw you strike for its heart . . .'

But suddenly I was overcome with shame at my lie and I hung my head low. 'No, I'm sorry,' I said. 'That's not true. I sneaked forward when you talked to the ghost of Naze. I heard everything you said.'

'And so you should be sorry, lad. You took a big risk. If the Bane had managed to read your mind—'

'I'm really sorry.'

'And you didn't tell me you had a silver chain,' he said.

'Mam gave it to me,' I answered.

'Well, it's a good job that she did. Anyway, it's in my bag and safe enough for now. Until you need it again . . .' he added ominously.

There was another long silence, as if the Spook were deep in thought.

'When I carried you up from the catacombs you

seemed cold and dead,' he said at last. 'I've seen death so many times that I know I wasn't mistaken. Then that girl grabbed your arm and you came back. I don't know what to make of it.'

'I was with the Little People,' I said.

The Spook nodded. 'Aye,' he said, 'they'll all be at peace now that the Bane's dead. Naze included. But what about you, lad? What was it like? Were you afraid?'

I shook my head. 'I was more afraid just after I'd read Mam's letter,' I told him. 'She knew what was going to happen. I felt that I had no choice. That everything was already decided. But if everything's already decided, then what's the point of living?'

The Spook frowned and held out his hand. 'Give me the letter,' he demanded.

I took it out of my pocket and passed it to him. He took a long time reading it but at last he handed it back. He didn't speak for quite a while.

'Your mother is a shrewd and intelligent woman,' the Spook said at last. 'That accounts for much of what's written there. She'd worked out exactly what I was going to do. She'd more than enough knowledge to do that. It's not prophecy. Life's bad enough as it is without believing in that. You chose to go down the steps. But you had another choice. You could have walked away and then everything would have been different.'

'But once I'd chosen, she was right. Three of us faced the Bane and only two survived. I was dead. You carried me back to the surface. How can we explain that?'

The Spook didn't reply and the silence between us grew longer and longer. After a while I lay down and fell into a dreamless sleep. I didn't mention the curse. I knew it was something he wouldn't want to talk about.

CHAPTER 22
A BARGAIN'S A BARGAIN

It was almost midnight and a horned moon was rising above the trees. Rather than approaching his house by the most direct route the Spook brought us towards it from the east. I thought of the eastern garden ahead and the pit that lay in wait for Alice. The pit that I'd dug.

Surely he wasn't going to put her in the pit now? Not after all she'd done to help put things right? She'd allowed him to blindfold her and seal her ears with wax. And then she'd sat there for hours in silence and darkness without complaining even once.

But then I saw the stream ahead and was filled with new hope. It was narrow but fast-flowing, the water sparkling silver in the moonlight, and there was a single stepping stone at its centre.

He was going to test Alice.

'Right, girl,' he said, his expression stern. 'You lead the way. Over you go!'

When I looked at Alice's face my heart sank. She looked terrified and I remembered how I'd had to carry her across the river near the Silver Gate. The Bane was dead now, its power over Alice broken, but was the damage already done beyond all hope of repair? Had Alice moved too close to the dark? Could she never be free? Never be able to cross running water? Was she a fully-fledged malevolent witch?

Alice hesitated at the water's edge and began to tremble. Twice she lifted her foot to make the simple step to the flat stone at the centre of the stream. Twice she put it down again. Beads of sweat gathered on her forehead and began to roll down towards her nose and eyes.

'Go on, Alice, you can do it!' I called, trying to encourage her. For my trouble I got a withering stare from the Spook.

With a sudden, terrible effort Alice stepped onto the stone and swung her left leg forward almost immediately to carry herself over to the far bank. Once there, she hurriedly sat down and buried her face in her hands.

The Spook made a clicking noise with his tongue, crossed the stream and strode quickly up the hill towards the trees on the edge of the garden. I waited behind while Alice got to her feet, then together we walked up to where the Spook was waiting, his arms folded.

When we reached him, the Spook suddenly stepped forward and seized Alice. Gripping her by the legs, he threw her back over his shoulder. She began to wail and struggle, but without another word he clutched her more firmly, then turned and strode into the garden.

I followed behind desperately. He was heading deep into the eastern garden, moving directly towards the graves where the witches were kept, towards the empty pit. It didn't seem fair! Alice had passed the test, hadn't she?

'Help me, Tom! Help me, please!' Alice cried.

'Can't she have one more chance?' I pleaded. 'Just one more chance? She crossed. She's not a witch.'

'She just about got away with it this time,' snarled the Spook over his shoulder. 'But there's badness inside her, just waiting its chance.'

'How can you say that? After all she's done—'

'This is the safest way. It's the best thing for everyone!'

I knew then that it was time for what my dad calls 'a few home truths'. I had to tell him what I knew about Meg, even though he might hate me for it and not want me as his apprentice any more. But perhaps a reminder of his past might make him change his mind. The thought of Alice going into the pit was unbearable, and the fact that I'd been made to dig it made it a hundred times worse.

The Spook reached the pit and halted at its very edge. As he moved to lower Alice into the darkness, I shouted out, 'You didn't do it to Meg!'

He turned towards me with a look of utter astonishment on his face.

'You didn't put Meg in the pit, did you?' I cried out. 'And she was a witch! You didn't do it because you cared too much about her! So please don't do it to Alice! It isn't right!'

The Spook's expression of astonishment changed to one of fury and he stood there, tottering on the edge of the pit; for a moment I didn't know whether he was going to throw Alice down or fall into it himself. He stood there for what seemed like a very long time, but then, to my relief, his fury seemed to give way to something else and he turned and walked away, still carrying Alice.

He walked beyond the new, empty pit, passed the one where Bony Lizzie was imprisoned, strode away from the graves where the two dead witches were buried and stepped onto the path of white stones that led towards the house.

Despite his recent illness, all that he'd been through, and the weight of Alice over his shoulder, the Spook was walking so fast that I was struggling to keep up. He pulled the key from the left pocket of his breeches, opened the back door of the house and was inside before my foot even touched the step.

He walked straight into the kitchen and halted close to the fireplace, where flames were flickering sparks up the chimney. The kitchen was warm, the candles lit, with cutlery and plates set for two on the table.

Slowly the Spook eased Alice from his shoulder and set her down. The moment her pointy shoes touched the flags the fire died right down, the candle flickered and almost went out, and the air grew distinctly chilly.

The next moment there was a growl of anger that rattled the crockery and vibrated right through the floor. It was the Spook's pet boggart. Had Alice walked into the garden, even with the Spook close by, she would have been torn to pieces. But because the Spook had been carrying her it wasn't until her feet touched the ground that the boggart became aware of Alice's presence. And now it wasn't best pleased.

The Spook placed his left hand on top of Alice's

head. Next, with his left foot he stamped hard three times against the flags.

The air grew very still and the Spook called out in a loud voice, 'Hear me now! Listen well to what I say!'

There was no answer but the fire recovered a little and the air didn't seem quite so cold.

'While this child is in my house, harm not a hair of her head!' ordered the Spook. 'But watch everything that she does and ensure that she does all that I command.'

With that, he stamped three more times against the flags. In answer, the fire flared up in the grate and the kitchen suddenly seemed warm and welcoming.

'And now prepare supper for three!' the Spook commanded. Then he beckoned and we followed him out of the kitchen and up the stairs. He paused outside the locked door of the library.

'While you're here, girl, you'll earn your keep,' the Spook growled. 'There are books in there that can't be replaced. You'll never be allowed inside but I'll give you one book at a time and you can make a copy of it. Is that understood?'

Alice nodded.

'Your second job will be to tell my lad everything that Bony Lizzie taught you. And I mean everything. He'll write it all down. A lot of it'll be nonsense, of course, but that doesn't matter because it'll still add to our store of knowledge. Are you prepared to do that?'

Again Alice nodded, her expression very serious.

'Right, so that's settled,' said the Spook. 'You'll sleep in the room above Tom's, the one right at the top of the house. And now, think well on what I'm saying. That boggart down in the kitchen knows what you are and what you almost became. So don't take even one little step out of line because it'll be watching everything that you do. And it would like nothing better than to . . .'

The Spook sighed long and hard. 'It doesn't bear thinking about,' he said. 'So don't give it the chance. Will you do what I ask, girl? Can you be trusted?'

Alice nodded and her mouth widened into a big smile.

* * *

At supper the Spook was unusually quiet. It was like the calm before a storm. Nobody said much but Alice's eyes were everywhere and they returned again and again to the huge, blazing log fire that was filling the room with warmth.

At last, the Spook pushed back his plate and sighed. 'Right, girl,' he said, 'off you get to bed. I've a few things that need to be said to the lad.'

When Alice had gone, the Spook pushed back his chair and strode towards the fire. He bent and warmed his hands over the flames before turning to face me. 'Well, lad,' he growled, 'spit it out. Where did you find out about Meg?'

'I read it in one of your diaries,' I said sheepishly, bowing my head.

'I thought as much. Didn't I warn you about that? You've disobeyed me again! There are things in my library that you're not meant to read yet,' the Spook said sternly. 'Things you're not quite ready for. I'll be the judge of what's fit for you to read. Is that understood?'

'Yes, sir,' I said, addressing him by that title for the first time in months. 'But I'd have found out about Meg anyway. Father Cairns mentioned her and he told me about Emily Burns too and how you took her away from your brother and it split your family.'

'Can't keep much from you, can I, lad?'

I shrugged, feeling relieved to have got it all off my chest.

'Well,' he said, coming back towards the table, 'I've lived to a good age and I'm not proud of everything I've done, but there's always more than one side to every story. None of us is perfect, lad, and one day you'll find out all you need to know and then you can make up your own mind about me. There's little point in picking through the bones now, but as for Meg, you'll be meeting her when we get to Anglezarke. That'll be sooner than you think because, depending on the weather, we'll be setting off for my winter house in a month or so. What else did Father Cairns have to say for himself?'

'He said that you'd sold your soul to the Devil . . .'

The Spook smiled. 'What do priests know? No, lad, my soul still belongs to me. I've fought long, long years to hold onto it, and against all the odds it's still mine. And as for the Devil, well, I used to think that evil was more likely to be inside each one of us, like a bit of tinder just waiting for the spark to set it alight. But more recently I've begun to wonder if, after all, there is something behind all that we face, something hidden deep within the dark. Something that grows stronger as the dark grows stronger. Something that a priest would call the Devil . . .'

The Spook looked at me hard, his green eyes boring into my own. 'What if there were such a thing as the Devil, lad? What would we do about it?'

I thought for a few moments before I answered. 'We'd need to dig a really big pit,' I said. 'A bigger pit than any spook has ever dug before. Then we'd need bags and bags of salt and iron and a really big stone.'

The Spook smiled. 'We would that, lad, there'd be work for half the masons, riggers and mates in the County! Anyway, get off to bed with you now. It's back to your lessons tomorrow so you'll need a good night's sleep.'

As I opened the door to my room, Alice emerged from the shadows on the stairs.

'I really like it here, Tom,' she said, giving me a wide smile. 'Nice big warm house, it is. A good place to be now that winter's drawing in.'

I smiled back. I could have told her that we'd be off to Anglezarke soon, to the Spook's winter house, but she was happy and I didn't want to spoil her first night.

'One day this house will belong to us, Tom. Don't you feel it?' she asked.

I shrugged. 'Nobody knows what's going to happen in the future,' I said, putting Mam's letter to the back of my mind.

'Old Gregory tell you that, did he? Well, there are lots of things he doesn't know. You'll be a better spook than he ever was. Ain't nothing more certain than that!'

Alice turned and went up the stairs swinging her hips. Suddenly she looked back.

'Desperate for my blood, the Bane was,' she said. 'So I made the bargain even before he drank. I just wanted to make everything all right again, so I asked that you and Old Gregory could go free. Bane agreed. A bargain's a bargain, so he couldn't kill Old Gregory and he couldn't hurt you. You killed the Bane but I made it possible. At the end that's why it attacked me. It couldn't touch you. Don't tell Old Gregory though. He wouldn't understand.'

Alice left me standing on the stairs while what she'd done slowly became clear in my mind. In a way she'd sacrificed herself. It would have killed her just as it had killed Naze. But she'd saved me and the Spook. Saved our lives. And I would never forget it.

Stunned by what she'd said, I went into my room and closed the door. It took me a long time to get to sleep.

Once again I've written most of this from memory, just using my notebook when necessary.

Alice has been good and the Spook's really pleased with the work she's been doing. She writes very quickly but her hand is still clear and neat. She's also doing as she promised, telling me the things that Bony Lizzie taught her so that I can write them all down.

Of course, although Alice doesn't know it yet, she won't be staying with us for that long. The Spook told me that she'll start to distract me too much and I won't be able to concentrate on my studies. He's not happy about having a girl with pointy shoes living in his house, especially one who's been so close to the dark.

It's late October now and soon we'll be setting off for the Spook's winter house on Anglezarke Moor. Nearby there's a farm run by some people whom the Spook trusts. He thinks that they'll let Alice stay with them. Of course, he's made me promise not to tell Alice yet. Anyway, I'll be sad to see her go.

And of course I'll meet Meg, the lamia witch. Maybe I'll meet the Spook's other woman too. Blackrod is close to the moor and that's where Emily Burns is still supposed to live. I have a feeling that there are lots of other things in the Spook's past that I still don't know about.

I'd rather stay here in Chipenden, but he's the Spook and I'm only the apprentice. And I've come to realize that there's a very good reason for everything that he does.

Thomas J. Ward